CONFLICT IN CALIFORNIA

KEN STUCKEY

Baker Books

A Division of Baker Book House Co
Grand Rapids, Michigan 49516

© 2001 by Ken Stuckey

Published by Baker Books
a division of Baker Book House Company
P.O. Box 6287, Grand Rapids, MI 49516-6287

Printed in the United States of America

Library of Congress Cataloging-in-Publication Data

Stuckey, Ken.
    Conflict in California / Ken Stuckey.
       p.   cm.
    Sequel to: Doubt at Daytona.
    Summary: Doug, Paolo, and their friends, members of the support crew for the Orly Mann Racing Team, attend a drag race and a stock car race in California, and depend on their faith in God to deal with various people there.
    ISBN 0-8010-4478-2 (paper)
    [1. Stock car racing—Fiction. 2. Drag racing—Fiction. 3. Emotional problems—Fiction. 4. Christian life—Fiction. 5. California—Fiction.] I. Title.
PZ7.S93757 Co 2001
[Fic]—dc21
                                      00–066706

For current information about all releases from Baker Book House, visit our web site:

http://www.bakerbooks.com

PROLOGUE

If the Lord delights in a man's way, he makes his steps firm; though he
stumble, he will not fall, for the Lord upholds him with his hand.

Psalm 37:23–24

"The whole deal about track position at Talledega is that you want to be
in front of the wrecks. Hopefully if there is a wreck mid-pack it happens
behind you."

Mike Skinner, Winston Cup driver, car #31

THE GREASY HOT DOG that he crammed down for lunch sat like
a hot piece of metal in the back of Bear's throat. His stomach was upset,
but it wasn't just due to the lousy food. Things were unfolding and it
was bound to happen and it could be soon. Bear could feel it along
with the hot dog. This was the fourth restart of the race, and the field
was bunched up getting ready to take the green flag. Bunched up was
a polite way of saying you could have hopped from the hood to the
decklid of the first thirty cars because they were running so close
together. That is, you could if you had nerves of steel and could maintain your balance at 180 miles per hour. Bear had eyes for only one car
in the midst of this mess—the yellow-and-orange Speed King Chevrolet driven by Orly Mann. Orly Mann, in Bear's opinion, was the greatest stock car driver on the face of the earth. Besides that, he was Bear's
best friend and co-owner of the Orly Mann Racing Team, Bear himself being the owner of the other half.

3

It was a bright, shiny Alabama Sunday afternoon, and they were at the Talledega Motor Speedway. Two and one-half miles of pure speed on a banked tri-oval that had long sweeping corners arching up 33 degrees. *Old Charlie Moneypenny outdid himself when he designed this place back in 1969,* thought Bear. He was the same guy that designed the Daytona International Speedway, which was also terribly fast, but Talledega was wider and smoother. Here the drivers ran absolutely flat out, sometimes three abreast, never lifting their right foot from the floorboards. That is if their cars were working right and they had the intestinal fortitude.

Bear hated this race and the other three just like it. It was a restrictor-plate race and it went against everything he believed in as a crew chief. NASCAR, in an effort to reduce speeds, which admittedly had gotten out of hand at the Super Speedways like Daytona and here, came up with a devilish device. It was simply a flat plate with carefully dimensioned holes that fit between the carburetor and the manifold. It restricted the amount of air and fuel going into an engine. Bear could tune all he wanted, but a normal 700-horsepower Cup engine was reduced to about 400 lathered ponies. It was still enough horsepower to push the car to nearly 200 miles per hour under the right conditions, but in essence, it equaled the playing field. It meant that nobody had the horsepower to really get away from anybody else. In fact, it put the whole racing game into the realm of aerodynamics. Drafting was the key. It was a known fact that the cars went faster during the race when they ran together than when they qualified by themselves. In order for a driver to stay in the hunt, he had to stay practically within touching distance of the cars around him.

It scared Bear to death to watch them run that close. *I don't understand how Orly and them other drivers can take that pressure lap after lap. But Orly does and that's because he's the best. I wish we had a better car for him today. I would feel a lot better if he could bust loose, 'cause it's coming. I can feel it.*

One of the offshoots of restrictor-plate racing, especially at Talledega, was called "the wreck." Every restrictor-plate race run here usually . . . almost always . . . just about every time . . . had a major crash that wiped out a bunch of cars.

So far it hadn't happened. But, just like Christmas, it was bound to come, and all Bear's senses told him it was gonna be soon. The laps were winding down, and a number of drivers that were caught back in the pack wanted to be up front, and they were running out of patience. Bear could see it in the way they were giving each other little taps and "leaning" on each other. "Leaning" meant shoving and pushing like a group of fifth graders lined up at the bus stop.

Unfortunately, Orly was right in the middle of this mess. The Speed King Chevy wasn't handling like it ought to, and Orly was trying to deal with a severe "push" going in the corners. A "push" meant that the car wasn't tracking like it should and had a tendency to go up the track toward the wall. Orly was having to work the steering wheel a little too much to get the car to turn, which scrubbed off speed. Not a lot, but enough to slow him down. Bear suspected what the problem was, but he didn't have a way to fix it now. The new rear-spoiler rule was making life difficult for the Chevrolets. So far they had made adjustments on every pit stop with tire pressures and such, but they could only do so much. The Thunderfoot Ballet was doing their usual fantastic job of getting Orly back on the track as quickly as possible, and he had been able to gain a few spots in the pits. But once the tires got hot and things settled down, Orly couldn't stay with the lead cars.

Bear quietly belched and felt somewhat better as the pack sailed by him on the front stretch. He mopped his sweating forehead with a red shop rag. Switching his attention to the video feed on the monitor built into the war wagon, he watched the cars head down the back chute. They would be catching the green flag next time by. *This is tough,* Bear thought. *We are sitting third in points right now, and we need to get out of here with a good finish. At this stage, anything in the top fifteen would be great. A top ten would be miraculous. But then, on occasion, with the Lord's help, Orly did pull off a miracle.*

Bear looked over at Doug Prescott sitting beside him on the war wagon. Doug was staring at the computer console as he kept track of some of the other cars. Bear regarded him fondly, then gave him a poke in the ribs.

"Whatcha think there, Doug my boy? Think we're gonna get out of here in one piece today?"

Doug didn't bother to answer or even look up. It was a question that he couldn't answer and Bear knew that. Doug had known Bear most of his life. Bear was fretting, which was what all good crew chiefs did during a race.

The tightly bunched pack gathered itself together for the restart. The leader brought them off the fourth turn, and everybody stayed in formation waiting for the starter to wave the green flag. He was perched high above the track in a little box that hung out over the fence. He studied the cars with his left hand in the proverbial "easy now" motion, and then with fluid grace whipped the green flag around his head with the right. The pack thundered by with earthshaking fervor as every driver's right foot went to the floor at the same time.

The pack disappeared from Bear's view and once again he looked at the monitor. He watched the cars jockey for position down the backstretch and focused on turn four, waiting for them to come by again. Bear saw it coming, groaned out loud, and stood up. The radio headset crackled in his ears as Jimmy, Orly's spotter, saw it coming too. Jimmy was high atop what was called the tri-oval tower and had a bird's-eye view of the whole track.

His voice rang sharp in Bear's ears as he spoke to Orly. "Watch it now, watch it, Orly," he twanged in his east Texas accent.

Bear could see that Orly was "watching it," but there wasn't a whole lot he could do. All of a sudden one of the lead cars was sliding sideways in a cloud of acrid tire smoke, and then the rest of the pack was coming apart like a clean break on a pool table.

Orly was hunkered down in his custom-fitted seat in a pool of sweat. It felt like this last pit stop had got some of the push out of the car, but it was still a handful in the corners. It was taking every ounce of his concentration and all of his skill as a driver to keep the thing off the wall. Every time he got serious about racing somebody, he found himself chasing the car up the corner.

Jimmy's voice rose an octave as he said, "Watch it now."

Orly was watching, and he caught just a quick glimpse of a car three rows ahead of him getting nudged sideways. Then his world dissolved into tire smoke and grease mud, as his windshield was instantly covered with oil and coolant. Somebody checked up in the corner and got tapped, which set off a chain reaction.

Orly held his line, hoping for direction from Jimmy.

"Low, low, low, stay low, Orly." Jimmy's voice reverberated in his ear.

Too late! A spinning car came out of the smoke across Orly's front end in a gentle pirouette that tagged him just hard enough to make him kiss the wall at 175 miles per hour. He banged it hard, ripping sheet metal and blowing the right side tires. Orly did his best to hold the car into the wall as he ground along it in a sheet of sparks and terrible grating noise. It sounded like a cat with six claws sliding across a chalkboard. The last thing he wanted was to slide back across the track in front of the rest of the pack. He couldn't do it. He got tagged again, this time in the rear as somebody punched him hard. Orly felt something pop in his shoulder as he watched his own decklid pop straight up in the rearview mirror. He spun into the wall again, and this time the front suspension and steering folded up. The car took on a mind of its own and came down the banking across the track. Now he was no longer driving but was along for the ride. He hunkered down as low as he could in the seat, hoping not to get hit again. He took another shot, but this time in the right door, and mercifully it spun him into the infield.

He slid across the grass doing slow lazy Susan donuts—bits and pieces of the broken sheet metal trailing along behind. Finally he came to rest. The silence was deafening. By instinct, Orly reached for the starter switch, but pulled his gloved hand back as he surveyed the crumpled hood of the Speed King Chevrolet. It was done. He could tell that for certain. There would be no getting this piece of junk back into the race. He started to undo his belts, but groaned out loud as his shoulder twinged in agony.

"Talk to me, Orly. Talk to me. You okay?"

Orly realized Bear had been calling him for more than a few seconds. Orly looked around the inside of the car and keyed the mike button on the steering wheel. "Yeah, I'm okay, guys, but I think we're done. Not enough left here to fix. Looks like the front end is a wash, and the radiator is practically in my lap. Oh yeah, one other thing. I think I broke my shoulder."

For I know the plans I have for you, declares the LORD, plans to prosper you and not to harm you, plans to give you hope and a future.

Jeremiah 29:11

"Running a racing business takes special people. . . . There are a lot of, let's say personalities involved."

Jimmy Johnson, Manager of Hendrick
Motorsports for 12 years

THE TOP FUEL DRAGSTER launched off the starting line with a blast of blue-orange flame and a howling bellow that literally shook the ground. Loren Janine slammed back in the thinly padded driver's seat as the g-force crushed her body. Right behind her helmet she could hear the engine building revs as the car accelerated on its 4.5 second run. The pass was good so far. The launch off the starting pad had been dead solid perfect as the huge racing slicks grabbed the asphalt. She eclipsed the 100-miles-per-hour mark in the blink of an eye. At half track she was well over 200 miles per hour, and in less than a second more, she'd hurtled her way to 300 miles per hour . . . *when it all went bad.*

The screaming engine detonated like a 1000-pound bomb, with a flash of brilliant orange flame filling the air with white-hot chunks of molten metal and smoking engine oil. In less than a heartbeat, the dragster was a hurtling, rolling, tumbling ball of fire, with the driver trapped in a suffocating cocoon filled with the stench of burning rubber and liquid heat.

Loren Janine screamed—fighting the covers from around her neck as she sat up in the darkness of the motel room. With a shaking hand she turned on the bedside lamp as she tried to get her breathing under control. "I'm okay," she constantly repeated to herself. As she calmed herself the tears flowed down her cheeks. "Not again," she moaned out loud. The recurring dream was getting more vivid each night.

"I can't take this anymore," she repeated to herself. She fumbled out of bed, throwing the covers back, and dove into her purse. She popped the cap on the pill bottle, shook the yellow tablets into her hand, and swallowed them without water. She lit a cigarette with her shaking hand and sat on the edge of the bed, waiting for the magic drug to do its job and numb her into the oblivion of sleep. After a moment she stubbed the cigarette out, snatched a blanket off the bed, and moved to the big chair across the room. She pulled her legs up and huddled in the chair with the blanket under her chin, staring at the floor with wide scared eyes.

The flight attendant took off her apron and patted her hair as she walked down the narrow aisle checking seat belts and tray tables for landing. The 747 began its descent into the San Francisco airport traffic pattern. She glanced at the three young people asleep in their adjoining seats. They had slept almost from take-off in Atlanta. *It is nice to be young and relaxed,* the flight attendant thought. The young man next to the window was a large guy with solid good looks and dark curly hair that went with his slightly olive complexion. *He looks a little Mediterranean,* she thought. *But he's a lot larger than the average guy and fills the seat to overflowing. Probably have to watch his weight as he gets older,* she thought as she unconsciously patted her own stomach.

Sitting next to him was a young Asian woman with beautiful features and long black hair that glistened in the afternoon sunlight coming through the window. Her head was resting lightly on the big guy's shoulder, and she seemed very petite sitting comfortably next to him. The fellow in the aisle seat seemed just as tall as the other young man, but he was thinner and had sandy colored hair and an almost "Aw shucks" handsomeness about him. *They make an interesting trio,* she thought as she made certain all three had their seat belts fastened.

The flight attendant didn't know it, but the three young people were experienced travelers who knew that the quickest way to get through an airplane ride was to sleep through it. They were used to traveling and flew somewhere almost two out of every four weeks. All three of them were part of the Orly Mann Racing Team and as a result spent a lot of time traveling to and from the various racetracks that made up the Winston Cup circuit across the United States. Most of the time they flew in the Orly Mann corporate airplane, but today was different.

The dark-haired guy was Paolo Pellegrini and even though he appeared to be asleep, he was really quite awake. He was trying not to fret, but he wanted this flight to be over.

Sitting was not easy for him, and he much preferred doing something that gave him freedom to move around as opposed to being still. He was cramped because of his size and bemoaned the fact that they didn't make commercial airline seats for real people. He was also afraid to move too much because he would wake Alicia, who had her head resting on his shoulder. His arm was asleep, but it didn't matter. He liked having her head on his shoulder and her hair fanned across his chest. He reached over to run a finger through the black, glossy strands. Her eyes were closed and she was breathing quietly as she slept. Paolo liked Alicia, always had. He just didn't know how to tell her.

What Paolo didn't know was that Alicia was not sleeping at all and was in fact wide awake. She had been for some time and was enjoying every minute of this flight with her head on his shoulder. They had a unique relationship. They had known each other practically their whole lives. They both used to live in San Francisco. They went to the same grammar school, middle school, and high school. They grew up together. Most important, they both attended the same church. Their families were very good friends and socialized together.

Alicia knew Paolo as well as anyone, and even though she didn't always understand him or what it was that motivated him . . . she loved him. They were both passionate people and also best friends, which meant that they often argued and disagreed with each other. But in the past couple of years she found her feelings toward Paolo changing. She no longer saw him as just a friend. In fact, she was wondering if she might be falling in love with him, and that thought scared her a little. She often found herself fantasizing about what it would be like to be married to him, but in the meantime she would wait on the Lord and be content with that. She knew Paolo liked her, but she just wished he wouldn't take her so much for granted. Most of the time she felt like his sister rather than anyone he might be attracted to. At least that was how it seemed.

In the meantime she was content to sit next to him and rest her head on his thick muscular shoulder. *Those workouts with the Thunderfoot Ballet Company are paying off,* she thought as she snuggled a little closer.

Doug, on the other hand, was genuinely asleep and snoring slightly. He wasn't from California at all, but from Charlotte, North Carolina. He was a slow talker with a thick Carolina accent. He possessed the coveted ability to fall asleep at will in almost any circumstance. Paolo, who was by nature a worrier, envied him. He and Paolo were not only great friends but roommates. Doug also had a great fondness for Alicia. But he knew that she was committed to Paolo. Even if Paolo didn't know it, everybody else did. It really showed when they were together, like right now. Alicia liked nothing better than spending time with Paolo and was always patting him or touching him in some gentle way. Besides, Doug had a lady friend of his own, and he was eager to see her.

Paolo and Alicia were on their way back to the West Coast from Charlotte to visit for a few days. Even though San Francisco was where she grew up, it was no longer home for Alicia. A few months earlier her family, including her Aunty Grandmother, had all moved to Florida where her dad was starting a new business. Aunty Grandmother and her two sisters had run the best restaurant in Chinatown for over twenty years, but now it was sold. Two of the sisters moved to Florida, and now the third was going to join them. It seemed strange because her family had lived in San Francisco Chinatown for two generations. It would be odd to be in San Francisco and not have family there. But then she still had lots of good friends and it would be great to see them. There was an unusual weekend break in the crowded Winston Cup schedule, and Alicia was going to spend nearly a week and a half with her friends enjoying the city, and then she would fly down to join the rest of the team for the California 500 in Fontana, California. She was the computer tech for the team, and she and Doug handled all the timing and scoring tasks during the course of a race weekend. She spent the rest of the week staying on top of the various software programs and answering phones in the Orly Mann Racing Team office. She shared an apartment with Helen, Orly's publicist and public relations person. It was working out great, and Alicia was enjoying her job very much. Bear often told her he appreciated her ability "to sort the marbles" and he didn't know how he'd gotten along without her all these years. She wasn't exactly sure what he meant by "sorting the marbles," but she felt she contributed to the team. After living practically her whole life on the West Coast, it was fun to see new places.

Living in Charlotte and working for the team gave her a certain notoriety. It was something she and Paolo talked about every so often. Stock car racing was so popular it seemed anybody associated with a team was seen as somebody special. Especially someone on the Orly Mann Racing Team. Orly, a past champion, was immensely popular. Besides, he was a good guy. Alicia had the utmost respect for Bear and Orly. They were honest and fair in dealing with their employees. They were men of integrity. Even Paolo was starting to get fan mail.

Paolo was a general mechanic and spent a lot of time chasing parts and degreasing things. In truth, he was Bear's protégé, and Bear treated him like an apprentice. Paolo was a quick learner, with a natural mechanical talent that lent itself well to the "racin' biz" as Bear liked to say. On race weekends, Paolo's job changed. He was a key member of the Thunderfoot Ballet Company. The Thunderfoot Ballet Company was the "over the wall gang" that serviced Orly Mann's car during a race. Their performance meant a great deal in Orly's ability to run with "the top dogs." Pit stops were an important part of any Winston Cup race, and the Thunderfoot Ballet Company was the best of the best. Paolo was the "jackman." He went over the wall with the thirty-five-pound jack in his arms. On a four tire stop he would sprint to the right side of the car, throw the jack down at the mark, and with two prodigious pushes on the handle, raise the car into the air to allow the tire changers to change the rubber. As soon as the new wheels were thrown on the car, Paolo would release the jack and sprint around the front of the car to lift the left side tires. The job took agility and strength. Paolo was strong with a natural quickness that lent itself perfectly to the job. He'd even been offered more money for a position with a couple of other teams, but he wouldn't dream of leaving. Bear was Paolo's mentor and friend, and their respect for each other was mutual.

Doug, on the other hand, worked mostly with paper and engineering. He was nicknamed "Bear's notepad." He kept track of the race setups on the twenty-some race cars in the shop. He also did a lot in terms of logistics to make certain the right parts went into the hauler so whatever was needed at the track was close at hand. That name had gradually been shortened to "Notes," which pretty much defined what he did. On race weekends, he worked with Alicia in keeping track of Orly's lap times, position, and pit stops with the help of a computer. It was Doug's job to keep an eye on the competition and the big picture as a race unfolded. Doug's dad, Bud Prescott, was second in command to Bear. He'd been with Orly and Bear practically from day one of the team's existence. As a result, Doug grew up in the racing business and knew practically everybody, which made him very good at his job. He had the ability to keep track of many multifaceted details at the same time. He and Paolo had met a few years back at Sears Point at a time when Doug was really hurting. Paolo had treated him like a brother, and now they shared a deep friendship.

Paolo was excited at the prospect of going home for a few days. He hadn't seen his mom and dad for several months and knew they'd be happy to see him. Some of his mom's good cooking would be great, but he was excited for another reason as well. His old '64 Chevy Malibu was out of the paint shop and ready to go. His uncle Rollie had given it to Paolo when he was learning how to drive not so many years ago. At that time, it was just an old "beater" Chevrolet, but Paolo had vision and a genuine love for cars. In the ensuing years, Paolo lavished much love and attention on the old car, so it no longer looked old.

It was restored and refurbished with new and updated parts. All the running gear was rebuilt, and Paolo had updated and modified a number of components in the brake and suspension systems. The paint job was the final touch. Just before he flew off to join the Orly Mann Racing Team, Paolo had wrapped up the engine rebuild and had done a few minor things that needed to be finished. It was purring like a kitten when he left. Well, that wasn't entirely true. Rather, it rumbled with a muted thunder that emphasized the balance and power of an engine that breathed through a big Carter four-barrel carb, a nice set of custom headers, and less than restrictive mufflers. He had even put on punched chrome wheels and a perfect set of tires. But the body still needed to be detailed to make it perfect.

When he arrived in Charlotte and was working steady for the team, with a good income, he asked his dad to take it to a special auto shop owned by a fellow in his church who did custom bodywork. With more than just a few phone calls and some explicit e-mails, Paolo directed the progress. The shop owned a digital camera and he received occasional pictures attached to his e-mail, but it wasn't the same as seeing it in real life. Just before he left, his pop called and told him the final work was done and it was ready to go. He also told him it was beautiful. The guys at the shop did a fantastic job and Pop had a hunch Paolo would be more than pleased. Paolo could hardly wait to see it. It would be like greeting an old friend coming home after cosmetic surgery.

It would be wonderful to have his own car again. He had put so much sweat and love into the thing it was almost an extension of his personality. The plan was for him and Doug to visit with his folks for a few days and then head south to Southern California with a leisurely cruise down I–5. He was looking forward to picking up "baby" and driving it down to Pomona, which wasn't very far from Fontana and the new oval track. It would be a great chance to get reacquainted.

He was excited for another reason. He and Doug and their friend Alphonse were going to hit the NHRA drag races next weekend at Pomona. The National Hot Rod Association (NHRA) is the biggest sanctioning body for drag racing. Pomona is a special nonpoints event involving only the top fuel dragsters in a winner-take-all shootout on the NHRA circuit. The timing was perfect for Doug and Paolo to join up with the Speed King team. It was a spectacular pressure-packed, pure nitro, drag race. The off-weekend for the Winston Cup Series freed up the guys to take a little holiday and attend the event. Orly's primary sponsor was the Speed King Oil Company, and they not only sponsored Orly's Winston Cup car but a top fuel car as well.

The Speed King team had a new driver, twenty-one-year-old Loren Janine. She was a natural. So far this season she had brought home two wins by being "top-fuel eliminator" at both events. She was also a beautiful natural blonde with a quick wit and vivacious personality. Doug met her at a drag race last year before she got her big break with the Speed King Team. He was smitten. To say that he was excited to see her once again was the proverbial understatement. He managed to date her a couple of times, but her schedule and his kept getting in the way. Once she hit the NHRA circuit she was crisscrossing the country as much as he was. It seemed like they were always talking on the phone, separated by at least two thousand miles. The coming weekend was a great opportunity for them to be together and Doug could hardly wait.

Paolo sat up and so did Alicia as the big plane made its final approach. Paolo reached across Alicia and poked Doug in the ribs, "Wake up, sleepyhead."

Doug just grunted and turned the other way, folding his arms across his chest.

"So, are you excited?" Alicia asked, looking up into Paolo's face.

"What? Oh you mean seeing the folks. Yeah, I think I am. I have missed them. They're good people," Paolo said.

"No. I didn't mean the folks. I meant are you excited about the other thing?"

"Who me? Nah. It's just a car, Alicia." It was a testimony to the level of his excitement that she knew exactly what he was thinking about. "You forget I work on cars all the time."

"Yeah, right," said Alicia. "Hey Pally, don't forget who you're talking to. I watched you put hours and hours into that thing." She said "thing" with a heavy emphasis on the "th." "I remember when Uncle Rollie gave it to you. I never said it to you, but I thought it looked like a worn-out pair of pajamas or something. Remember when I spilled a Coke on the raggedy old upholstery? I was sure you were going to stop on the side of the road and make me get out and walk."

Paolo laughed. "Yeah, I was a little ticked. It was my first car, Alicia. Guys have a thing with their first car. I was just blessed enough to be able to make it sharp. Yeah, I'm excited about it. I chose that deep purple color that's almost black. Pop dropped by the shop and checked it out. He says the color is so deep it looks like you could fall into it. I know Arnie did a good job. I just hope Orly doesn't mess up the primary car, so they can sell the backup and I can get it back to Charlotte okay. I'll look good riding around in it."

What made the deal exciting was a big chance that he could get his car back to Charlotte without driving it across country. He didn't have time to do that anyway. The team was bringing a primary race car and also a backup (or secondary) car to Fontana for the California 500, but Orly and Bear had made a deal to sell the backup if it wasn't needed for the race. If they sold it, there would be room in the team hauler and Paolo's car would get a free ride back to Charlotte. It would sit up high in the hauler covered by a protective cover, and he wouldn't have to worry about road damage while it crossed the United States.

He laughed again. "Say, speaking of cars, is that little econo-box you bought in Charlotte running okay?" Paolo laughed again because they both knew Alicia possessed absolutely zero mechanical aptitude.

"Yes, it's running fine, and don't you laugh at my little car. It gets 32 miles to the gallon, which is good for the health of the planet as well as my pocketbook. Not like that gas hog thing you have."

Doug spoke with eyes closed, "You tell him, Alicia. Those racer guys are all the same. Think the whole world revolves around cars."

Alicia turned to face Doug. "You! You're no better. You have that Camaro thing that hurts my neck every time you step on the gas."

Doug smiled and kept his eyes closed as the big airplane gently touched down.

The flight attendant was out of her seat as soon as the pilot gave the okay. She glanced down the aisle to see Doug doing his best to stretch his arms and stifle a yawn at the same time. It was evident that the three young people were wide awake and ready to get going. *I wonder where they are off to?* thought the attendant. *They look eager.* One of the other crew members caught her looking.

"Do you know who those folks are?" she asked.

"No, I don't, but I wish I had their energy and youth. They look like they're heading to a fun time somewhere."

"Those guys are part of the Orly Mann Racing Team. I saw them on TV last week at Talledega. I don't know what they are doing in San Francisco, but I bet they will be down in Fontana next week for the California 500."

"Some life," she replied as she looked at them with renewed interest.

A few minutes later she was standing at the door bidding folks farewell. Doug, Alicia, and Paolo came down the aisle carrying their Orly Mann travel bags. She flashed them a smile and said, "Thanks for flying with us. You folks have a wonderful time in San Francisco and tell Orly to do good in Fontana."

Doug smiled back and said in his deep North Carolina accent, "Why, thank you, Ma'am. Thank you very much," as they headed down the jetway.

Paolo looked over at Alicia. "Thank you, thank you very much," he mimicked. "He sounds just like Elvis Presley, doesn't he?"

Alicia's reply was lost as they were met at the gate by a noisy group of friends and relatives. There were lots of hugs and back pounding. Paolo's mom hugged everybody and clucked her tongue over Alicia's beauty and how much older the young people looked. She managed to reach up and pinch Paolo's cheeks two or three times. Doug did his best to stay out of range but was finally trapped and given a warm hug and a wet kiss as well.

When the bags were picked up, the group sorted itself out as Alicia took off with her friends and Doug and Paolo headed home with his folks.

Two hours later Paolo was standing in the body shop, speechless, as he rubbed his hands across the satin smooth finish. It was dead solid perfect. It was even better than he thought it would be. The deep dark purple color shimmered and looked so deep that you could plunge your hand into it.

"Cool! Man, Pally, this is beautiful. They did a fantastic job. The wheels and tires set it off perfectly. It looks so rich. Man, it looks good," Doug said as he stood, hands on his hips. "I wish it wasn't so far 'cause I'd bring the Camaro out here for you to paint, Arnie. You guys do great work."

Arnie, the owner of the body shop, stood to the side, scratching his ample belly with a satisfied look on his face. "Yeah, Paolo, that was a good choice in colors. It looks good here in the shop, but you should see it in the sunshine. It kind of changes a little as the light hits it. We rolled it out yesterday to wash it and detail it, and the color just kept getting deeper and deeper. The guys did a real nice job."

"Yeah, they sure did, Arnie. Thanks a lot, man. You guys did a great job. I'm really grateful."

"We charged the battery up for you, but you better put a little gas in it. Thanks for giving us the business, Paolo. Been fun working with you," Arnie said, marking Paolo's invoice "paid" and putting Paolo's check in the cash drawer.

Paolo slipped into the Chevy and ran his hands across the tucked and rolled upholstery. The inside of the car was immaculate and everything looked new and clean. Finally he put the key in the ignition and started it up. He looked around the interior again, then sat listening to the engine gently idle. The sound was perfect. It wasn't any wimpy exhaust whisper, but it wasn't so loud as to be annoying either. It spoke of restrained power. The new upholstery looked wonderful, and the color blended perfectly with the pristine purple exterior. It was a car that would turn heads. Paolo looked down at the custom dash with its array of gauges. Everything looked good as he shifted into gear and headed out into Van Ness Avenue traffic. He turned onto Geary and drove carefully to 19th Avenue and headed home. He stayed in the right lane, keeping a wary eye out for "idiots" as he made his way through traffic. He noticed that at nearly every traffic light people stopped to take a good look at the deep purple classically styled machine. He sat up a little straighter, grinning from ear to ear. *I feel good.*

Doug followed at a respectful distance in Paolo's parents' car.

Ah right, thought Paolo. *Thank you, Lord. What a great piece of iron this is, as Bear would say. Speaking of Bear, I wonder what he'll say when he sees this baby come purring up. I bet he likes it. He sure has heard enough about it.*

That was Tuesday. Early Friday morning the guys loaded up, and amidst tearful good-byes with Mom and Pop, headed out to pick up Alphonse. He lived in another part of San Francisco and, at Doug and Paolo's invitation, was joining them for the trip to SoCal. The plan was for the guys to do the drags in Pomona over the weekend, then knock around in LA for a few days and ultimately join the team in Fontana on Thursday to get ready for the California race.

Alphonse was throwing stuff into his bag as quickly as he could. He was excited. This was going to be a great few days with Doug and especially Paolo and Alicia. They were good friends and he missed them. He was sad when they moved to the East Coast, but now they had a chance to be together again. Alphonse wasn't a real "car" guy like Doug and Paolo, but they knew that. They didn't expect him to be anything other than what he was—a hard-working African-American young man doing his best to go to school while he helped his mom support his little brother and sisters. Most of the time he worked at least two part-time jobs and was forever burning the candle at both ends. That was okay because he always had a lot of energy. He zipped up the bag as he checked the clock. *Be here any minute,* he thought.

"Hey, Mom, you need anything before I head out?" he yelled to his mom in the kitchen.

"No, son, we don't need a thing. You go on now and have a good time with your friends. I'll be praying that God uses you in a special way."

"Thanks, Mom," he said as he headed out the door.

Alphonse was dutifully impressed when Doug and Paolo rumbled up in front of his flat in the Chevy. He gave a low whistle as Paolo got out and popped the trunk.

"Yo, Paolo, we are styling now. Man, that is a nice color. Eye-popping deep . . . but not overstated. Makes a nice comment about class and the maturity of vintage . . . looks like a fine deep burgundy wine—"

Paolo interrupted him, "Get in the car, Alphonse."

Alphonse ignored Paolo and continued his verbal appreciation of the Chevy. "We are the epitome of coolness now. SoCal, here we come. Little ladies, look out. The boys are looking good. Wooeee this looks nice. This is definitely a ten-plus on the spectrum level of the upper-class appreciation chart. Looks like all your work has paid off, man. We are looking good. This is what I call a major ride. Yo, Doug. Good to see you, man."

Doug was out of the car with his hand outstretched. "Good to see you, Alphonse. How's it going?"

"Going good. Even better after seeing Paolo's ride. I got a feeling this is going to be some sort of vacation."

They threw Alphonse's stuff in the trunk and Doug jumped into the backseat.

He who is pregnant with evil and conceives trouble gives birth to disillusionment.

Psalm 7:14

"Personalities will build any sport. You've got to have it. You need somebody who you can talk to who will give you a comment worth printing, not some driver who can't tell you this or that because he's afraid he can't get through inspection."

Bruton Smith, Chairman of Speedway Motorsports
and owner of six Winston Cup Racetracks

CLEAR ACROSS THE COUNTRY in a suburb of Charlotte, North Carolina, Orly Mann and Bear Erickson were in heavy conversation. Talledega was a memory, just a series of numbers in Bear's race book. The NASCAR schedule is too packed to dwell on any one race. In Bear's scheme of things, looking backwards didn't pay any money or add to the overall points. There is always another race lurking just over the horizon. A race that requires planning, preparation, and attention to the smallest detail.

They were sitting in Bear's office near the large picture window looking over the expansive and "so clean you could eat off the floor" Orly Mann Racing Team facility. Several race cars were in various stages of construction, and the wrecked car from Talledega had already been stripped of its outer skin. The chassis would be straightened and every weld and seam meticulously inspected. If it was found to be too damaged to save, it would be cut up and sent out with the next load of scrap.

Even as Bear talked with Orly he kept one eye on the twenty-some employees efficiently doing their jobs. The shop resounded with the sounds of fabrication. Occasionally the flash of an arc welder blinked in the modern, well-lit shop. One had a sense that the work done here was precise and done with pride. Printed on one wall of the shop in large letters were the words:

> Do you not know that in a race all the runners run, but only one gets the prize? Run in such a way as to get the prize.
>
> 1 Corinthians 9:24

The foundation of the Orly Mann Racing Team was excellence, and every man that worked for the team knew two things for certain. First, it was expected that he would give his best and nothing less, and that might mean long hours and sometimes herculean effort. Second, he knew when the team won he was part of the victory and compensated for his efforts. An employee also knew that when Orly or Bear said something they meant it. In a business that had its share of hype and false promises, Orly and Bear kept their word. Their handshake was their bond. Those were some of the reasons Orly and Bear had little turnover in the shop. Guys came and stayed because they were treated with respect and paid well for honest hard work.

Bear's thoughts were never far from the activity in the shop, but as he glanced out the window, then back at Orly, he decided he needed to keep his full attention on what Orly was saying. They were good friends and had been together a long time, sharing a good deal of success in the "racin' bidness," as Bear liked to say. The "bidness" had changed and become more corporate in nature, but Bear and Orly were different. They worked hard and raced hard and both had the utmost respect for the other's talents and abilities. Orly was not only a good Winston Cup driver, he was a great one and had two NASCAR championships to prove it—championships he never would have won without Bear's brilliant mechanical expertise and his organizational capability.

Bear knew what it took to build a winning car, no matter what the racetrack, and more important, he knew how to inspire a team to give its best effort in the process. It took enormous commitment to create a winning combination in the Winston Cup Series. A team had to have a facility that manufactured the cars and serviced the equipment to make running the circuit possible. The cars not only had to be perfect, but built to a very stringent set of rules and guidelines that incorporated the elements of safety and competition. Bear built good cars that were always competitive, and he did it by utilizing the skills and talents of the best people he could hire. But building the cars was only half the equation, and it was here that Bear truly excelled.

Once the cars were built they had to be raced. Racing always involved adapting the team and cars to the ever-changing circumstances of a particular racetrack. Bear was a master of the fine-tuning it took to make a car a bit better than the competition. He was always looking for an edge that would help put Orly up front.

Orly's pit crew, the Thunderfoot Ballet Company, was a prime example. There were seven guys that went over the wall to service the car during a race. They could make or break a driver's chance to finish up front. Bear handpicked the Ballet Company, then worked at shaping and molding them into the fastest pit crew on the circuit. He was not only their boss, but their coach as well. He drove them hard to attain perfection and they respected him for it.

Because Orly and Bear were friends and confidants, Bear recognized the look on Orly's face. He gave him his full attention and watched as Orly stood up and paced the length of the office, then sat down again.

Orly stretched out his long legs as he relaxed in the overstuffed chair facing Bear's desk. He started to put his hands behind his head but grimaced in sudden pain and thought better of it.

"Still hurting that bad, huh Orly," Bear said with a look of compassion on his face.

"Yeah, it still pains me some. I never thought a bone chip off a shoulder blade could hurt so much for so long."

"Did I tell you I'm working on some seat modifications that might eliminate this type of injury? Me and some of the other guys in the Crew Chief Club have some ideas. It's time to do something about this."

The injury Bear was talking about was a broken shoulder blade. It happens when drivers take a hard shot in a crash. Because of the nature of the driver's seat, shoulder harness, and the configuration of the driver's body as he holds the wheel with his arms slightly outstretched, it was a common injury. For that very reason, some drivers liked the steering wheel as close to their chests as possible for better leverage, but Orly was from the old school. He liked a medium extension of the arms, and now maybe he was paying the price.

Getting beat up in a race car is not an unusual experience for a driver. Winston Cup racing is competitive. Crashes are more common than folks expect. Orly had groaned his way through his share of injuries. Bear had helped Orly climb in and out of a race car because of some debilitating injury more times than he cared to remember. This latest one from Talledega was not really serious, but it was very painful nonetheless. It was one of those nagging injuries that would take a while to heal. Every wrong move zapped an immediate bolt of pain to the nerve endings. Fortunately he had two weeks off to heal a little before climbing back into a race car.

In fact, three other drivers on the circuit were rehabbing, just like Orly. Some guys just seemed prone to this type of injury. But it was Orly's first go-round. He was willing to make whatever modifications it took to not have it happen again.

"Well, I wish you'd get with it, Bear, then we'll patent it and make some money off it. Way things are going we are going to need it. I just came from talking with Harry and we got some serious problems," Orly said.

Bear got up and closed the door to his office and reversed the blinds on the big window so no one could see in. He sat back down, placing both palms on the arms of his desk chair, and sat silently looking at Orly.

Bear was concerned. Harry Hornbrook was the owner of the Speed King Oil Company, which was the major sponsor of the Orly Mann Racing Team. Harry was a good man. He, Orly, and Bear had been friends for many years. He started sponsoring Orly way back when he was running modifieds and sprint cars fifteen years ago. As Orly went up through the ranks, Speed King Oil went with him. Now the company's involvement in Winston Cup ran several million dollars a year. Harry's company also grew with the national attention, and it was now a very successful corporation that produced several automotive-related products. But now Harry was in trouble; he was facing a serious hostile takeover from a major global oil consortium.

Orly explained the details to Bear and then added, "These guys are playing for keeps and they got the cash to back up their move."

"Well, I'm sorry for Harry. Sounds like a serious challenge for his company. I know he came up the hard way and has built that business from nothing. Didn't he start in the Oklahoma oil fields when he was just a kid?" Bear asked.

"Yeah, he sure did. He hit it big time when they pioneered the additive business. That is where most of his profit is right now, but he has other stuff in the development stage. He was very apologetic and said he would do everything possible to uphold his end of the contract, but if he gets bought out, or I should say 'took over,' things could change in a heartbeat." Orly sat up straight and put his elbows on his knees and cupped his chin. "The truth is, Bear, it doesn't look very good. Harry says he just hasn't got the strength. He's no spring chicken you know. He was thinking that maybe he would counter their offer and take the money and run. If he doesn't, they could buy the minority stock in the company and put enough pressure on him to make him quit. He would end up going out to pasture with hardly anything to show for his years of hard work."

"Where are these guys from?"

"Well, as I understand it, they're a mixed group and it's the same old story. They buy a company that has a record of making money by selling a good quality product. Something folks buy because they know it works. They strip the company down to the bare nubbins in regard to people and downgrade the quality of the product. The product still sells for a while on its previous reputation, and during that time they make a lot of money. Then when the sales start dropping they sell the company off. Sometimes someone will come in and reestablish the business, but not often. By then the damage is done and the raiders have got the cream off the top, so to speak. Harry is really stuck. He could fight these guys, but it would take nearly all his assets. There goes the advertising that he needs to sell his products and so goes the business."

"Yeah, and so goes us, being that we are heavily connected with his advertising budget. Everything we got, practically including our underwear, is painted orange and yellow with purple lettering, which ties us in pretty close to Speed King. Whew, Orly, what do you think we ought to do?"

"We won't do anything for right now. Harry has been incredibly loyal to us, so I think we ought to hang in there. Besides, Bear, we're in the middle of the season, which is the worst possible time to try to find a new primary sponsor. We'll just have to play it out and see what happens."

"What about Hildy?" Bear asked.

Orly shifted his weight and looked at Bear, eyebrows lowered.

Bear looked back with an innocent look.

"What about Hildy?" said Orly.

"Well, you and I both know she's just like her old man Harry. She isn't gonna roll over and let this happen to her father's company. She doesn't have that law degree for nothing."

"I don't know about Hildy. Harry and I didn't talk about her. You know she doesn't like racing much anyway and thinks Harry would be better off spending his promotional money in different ways. Probably come up with some idea involving a stuffed animal hugging a tree or something."

"Not likely. If it was a stuffed animal, it would be a lion or tiger or something big—maybe a dragon," responded Bear.

There was more here than met the ear. Bear knew that when he asked the question. He also knew what Orly's answer was going to be. At one time, Orly and Hildy were much more than business associates. In fact, they had been what the gossipmongers call an "item."

It appeared they were on the way to establishing a permanent relationship, but for reasons known only to a few, they abruptly called it quits. Bear more than anybody knew why they had split, but he was helpless to do anything. The separation had been a painful time for Orly, much worse than any racing injury. Bear suspected it was equally painful for Hildy.

Now Orly and Hildy seldom saw each other and when they did, they hardly spoke. In his heart, Bear had hoped there might be just a little glimmer of hope for the relationship. Bear loved Orly, but he knew Orly could be stubborn. Orly was a driven man. That was one of the things that made him one of the best, if not *the* best, stock car drivers in the world. When he wanted to, Orly could narrow his focus so that every ounce of energy was targeted on the task at hand. Bear also knew Orly was haunted by ghosts from the past. It was these ghosts that refused to leave him alone and often tormented his thoughts with guilt and unspeakable pain. But above all, Bear knew that Orly was also incredibly lonely.

Orly was a public figure and could hardly go anywhere without drawing a crowd of autograph seekers and glad-handers. His tall well-built profile was recognized all over the country. He had a public image of being a quiet, confident man—articulate and personable. He was a favorite interview target of the media because he was honest and forthright with his comments and laid things out the way he saw them. He could also back up his comments with his driving ability, and no one was more consistent on the racetrack.

Bear was Orly's greatest fan, but he knew that behind that facade was a man who seldom let people inside his private world.

Bear was his best friend, and his second best friend was Pastor John, the Winston Cup chaplain. John and his wife, Martha, traveled the Winston Cup Series in their new motor home and offered spiritual leadership to the traveling circus that was Winston Cup racing. They led weekly Bible studies for adults and kids. Pastor John always held an early morning chapel service on race day for drivers, teams, and their families. Through the years, Orly and John had become good friends and Bear was glad. John was Orly's spiritual mentor. Sometimes when the black clouds descended, he was also Orly's life raft.

Bear came out of his reverie to listen to Orly.

"At any rate, Bear, that is where we stand. In the meantime, what kind of junk have you got for me to run in the California 500? I'm glad to be done with restrictor-plate racing for a while and get back to horsepower. We going with last year's setup or are we starting fresh? You know the key to running there is being able to get off the corners. It's a two-mile track, and it's still new and can get pretty slick, 'specially if it's hot. The corners are pretty flat. Tell me what you think," said Orly.

Bear scratched his stomach through the buttonhole of his white Orly Mann Team shirt and said, "Well, I been thinking. . . ."

The ensuing conversation lasted an hour as the two friends made decisions that would have important ramifications for the upcoming California 500.

Most teams and drivers enjoyed the West Coast trip to the new race-track, the California Speedway in Fontana. It was just two years old and state of the art. It had been built on the foundation of the old Kaiser Steel Mill site, located forty miles east of Los Angeles, near the base of the San Bernardino Mountains. Corners were banked only 11 degrees, which was a far cry from the 33-degree banking of Talledega. The track was wide and racing could be fierce, as the cars run two and sometimes three abreast. Everything about the place was new and fresh and done with a major Southern California flair. Luxury boxes backing up the pit lane gave a broad panoramic view of the 530-acre facility. The place seated over 100,000 people. They already had plans in the works to add another 15,000 to 20,000 seats. Orly liked the place a lot. It was a racer's track that required the proper mix of handling and horsepower.

"Oh man, he's not going to be happy when he gets back in this car. This is not cool," Doug said to Alphonse as they both looked out the windshield at Paolo standing dejectedly in front of the California High-way Patrolman writing out the citation. It had started innocently enough. Paolo was just cruising down I–5 at the speed limit and doing his best to stay out of the way of the kamikaze truckers on the Frisco to LA run. They were loafing in the right lane, listening to some tunes and debating amongst themselves whether to pull off at Buttonwillow and bag a burger or two, when the Camaro pulled up alongside. There were four guys riding with the windows down and the radio turned up as loud as it would go.

"I think they want to see what you got, Pally," Doug said.

"Yeah, I know. I'm trying to ignore them. I could blow their doors off in a hot minute." Paolo looked out the side window and said, "I'm tempted to give them a run." The truth was Paolo was more than tempted. He wanted to blow these guys off bad and show them just how loud a well-tuned, ported, polished, and balanced 350 could sing. He looked up the interstate, and for once there was no traffic around. It would be easy. He could smoke them off for a mile or two and then slow back down to the limit.

"Hey, Paolo," Alphonse said, "show these guys who they're messing with."

"Yeah. Come on, Pally," Doug chimed.

Paolo looked over to the left and downshifted, then stood on the gas. It was no contest. The Camaro tried to keep up, but the Malibu simply hunkered down and ran away from them. Paolo ran it up to 110 miles per hour, then backed off of the throttle and slowed down to the limit again. The Camaro came screaming by with all four guys waving for Paolo to come on. He just smiled as they flashed by. A half mile later he wasn't smiling at all when he saw the black-and-white CHP car coming up behind him with its flashing lights. His stomach sank. Maybe the cop was chasing the Camaro and would go right on by. It was a small hope that was immediately dashed as the black and white pulled up on his rear bumper. Paolo put on his right blinker and pulled over onto the shoulder.

When he got back into the car, nobody said anything for a while. Finally Doug said, "How bad is it?"

"Well, he gave me a break because he didn't cite me for reckless driving or being involved in a speed contest. He just cited me for excessive speed. Then he hassled me for having a North Carolina driver's license with a car registered in California. Then I told him who I worked for and that all three of us were headed to the races in LA. Told him we were doing the drags for Speed King then heading to Fontana, but he wasn't much impressed. I didn't think he knew anything about racing at all, but when he gave me the ticket he told me that he liked Orly's new colors and paint job and asked me about his shoulder. Then he told me what a nice looking ride I had and how nice the paint looked. He still gave me the ticket though. Man, I can't imagine what this will do to my insurance. I was gonna ask him why he didn't go after the Camaro, but I thought for once I better just keep my mouth shut. Didn't want to make it any worse. There's no justice in this world," Paolo concluded.

"Well, on the other hand, there might be a little, Paolo. Look there," said Alphonse. They waved as they passed the Camaro on the side of the road with yet another CHP writing out a citation.

The rest of the trip down I–5 was uneventful, and they even managed to get through the LA basin without getting tied up in any major traffic jams. An hour later, they hit the hotel a few blocks from the Pomona Fairgrounds and checked in. It was a big, spread-out, typical Southern California place with large parking lots. It was the main base of operations for most of the teams racing at Pomona, but right now virtually everybody was out at the track for the night qualifying sessions. Helen, Orly's publicist, had made all the arrangements for them, and their passes and parking permits were all set and waiting at the front desk.

As Paolo signed in, the desk clerk handed him a package and said, "Here, this came for you yesterday."

"Yeah, thanks, I was expecting it," Paolo said. They threw their stuff in the room and Paolo threw the package at Alphonse. "Orly said that for this week you are an official member of the team and he wanted you to wear the same stuff as me and Doug all weekend and next weekend too at Fontana. Good advertising and all that."

"Cool," Alphonse said.

"Hey, guys, whatta you say we just wear the jackets tonight? We can do the whole thing tomorrow. Let's meet the other team first before we get too carried away," Doug said, pulling his orange-and-yellow team jacket from his travel bag. "I'm thinking we might look a little . . . uh, you know, if we go all decked out . . . you know what I mean."

"No, Doug, we don't know what you mean," Paolo said with an innocent look. "You mean you don't want to try to impress Miss 300-mile-an-hour Loren Janine?"

Doug replied by picking a pillow off the bed and heaving it at Paolo.

"Wow! Do those things really go 300 miles an hour?" Alphonse asked. "How do they do that in just a quarter mile?"

"Yeah, they do," Paolo said. "That and some change, and the funny cars are right up there with them, even though they've got a shorter wheel base. They get it on, Alphonse. You've never seen such acceleration and noise . . . man, they make stock cars sound like nothing. When they light those things off, you can't believe what it sounds like . . . in fact, you can even feel the sound in your gut. Come on, you guys, let's get out of here. I'm getting excited just thinking about it. If we hurry, we won't miss much of qualifying. These guys are awesome in the dark. You never saw so much flame in your life. Those headers are horkin' gouts of fire like flame throwers that light up the sky, and when you get two of them side by side . . . man, is it purely awesome." Paolo waved his arms to emphasize his point.

A few minutes later they were walking quickly across the hotel parking lot when Alphonse nearly tripped on his shoelace. He stopped to tie it. As he kneeled down on one knee, a young man sidled over to him from between two parked cars. Alphonse looked up and then looked down again, his brows furrowed in anger. He knew what was coming.

Alphonse muttered a silent prayer. *Please, Lord, help me keep my cool here. You know, Lord, I get real angry.*

The young man kneeled down next to him with his hands in the pockets of the black stadium coat he was wearing. The night was warm, but this guy looked like he was ready for winter in Chicago. It was hard to tell, but he could have been Hispanic or African-American or maybe even Asian. He looked about fifteen or sixteen, but that was also hard to tell; he really could have been anything from fourteen to twenty. He was wearing a black stocking cap pulled low on his head and wore a flannel shirt that buttoned all the way to the collar, giving him a distinct familiar look.

"Hey, bro, you want to buy some blow, man? I got some good stuff. Can slip you a dime bag just like that and no one will see, man. Just slip me the money and I'll pass it to you, man. It's real good stuff. You won't get none better, my man." His low voice didn't carry any farther than the next parked car.

Alphonse said nothing and just kept tying his shoe. Finally, when he was finished, he stood up. The young man stood up with him. "Come on, brother, what you say? You can go watch the cars and get mellow at the same time."

Alphonse controlled himself for a minute and then lost it. He reached out with both hands and pushed the young man in the chest, forcing him to fall back a step. "Listen, you punk. I'm not your brother and I am definitely not your 'man.' Just 'cause I'm black doesn't mean I do drugs, punk." Alphonse shoved him again. "I'm not interested in buying any of that junk you're carrying, and if you don't beat feet, I'm going to really lose my cool."

The young man backed up and threw his hands in the air. "Hey, man, be cool. I'm just trying to help you out. I'm just trying to make an honest living. I'm just a poor kid from the hood, man. I didn't mean nothing by it."

Another voice spoke from behind Alphonse. "He didn't mean nothing by it, man."

Alphonse looked over his shoulder to see four or five guys all dressed in the same black coats with flannel shirts buttoned up to the collars and their pants hanging off their hips. Some had skull rags on their heads, and a couple were wearing black stocking caps like the kid in front of Alphonse. Others had their hands in their coat pockets like they might be holding a weapon of some kind.

In ordinary circumstances Alphonse might have been scared, but his anger overrode his fear. He was an inner-city kid and knew all about the projects in Hunters Point in San Francisco and what it was like to grow up in gang-infested areas. He also knew how dangerous it could be to find yourself in a situation with a load of gangbangers carrying knives; a couple of them might even be carrying guns. He also knew what it was like to be hassled by the cops just because you were young and black and what it meant to walk the fine line between values and survival. He had his share of struggles, and were it not for his faith, he could just as easily be hanging with a group like these guys. But the thing that affected him the most was how guys like these made it so difficult for anyone who was trying to play it straight and stay out of trouble. He had seen too many friends succumb to the temptation and go down in flames with drug habits and the resulting sickness that went with the whole bad scene.

Good sense said turn your back and walk away from it, but his anger overcame his good sense. He grabbed the young man in front of him and turned him around and threw him back toward his friends.

"Why don't you punks get out of here. I'm sick of you people and your poison. Your lives are useless and wasted. You know what you punks need? First of all, you need a good butt-kicking and then you need the Lord. That's what you need. You need Jesus as your Master and He'll teach you a little discipline."

This brought an angry response. A couple of the guys brought their hands out of their pockets, and Alphonse thought he saw the glimmer of something metallic in the early evening darkness. Suddenly he was aware of Doug on one side and Paolo on the other, standing shoulder to shoulder with him. Paolo's brow was furrowed in anger and his large bulk added a sense of size and presence to Alphonse.

"Holy cow, Alphonse, what have you got going on here?" Paolo asked out of the corner of his mouth.

"This banger tried to sell me some dope and I'm getting ready to . . ."

About that time a black-and-white police cruiser eased into the parking lot. The young men in black quickly turned on their heels and melted away between the cars. The kid who tried to sell Alphonse drugs looked over his shoulder and pointed to his own chest with his thumb. "Yo, Ricky. That's me, man. Ricky! I'll see you again." Then he was gone between the cars.

The police car pulled up to the three and a lady cop looked them over carefully and asked them if they were okay.

Paolo took the role of spokesman. "Yeah, we're okay. Those guys tried to sell us some dope and my friend here took exception."

"Well, watch yourselves. Those guys are part of a local gang here. They cause nothing but trouble. Call themselves the Pomona Rangers. They have staked out this place as their turf and have been hassling some of the guests. We're trying to keep track of them, but that is hard to do. Watch yourself after dark around here. These guys are trying to take advantage of the race crowd. Don't be afraid to yell for security if you get in a tight spot." About that time her radio crackled and she spoke quickly into the mike. She gave them a nod as she put the car in gear. "You guys be cool and call us if you need help. You'll probably see these guys again. That's their style."

"Yeah, thanks," Paolo said.

After she had gone, Paolo patted Alphonse on the back. "You okay, man? What am I going to do with you? Leave you alone for thirty seconds, and the next thing we know you are ready to take on the Pomona Pomegranates or whatever they're called. Bangers for sure. No doubt about that."

Alphonse was taking a few deep breaths as he got his adrenaline under control. Doug was looking at him with a concerned look.

"What are you looking at?" Alphonse asked with an irritated bark to his voice.

"Hey, be easy. I'm your friend, remember. I was standing beside you, not in front of you, man."

"Yeah, yeah, I'm sorry, Doug. I'm okay. It gets me though. They think just because of who I am and what I look like I do certain things. It gets tiresome. I been dealing with that ever since I could remember. I been approached so many times by dealers it's not even funny."

Doug blinked his eyes and realized that he had forgotten Alphonse was black. He was just Alphonse and he looked like what he looked like, just like Paolo or Alicia or Bear or Orly or anybody else. *It's amazing how race or ethnic origin pales into insignificance when friendship takes hold.*

Paolo threw his arm around Alphonse again and said, "Yeah, I know, Alphonse. There isn't any justice in the world. Hey, man, I got to teach you a better way to share your faith, man. You don't offer to go kick someone's butt and then tell them they need Jesus. Probably not the best way to win them to the kingdom, if you know what I mean." Both Paolo and Doug laughed out loud as they slapped Alphonse on the back again.

"Well, you and I know that is exactly what these guys need. They need the Lord. Then they could stop making it so hard for the rest of us," Alphonse said hotly. "Yeah, I guess it did sound a little odd considering the circumstances." Then he smiled and joined in the laughter.

"Come on, forget it. Let's go watch some wild machines do their thing at three hundred miles per hour," replied Paolo, reaching for his car keys.

He raises the poor from the dust and lifts the needy from the ash heap.

1 Samuel 2:8

"We'll be the brunt of rumors again with my contract being up and Pennzoil's contract being up, but we are hoping the performance we are going to have on the race track will put all that behind us."

Steve Park, Winston Cup driver
car #1 Pennzoil Chevrolet

THEY PILED INTO PAOLO'S CHEVY and a few minutes later pulled into the VIP parking lot at the Pomona County Fairgrounds. Paolo flashed his pass and chose a carefully selected parking spot that would keep the Chevy from getting dinged. Paolo locked the car as they gathered their stuff and quickly joined the crowd headed toward the ticket gates. Their yellow-and-orange Orly Mann Racing Team–Speed King Oil jackets drew people's attention as they walked toward the entrance gates.

A young boy ran up to Paolo and stuck a program with a pen in front of him. "Are you guys part of the Speed King crew?" he asked, trying to catch his breath.

"Well, not this team. We are part of Orly Mann's stock car team. But we will sign your program if you want," Paolo replied.

"Sure! Here, sign it here." The kid pointed to a spot.

Paolo signed it, then passed it to Doug. Doug signed, then gave Alphonse a wink as he handed him the program and pen. Alphonse signed his name, then sheepishly gave it back to the boy.

"Thanks," he yelled over his shoulder as he headed off to get more autographs.

They went through the turnstile, flashed their pit passes, and headed toward the pits. They walked down the line of big semi-trucks similar to the haulers the Winston Cup teams used. With professional interest, Doug and Paolo checked out the activity taking place in the various pit areas. Each hauler had a big awning coming off the top of the trailer section that shaded a roped-off area beside the truck. This was the pit area, and the hauler acted as a mobile shop. The activity seemed frenzied at first glance, but to their trained eyes it was clear that these guys knew what they were doing.

It wasn't long before they spied the familiar yellow-and-orange colors splashed across the side of the Speed King team's hauler. A large crush of people gathered around the roped-off section at the end of the trailer. Just on the inside of the roped-off area, a media team from *NHRA Today* was interviewing a slim blonde girl dressed in a thick purple driver's suit. She had slipped the top part of the fireproof suit off her shoulders and tied the arms around her waist. Her long hair was tied up in a scrunchy, her ponytail hanging down over the long-sleeved fireproof shirt she was wearing under the suit. She was animated and vivacious as she responded to the interviewer's questions, and occasionally flashed a brilliant smile, showing perfect white teeth.

The interview was winding down as the three guys worked their way through the crowd and slipped beneath the rope holding a sign that read: Entry by Invitation Only Please.

Loren Janine looked over the interviewer's shoulder and saw the three young men. She said the appropriate things to end the interview. As soon as the camera was shut off, she rushed over to Doug and threw her arms around him, much to the delight of the crowd that was being restrained by the rope.

"Doug, I'm so glad to see you. I've been waiting for you guys to show up." Doug blushed as she disengaged her arms and stood back to get a better look at him. "You look good, guy. How are you?"

Paolo exchanged a knowing grin with Alphonse.

"You look good, too, Loren. How you been?" Doug replied.

Paolo cleared his throat in a theatrical manner.

"Oh, these guys are my friends. This is Paolo and this here is Alphonse."

Loren extended her hand and shook hands with them. Her grip was gentle and her fingers cool to the touch.

Loren always drew a crowd around the Speed King Oil Company pit stall. Part of her popularity was because she looked far too feminine to pilot a dragster, yet she had the reputation of being a very serious competitor. She was, as one reporter said, a foxy lady. Several guys in the crowd were whistling and making comments as Doug and Loren stood looking at each other. Suddenly both of them were aware of the people staring at them. Loren took Doug's hand and walked him to the back of the pit area toward the front of the hauler and away from the hundreds of watching eyes.

Alphonse touched Paolo's arm. "Are you telling me this little girl, who don't weigh more than 110 pounds, drives that big monster?" Alphonse motioned to the top-fuel car on jackstands. It was indeed impressive, and the huge engine dominated its profile.

"Yeah, she sure does. She's been driving dragsters for some time now and does a pretty good job."

In the meantime, Paolo stared at the race car with professional curiosity. The strange-looking machine was sitting in the air with all four tires off the ground as the busy crew made the final adjustments to button it up and get it ready for the qualifying session. A short gray-haired man climbed down the steps out of the hauler, carrying a large funnel. He looked over at Paolo through thick glasses and gave him a wave. Then he motioned for Paolo to follow him.

He popped the top off the dragster's fuel tank and motioned for Paolo to pick up the five-gallon plastic fuel can. "Here, pour that in here while I hold the funnel."

Paolo was used to being told what to do by Bear and the rest of the crew back home, so it seemed only natural to him to do exactly as he was instructed.

"Look away when you pour that stuff. Nitro methane fumes can be rough on your nose and eyes."

Paolo did so and gently poured the fuel into the tank, while the old guy held the funnel.

"That's good. We got enough for this run. No sense in carrying the extra weight," he said.

Paolo set the plastic fuel can down as the old man wiped his hands with a rag.

"My name is Brewster, and you must be Pellegrini or Prescott." He extended his hand.

"My name is Paolo Pellegrini, Doc, and that's Doug Prescott over there. This guy here is Alphonse McCarty," Paolo said as he motioned to Alphonse. "Do you mind if I call you Doc? I seen you so many times on TV I feel like I know you."

"Nah, you can call me Doc. Everybody else does," he said.

Doc Brewster was one of the most renowned men in drag racing. He was one of the old-school guys that started with the sport way back in the '50s, when guys were racing Ford Flatheads installed in old airplane wing tanks on airport runways. He also had a reputation for a quick fuse and short temper. He made it plain that he didn't like the media much and suffered fools not at all. He was a public relations person's nightmare. Some of the older competitors said he had toned down in his old age, but it wasn't true. If anything, he was even more short-tempered.

Others wondered why he was still around and why Harry Hornbrook stayed with him. Most thought it was because he knew how to win. Doc might be testy, but he was no dummy. As the sport evolved and changed, so did he. He was a mechanical genius and stayed on the cutting edge of the technological aspects of the game. He had seen the records come and go and was personally one of the first to break the 200-mile-per-hour barrier in an old hemi-powered slingshot dragster. He reluctantly gave up driving a number of years ago when age and arthritis caught up with him. Doc didn't know much other than drag racing. If the truth be known, he didn't want to know much other than drag racing. He had his own team that he could dominate and control, and he was pretty much a threat to win every race he ran. Much like with Orly, Speed King Oil had been with Doc a long time, and he had served them well. Like all racers, he had good times and bad times, but this particular year was working out great.

Doc also had little respect for drivers. Particularly the younger generation. Loren Janine got the opportunity to step into the driver's seat of his car at the beginning of the year when Doc refused to renew the contract of the talented young man driving last year. He had the temerity to ask Doc for more money and Doc fired him. Right now, Loren Janine was hot, and even though Doc had little patience with the media, he knew the value of image. As long as Loren listened to him and won, she would have a ride. If she didn't . . . well somebody else would come along.

Loren Janine was a natural drag racer, with lightning-quick reflexes, and Doc was the perfect team owner to give her a quick car and help her reach her potential as a driver. Drag racing was a unique combination of skill and experience mixed with technological innovation. Doc had a lifetime of experience and he knew the tricks and the secrets that made these big monsters run. Just setting the clutches was a ticklish business, and it took the wisdom and skill of a demolition expert to read track and weather conditions. The big motors gulped huge quantities of air through their superchargers, or blowers as they were called. Humidity changed the density of that air, which in turn changed fuel settings and other important calibrations. Doc provided that wisdom and skill. He was also one of the innovators of the new pneumatic multidisk clutch system that kept the wheels connected to the track to produce speeds of over 300 miles per hour. Used to be that 300 miles per hour was unthinkable. But now it was common and, like always, was due to fresh innovation with technology mixed with sweat and brains. Doc brought the whole package, even though the wrapping might be a little tattered . . . and disagreeable.

Doc looked at the big clock mounted on the side of the hauler by the side door. "Here, Fettuccini, help me pop this cowling on. Don't have time to talk right now. We got to get this thing to the line."

"It's Pelligrini, Doc." But once again, Paolo did as he was told and Alphonse jumped in to help. They popped the zeus fasteners and Paolo reached in his pocket to grab a quarter to give them a half turn to lock them in.

Doc was impressed. "You must be a natural. Most guys would be whining for a screwdriver to lock the fasteners, but it's obvious you had some training."

Paolo didn't reply. He watched Doug talking with Loren, ignoring Doc for the moment. She flashed Doug yet another brilliant smile, patted his shoulder, and turned to disappear into the hauler to get her stuff for the qualifying run. *I've never seen that look on his face before,* thought Paolo.

Doug had his hands in his pockets as he followed Loren with his eyes, then he caught Paolo looking at him and smiled . . . then frowned.

"Don't you say nothing," he mouthed at Paolo.

Paolo shrugged his shoulders in an innocent fashion as if to say, "Who me? Why would you think such a thing?"

The crew dropped the machine off the jack stands while everybody did a quick double check on nuts and bolts and gave the yellow-and-orange body a quick wipe down. The crowd parted as the crew, along with the three newcomers, pushed the car out of the pit area. One of the crewmen motioned for Alphonse to slip into the cockpit.

Alphonse was a little less than average size and as he looked in, he wondered how he was going to fit. He wasn't about to miss this opportunity, though, and carefully threw his leg over and slipped into the car. He wasn't quite sure that was the proper terminology. It was more like he put the car on. He noticed several things right from the get-go, and the first was how long the front end of the thing looked. The chassis seemed ten miles long and the little bitty wheels hanging off the front end looked totally inadequate to support this much body. He sensed the ominous presence of the enormous motor block just inches behind his head. He looked down at the gauges and realized the dash was pretty simple, which made sense. The driver didn't have a lot of time to check stuff in a 4.5-second run. Everything was recorded in a computer box located beneath the cowling anyway. He worked his shoulders back into the seat and once again felt like he was wearing the car. He looked around and suddenly realized there were several hundred people watching him, and a number of them were taking his picture. He smiled while a crewman on a quadrunner pulled up in front of him and another crewman passed a tow strap around a special hook on the front end. He yelled in Alphonse's ear, "Just hold it straight and I'll tell you when to turn the wheel."

That was another realization. There was no steering wheel as such. Just a little set of handles connected to a steering shaft. The handles were open so the driver could wrap his hands through them. The quadrunner gently took off, and Alphonse used all his concentration to keep the machine straight. As soon as it started to move, he felt the frame flex and bounce, and the great big wheels and tires behind him made crunching grinding noises on the asphalt as the crew slowly worked their way through the crowd to the starting grid.

Doc Brewster and Loren walked along behind. Paolo could see that Doc was talking into her ear and she was listening intently as he spoke. A man approached with a program for an autograph, but Doc waved him away with an abrupt motion. The entourage rounded the corner, with Alphonse doing his best to get the car turned. It was settling into full darkness as they stopped the car and joined the line of similar cars in the prestage area. Alphonse unclamped his hands from the steering handles and gingerly climbed out of the car to the safety of the asphalt.

There were over twenty top fuelers in line waiting to run. The first two strange-looking machines sat mute in the staging area, with their elongated snouts pointing to the finish line a short quarter mile away. They were ungainly in appearance. They resembled spindly radio towers laying on their sides, with a thin coating of brightly painted sheet metal covering a tubular interior. They were supported by two tiny bicycle wheels in the front and two enormous wide tires in the rear, which made them look unbalanced. Just in front of the two rear tires sat the chrome-and-black engine of monumental dimensions. It looked out of proportion as it perched on the spindly chassis. It had four short deadly looking exhaust pipes curving out of each side, which swooped in sharp arcs before pointing straight into the air. *Wow! Look at those killer headers,* thought Paolo. They were immense and looked like six-inch sewer pipes that belong in a ditch rather than bolted to the gargantuan motors. Some said these engines made over 6000 horsepower, but no one knew for certain because there was no dyno capable of measuring what they produced. As Paolo watched Alphonse steer the car, he realized that the pilot of this land-rocket sat in a small cocoon, just in front of the power plant, with the crankshaft pulleys and blower belts scant inches from the back of his helmeted head. That was a lot of potentially lethal horsepower looking down the driver's neck. He or she, as there were a number of top fuelers driven by women, was strapped into a form-fitting seat and surrounded by a series of molly steel tubes that formed a bulletproof safety enclosure. The tubing looked slightly bigger even than what they used in the Winston Cup cars, and that was strong stuff. Paolo glanced at Loren still in deep conversation with Doc. She looked pretty tiny compared to the engine and huge tires. As Paolo studied the car, he looked up at the immense wing sticking in the air over the rear of the chassis. It looked strong enough to give lift to a Boeing 747. It was not designed to lift, however, but was instead inverted and designed to keep the back wheels pushed firmly into the pavement as the car rocketed down the quarter-mile concrete strip. Paolo whistled as he calculated the amount of downforce the thing must generate at top speeds.

It was a wonder that the tires didn't cut grooves in the concrete at the fast end of the track. But the truth was that power was useless if you couldn't translate it into grip. Otherwise it just produced wheel spin and a lot of burnt rubber and tire smoke.

For the moment the monsters were caged. The crowd of several thousand people murmured in excited expectation and restless agitation as they waited for the show to begin. In just a few minutes qualifying would start for Sunday's final. The top-fuelers were getting set to perform their particular brand of heart-stopping excitement. Every competitor had three chances to qualify. The final sixteen fastest cars would begin eliminations on Sunday morning. There would be eight races with eight winners. Then there would be four races with four winners. Then two races with two winners and then the final race between the two survivors Sunday afternoon.

Drag racing is simple. When the light turns green, go as fast as you can for a quarter mile and get to the finish before the other guy. The winners go on . . . the losers go back in the haulers and head for the next race.

42

Paolo stood at the back of the staging area with Doug and Alphonse, watching everything with his hands in his jacket pockets. It was cooling down some. This was good because cooler air made the engines run better, and better running engines made more horsepower. Horsepower, when it was distributed correctly, equaled speed . . . and a lot of it. One of the Speed King crewmembers threw each of them a set of ear protectors as they impatiently waited with the rest of the crowd. Paolo sort of knew what was coming, and his stomach churned in excitement as he looked at Doug and Alphonse with a large nervous grin. Paolo caught Doug glancing anxiously over his shoulder to look at Loren as she put on her helmet. Even from here, he could see her hands were shaking a little as Doc helped her fasten the chin strap.

Over to Paolo's right, the NHRA starter stood silently, contemplating his fingernails in nonchalant indifference in front of the "Christmas Tree." "Guess he's waiting the go-ahead," Paolo said. "Someone up there," he pointed to the tall press building that faced the starting line, "will give him the signal to get this show on the road."

The "Christmas Tree," slang expression for the light tower that split the two starting lines, would be used to unleash these guided missiles on their incredible journey down the quarter-mile drag strip. It was the starter's job to push the button that began the sequence of lights. As Paolo watched, the starter pressed one hand against the earphone on his head. He nodded to no one in particular and looked over at the two crews surrounding the first awkward-looking machines and gave them the "start 'em up" sign. An audible sigh rose from the crowd, and the murmur of excitement erupted into cheers and exclamations of anticipation.

Both teams jumped to the task at hand as each member took his place around the cars. The portable starters were slammed up against the back of the enormous engines and electrical power was applied. Begrudgingly, the huge crankshafts began to turn. Slowly at first. The two drivers sat hunched and gripped the small steering handles in nervous anticipation. Switches were thrown and magnetos began to generate voltage that would ignite the nitro methane fuel. To help the process, another crewman squirted raw fuel into the intake of the blower as the motor began to whine in protest as it turned faster revolutions. The starter ground away with a high pitched growl as it labored to bring life to the engine. Then suddenly the universe erupted in a bellow as the engine caught and began to run on its own. It idled slowly, belching flame from each exhaust header into the darkness as each of the eight cylinders fired.

The ground literally shook beneath the feet of those standing around the cars. The noise of the first car drowned out the sound of the crowd. It overwhelmed all sound except its own throbbing pulse. For this moment of time, it was the focal point of the universe and did not ask, but literally demanded everyone's attention. A few seconds later the second engine caught and the noise level was intensified and the universe expanded. Huge gouts of flame shot out of the short header pipes, and the air became wavy with the thick nitro fumes as the drivers racked the throttles clearing the plugs. Anyone within fifteen feet of both cars immediately felt their eyes burn and their noses begin to run as the volatile exhaust fumes filled the air with unspent fuel.

Despite knowing what to expect, all three young men jumped when the first motor caught. They were close enough to feel the throbbing exhaust in their chests and stomachs as the cars warmed up. The crews made a couple of last minute adjustments and stepped away from the cars. Suddenly, without warning it seemed, both cars erupted in a howling cloud of smoke as the drivers warmed the tires in the water box. The low-slung fat tires suddenly changed shape as the centrifugal force elongated and narrowed their form. They were designed to do this. At low speed they looked like fat black wrinkled marshmallows, but when the driver stepped on the throttle they grew in height, which gave them better contact with the pavement. The tires spun, burning rubber in friction, then caught traction and continued to burn fifty yards down the track as the cars trailed an acrid cloud of thick smoke. This procedure was called a "burnout." The whole purpose was to bring the tire temperature up to the point that the immense rolls of rubber would turn sticky to grab a better purchase on the racing surface. It also brought up the temperature of the crowd as nearly everyone jumped to their feet. The smoke rolled across the starting line in a blue haze, bathing the lower rows of the grandstands in the smell of hot rubber and fuel. It was a unique sight and smell. Drag racing has a dramatic beginning like no other motorsport. The crowd was yelling and pounding each other on the back in excited anticipation.

As soon as the burnout ended, both crews leaped into action in preset motion. The cars were shifted into reverse. The drivers backed them up, with directions from a crewmember in front of the spindly front tires, who took his direction from another man in the back. They were careful to back the cars exactly into the black strips of rubber laid down on the starting line. The crew chiefs made a final adjustment to the motors, switching them from a burnout mode to a full-race, power-down, setup. They then gave their drivers a pat on the helmet and hurried back out of harm's way.

The starter, who now was anything but nonchalant, held the starting box in his hand. First one car then the other carefully inched forward as the drivers worked the handheld braking levers. The motors idled with a lazy crackling thunder. The top staging light blinked on one side and then the other as the cars broke the invisible electronic beams. Both drivers waited what seemed like an eternity and then crept forward once again, easing into the starting box. Both bottom staging lights blinked on at almost the same time. Both cars were staged and completely in the starting box. Every eye focused on the Christmas Tree. The starter, holding the button behind his leg so no one could see, quickly pushed it and closed his eyes. Three amber lights flashed like old-time flashbulbs popping and then the green one flashed. The universe disappeared in a cloud of tire smoke and clutch dust, in a wave of sound that reverberated off people and structures alike. The cars leaped off the starting line with power that lifted the front ends as they literally blasted down the track. The drivers sat pressed flat in their seats from the awesome g-force, hanging on for dear life to the small steering handles, with their right foot buried on the floorboards. At half track they were running well over 200 miles per hour, and the drivers were pressed back in their seats even harder. Steering was minimal. The goal was simply to keep the thing as straight as possible. Drift over the center line and you were immediately disqualified. Drift to outside and hit the wall . . . well, that was worse.

The roar of the engines reached an agonizing crescendo and then went suddenly silent with a discrete popping. The drivers blurred across the finish line, trailed by the huge parachutes that acted like brakes to slow them down. When the chutes opened with an audible bang, the drivers were thrust forward in yet another violent motion. The chassis flexed in gentle bounces as the cars lost speed and coasted to a stop. It was over, and for just a brief moment there was silence.

Down at the end of the strip, Paolo saw the win-light flash over the left lane, and the numbers 316.05 miles per hour and 4.74 stood tall for all to read. In the right lane, the numbers 306.03 miles per hour and 4.81 flashed, but it was all for naught. The crew of the car in the right lane stood dejected, with their hands on their hips. It was a good time and might get them in the show, but it wasn't what they had hoped for.

Paolo turned and clapped Doug on the back with a whoop. "Man, Doug, those suckers are just pure awesome. Cool! Did you see that, Alphonse? Man, those things go."

Alphonse was stunned. He was speechless and could only nod his head in reply. He still had his hands over his ear protectors and was blinking the nitro fumes from his eyes. He had thought he was prepared for the noise and the sheer gut-wrenching power of the dragsters, but it had been overpowering and more than a little frightening. That was pure mechanical mayhem unleashed, and that little blonde-headed girl was going to drive something like that. He shook his head in wonder.

After the noise died down, Alphonse said to Paolo. "Wow! I thought I was prepared for the noise and power, but it's overwhelming. What do you know about her . . . little blondie?"

Paolo responded, "She's young, but she isn't a rookie. Doug told me Loren has been driving dragsters since she was fifteen years old. She knows what she's doing. She's been to Frank Hawley's school twice and has driven alcohol fuelers for two years, which are almost but not quite as fast as top fuel cars. She's been pretty successful and knows what it takes to go fast and win. No one on the circuit treats her lightly. In fact, everybody races her real hard. She has quick reflexes and Doc's mechanical skill makes the Speed King car a challenge to anybody. You know, Alphonse . . . on any given Sunday, anybody can beat anybody and all that stuff. Like I said, they're having a pretty good year. The time was when the older guys would give a woman driver a bad time but not anymore. 'Course, Doc is one of the older guys, if you know what I mean."

"Well, what makes a winner in drag racing? Seems like all you have to do is hang on," Alphonse said.

"No, there is a lot more to it than what meets the eye. It's not so simple. The key to winning a drag race is reaction time and knowing how to drive the car. Loren can do both. See the Christmas Tree there?" Paolo said as he pointed to the light stand. "It takes four-tenths of a second for the car to leave the starting line if it starts exactly the instant the Christmas Tree flashes the green light. Four-tenths of a second is the absolute dead-solid perfect reaction time because it is the time it takes the car to react mechanically to the light. You know the time it takes the fuel to be turned into power and the slack to come out of the clutch and the tires to catch hold? Four-tenths of a second."

"Four-tenths of a second doesn't seem like much," said Alphonse.

"Yeah, I know, but if a driver is slow reacting to the light, he adds his own reaction time on top of that four-tenths of a second, which can cost him the race. If you are sitting there and the guy next to you cuts a .45 reaction time and you cut a .48, he already has a head start on you. You could even run a faster top speed and still get beat, because he got to the starting line ahead of you because he left before you did. These cars are so close in horsepower and speed, reaction time is really critical," said Paolo.

"So Loren must be quick, right?" Alphonse asked.

"Loren is bottled lightning, and that's why Doc has her in the car. Believe me, from what I know about Doc, if she slows down any she'll lose her ride in a hot minute. You see, that elapsed time of the run, or in the slang of the sport, the ET, is really what wins or loses the race. Like I said, Alphonse, a driver could be faster than the guy he is racing and run a higher top speed but lose the race because he was late leaving the line.

"Oh yeah, I forgot to mention, if a driver leaves too early, a red light comes on and that means you are instantly disqualified and lose, no matter what kind of time you run. The light goes green in both lanes at exactly the same instant. Leave too early and bingo . . . red light . . . you're done."

Alphonse nodded his head. He was beginning to understand that there was a lot more to this sport than what there seemed to be. He watched as Doc bent over the cockpit to tighten Loren's belts.

Loren was locked in the cockpit. She was so nervous that she had tears in the corners of her eyes, but she ignored them. Besides, nobody could see them through the visor of the helmet and the confines of the flame-arrester mask she was wearing. *I used to love this sport and everything about it. I liked being the center of attention and the money is pretty good, even though I haven't seen much yet.*

Doc gave her the best equipment and she gave it the best ride she possibly could. She always listened carefully to everything he said and did exactly as he told her. That was the main reason she was driving for him and she knew it. He'd forgotten more than most crew chiefs knew.

But she was scared. She was afraid of the car and the speed. It was just too terrifying now. It used to be fun and was the biggest rush you could ask for . . . but not anymore. Now the fear seemed to permeate her life. She was scared of nearly everything and her anxiety made her even more anxious. Lately the fear had become more than she could handle—sometimes the pills helped, but she was having to take more of them and she was afraid of getting hooked. There was a little voice inside saying she was already hooked, whether she wanted to admit it or not. Doc and the crew usually stayed in a couple of motor homes parked at the track instead of hassling with a hotel room. It made their jobs easier and gave them more prep time on the car. She was a girl and couldn't stay with the guys, so she usually stayed in a nearby motel or hotel in a room by herself. Most of the time she was alone and it was getting to be more than she could handle. It seemed the weight of the world was leaning on her thin shoulders. Doc was good, but he was tough, and in truth she was afraid of him. *I have to perform. I can't let Doc down and I can't let the crew down. I can't let my fans down either.*

She felt a sudden almost uncontrollable surge of bile rise up the back of her throat and immediately swallowed it down. The waiting was the worst, it seemed. She wrapped her arms around her body in the cockpit and cupped her elbows with her thickly gloved hands.

Two by two the fuelers blew holes in the night air, until it was time for the Speed King car to take its turn. The guys pushed the car into the staging area and at the starter's command, slammed the gear drive of the starter motor against the crankshaft of the big block power plant.

The engine complained with cranky growling, like they all do, and then exploded into life with an angry rumble. The crew gave a collective, if inaudible, sigh of relief as the engine caught, and immediately began checking for leaks. These big motors could be balky, unpredictable, and sometimes just plain obstinate. Everything about them was stressed to the max, and sometimes just getting them to fire up was a major hurdle. Loren stared down the track, then looked up at Doc as he put his head in the cockpit to check the gauges. He nodded his head and patted the top of her helmet. She gritted her teeth behind the flameproof protection of her helmet and performed the burnout in the usual fashion. She brought the car to a stop and waited to be guided back to the starting line. One of the crewmen ran by her and stood in front of the car with his arm out. She reached down between her legs and lifted the reverse lever and guided the car backwards at a slow idle under his direction. Doc was waiting for her at the starting line.

Doc reached down into the depths of the motor and switched the computer from a burnout mode to full race. He looked the engine over carefully, then moved up to the cockpit and checked the gauges again. Then he looked into Loren's eyes through the visor of her full-face helmet. She blinked several times, knowing that he couldn't see much through her flameproof mask. He checked her belts and studied her for a minute, then he gave her a quick thumbs-up and stepped back out of the way. She tried to empty her mind of everything except the Christmas Tree, but beneath her mask her jaw was trembling.

She crept the car up to the starting box until the top light blinked on. She tried her best again to clear her mind and moaned a quiet prayer for protection. She wasn't sure who she was praying to, but right now it didn't matter. She was the most frightened she had ever been in her whole life. The adrenaline was shooting through her veins like a big wave rolling in on the north shore of Maui, threatening to engulf her and throw her down on the sharp coral. She moaned out loud inside her helmet. *Nobody could hear even if they cared,* she thought. She willed herself to concentrate. If she didn't she could easily make a mistake that could kill her. She physically squeezed the fear to the back of her throat and remembered to unclench her jaw. The vibration of the car at speed could cause her to chip her teeth.

Finally the Christmas Tree became her total focus. She inched the car forward until the lower staging light blinked on. She brought the throttle up, holding the brake lever in her left hand. The lights went amber, and then the bottom one went green. By the time the green was showing, Loren was gone in a split-second reflex. A half a thousandth too soon and she would have red-lighted, which would have meant an expletive-filled, finger-pointing harangue from Doc. She had to be dead solid perfect, and indeed she was. She slammed back in the seat as the clutch hooked up and the front end of the car lifted slightly. It rolled in on itself like a large bicep as the big tires in the rear expanded with centrifugal force and gripped the pavement. As the chassis flexed and began to unwind it forced the wheels down, making contact with the pavement even more solid. Small bits of rubber flamed off the tires in blue smoke. At the hundred-foot mark, the car was in full song with eight feet of pure blue-orange flame shooting from each of the exhaust headers into the night sky.

The world went into slow motion for Loren. She could tell immediately that the car was hooked up and that this was going to be some run. The engine continued to scream as the sophisticated five-disc clutch system engaged plate by plate, transferring more power to the wheels.

Loren saw the finish line sucking her to itself like some huge vortex in a science fiction movie. Then, when the car was at the peak of the run, at top acceleration and maximum stress, the blower belt kicked off as the crankshaft broke and blew the side of the engine block out in a tremendous ball of flame and debris. The explosion instantly shredded the right rear tire and the car slewed sideways in a sickening lurch just the other side of the timing lights. Loren tried to pop the chutes, but they had already opened of their own volition, slamming her forward in her belts. She immediately took her hands off the steering grips, knowing that it would be useless to try to steer this out-of-control monster. She hunkered down as low as possible in her seat and held on—waiting in sheer breathless terror for the car to stop. As the tire shredded, the chutes kept it upright and semi-straight as it slid down the shut-off lane in a shower of flame and sparks. At one point it tipped up, and Loren screamed in fright, thinking it was going over, but the drag of the chutes brought it back down and it gently turned sideways across both lanes and then came to rest against the wall. Fortunately, the car in the other lane had engine problems off the line and was well behind the Speed King car when it blew. The NHRA Safety Safari crash truck was already in motion before the car came to rest.

At least it stayed upright, thought Loren, as she fought to catch her breath. As soon as the car stopped, she could smell the hot oil and literally tasted it in her mouth. She did a quick mental check of her physical attributes and decided she was okay. She popped her belts and started climbing out of the car. She stood up in the seat and then collapsed into the arms of the first safety worker to reach the car. Her tears wet the inside of her flameproof mask as she tried to get her breathing under control.

Doc watched the car disintegrate at the end of the strip with a tight look on his face. He waited for it to stop and then saw the numbers flash up on the tower at the end of the track. He knew it was a good run, but it was better than he hoped when he saw 328 miles per hour and an elapsed time of 4.59. He also knew that the power plant would probably self-destruct. His tune-up on the motor had taken it beyond the dangerous to the extreme level of performance. He had put all his eggs in one basket for a kamikaze, go-for-broke run that would either put them on the pole with the fastest qualifying time or send them up in a ball of flame and smoke. Somehow he had managed to accomplish both. He smiled to himself. *That was a good run . . . but boy, what a mess.* He was already thinking of who he might get to drive if Loren was hurt. Then he turned and walked over to the van, joining the rest of the team to make the run to the end of the strip to assess the damage.

And we know that in all things God works for the good of those who love him, who have been called according to his purpose.

Romans 8:28

"Talk is cheap . . . we're committed to working together. We're going to win together and we're going to lose together, but we're going to be together."

Rick Hendrick, owner of three Winston Cup teams,
including drivers Jeff Gordon and Terry Labonte

NO, DAD, I WON'T ALLOW IT. You slaved your whole life for this company and we can't allow these guys to just walk in and take over. It isn't right. It isn't fair and there is nothing that says we have to do this." Hildy was walking back and forth across the carpet of the big paneled office of Harry Hornbrook, owner and major stockholder—at least for the moment—of the Speed King Oil Company.

It was an impressive office with beautiful paneling on three sides and a deep pile carpet that blended nicely with the bookshelves and personal photographs decorating the walls. She stopped briefly in front of the two oil paintings on the wall across from the massive desk. One was a picture of a top fuel dragster in full song blazing down the strip. The Speed King Oil Company logo stood out prominently on the side and top of the elongated body. The other picture was of a Winston Cup stock car painted in the company colors of yellow and orange with deep purple lettering. The Speed King Oil Company logo was in plain view on the hood, and there was no doubt that this was a Speed King car. One could also make out the logos for the Orly Mann Racing Team, as well as the Thunderfoot Ballet Company. Hildy stood in front of the pictures for a moment and then snorted and continued her pacing back and forth. The drapes were open and the sunshine streamed in from outside—a glorious California day. The office looked like it belonged to the powerful head of a large company that was doing well in sales and promotion and had nothing but happy trails ahead of it.

Its owner and major stockholder did not look anything like the powerful head of a successful company. Harry sat behind the beautiful mahogany desk in his overstuffed leather swivel chair and contemplated his daughter and only child as she paced back and forth with quick deliberate steps. He looked tired, old, and unhealthy. His skin had a sallow, yellowish look and his tailor-made dark blue suit looked a trifle too large on him. Even his starched white shirt looked one size too big. His eyes were dim behind the bifocals, and he sat at an awkward angle in the imposing chair that seemed to dwarf him. He wasn't really listening to Hildy's words. He had heard them all before, and that wasn't why he had asked her to meet with him. He was watching her and wondering how he was going to give her the news that he had received yesterday. It wasn't good news. But to be truthful, he really wasn't very surprised when he heard it. It was what he had been expecting. Now he must make a decision—one of the most important decisions he had ever made in his life. He watched as she walked back and forth across the office yet again.

She was beautiful but not in the classic sense. She was a big woman with dark black shoulder-length hair and piercing hazel eyes. She was just over six feet tall with an athletic build, but moved around the room with a fluid grace. Harry knew from a lifetime of experience that she was strong physically, and also knew she could be tenacious as a bulldog. When she made up her mind to do something, she refused to acknowledge the word "quit." She was a lawyer and an exceptionally good one. She had heard all the lawyer jokes, laughed politely, and then went about her business in a way that gave credit to the profession. She worked mostly with the underprivileged and downtrodden and did a large amount of pro bono work out of a modest office in downtown San Diego.

She worked independently and sometimes handled special cases for other firms. She spoke fluent Spanish, and it wasn't unusual for her to work fourteen- to sixteen-hour days on some situation that invariably involved the violated rights of an immigrant. She was a strong advocate for victims' rights and woe unto him who persecuted the helpless or the disenfranchised. Once she locked her teeth into a case, she was ruthless. Harry was secretly proud of her tenacious attitude and it was this quality of her personality that he needed. *She has always had a strong sense of justice,* thought Harry.

When she was barely four years old, the family dog was killed by a hit-and-run driver in the street in front of the sprawling house in the Claremont Hills. She had asked her father if it was a law that animals had to die. He had replied that it was and that everything that was alive ultimately died. She pondered that thought in her child brain for a while and then responded with the firm statement that somebody ought to change it and when she grew up she would.

Perhaps it's her eyes that keep her from having a relationship with a man, he thought. *She can be downright intimidating and sometimes as direct as a Mack truck.* She was thirty-two and had never been married. In love twice that he knew about, although she didn't talk much about her personal life. Occasionally she brought a boyfriend by to meet him, but as the years went by that seemed less common. She was named after his wife, Hildegard, who died when Hildy was nineteen years old and a freshman at Stanford. It had been hard for Harry to lose his wife of thirty-five years, but it had been exceedingly difficult for Hildy to lose her mother. Hilda was the stabilizing influence in both their lives. She also was the ever-present referee between them, because they often clashed. Hildy was opinionated and vocal about how she felt.

Through her teens, she bordered on the edge of disrespect and was constantly on him about environmental issues and how his company, Speed King Oil, impacted the earth. There was a period in her early twenties in which they barely talked, and when they did it usually resulted in a shouting match. It was a very tough time of adjustment for both of them. It seemed just when they needed each other the most, they beat each other up. Perhaps it had a lot to do with the way both of them handled Hilda's death. *Lord, I sure miss her,* he thought.

But now the relationship between himself and Hildy had warmed somewhat. They were older and what seemed so almighty important before was now less consequential.

"I don't know why I'm talking to you, Dad; you aren't even listening to me." She stopped and faced him across the desk with her hands on her hips.

"I am too listening to you, daughter. I've heard everything you've said and I couldn't agree more." He gave her a weak smile and a wave of his hand, as if to confirm the honesty of his words.

Hildy studied him closely and realized that since she had come into his office, she had really not stopped to look at him. She'd driven up from San Diego this morning to see him at his request. She knew what was going on with the takeover attempt. She knew who wanted the company and why they wanted it. She also knew how much Speed King Oil meant to him. There were over four hundred employees working in this plant just out the window, and several hundred more salesmen and suppliers scattered across the country relied upon Speed King for a living. Her father was not only an astute businessman, but he was fair and honest. This whole takeover thing was incredibly unfair and it upset her sense of justice. She continued to look at him without speaking, and the realization took hold that he did not look well. In his prime, he had been a strong man with thick powerful shoulders and strong hands. Now he was slumped and thin, his hands gnarled and misshapen. Her brow furrowed as she studied him. He had aged even more since she had last seen him and that was just a month ago.

"Are you all right, Dad?" she asked.

"No, Hildy, I'm not," he said as he looked up at her from the chair. "That's why I asked you to come up. You are all I have in the way of family and we need to talk." He had been waiting for her to wind down so he could have a turn to speak.

"I have been under treatment for prostate cancer for the past few years. Now it has the best of me and has spread to my bones. I have kept it from you until now because I didn't want you to worry. The doctors told me yesterday that there really isn't much more they can do except keep me comfortable. Whatever that means."

As he spoke, the air seemed to go out of Hildy and she sought refuge in one of the overstuffed chairs in front of the desk. Tears started to well up in the corners of her eyes.

"Now, don't say anything just yet. Let me finish. This isn't any easier for me than it is for you. I don't know how much time I have left. It could be weeks or it could be months. Doctors don't give you a time frame, you know, despite what some folks might think. At any rate, I don't have much strength left. Here is my dilemma. This takeover bid couldn't have come at a better, or perhaps I should say a worse, time. If I sell the company, I will be able to leave you a very substantial inheritance, and you can pursue your just causes through the court systems, unencumbered by any financial burden. As a matter of fact, you would probably have an estate that will allow you to support several benevolent organizations. You know that because you helped me set it all up." Harry paused for breath.

"As Chairman of the Board of Directors, I have discussed our options with the board, and they have agreed to abide by whatever decision I make. One possible option is this: I could turn over operation of the company to you, and you could take over as CEO and we might fight these guys. I'm not sure what you want or what I should do." Harry paused and pulled a handkerchief from his pocket and blew his nose. "You have the moxie to take these guys on and you certainly have the energy . . . but I'm not sure where you are and if this would be what you want. I know that you have your own life and career, of course. It would mean you might have to put other things on hold for a while, but it would mean a great deal to the employees and those that rely on making a living from Speed King. You know this business, you grew up with it."

Hildy stared at him while she internalized his words. *He has a terminal illness and is dying. Hang the company! What does it matter at this moment?* He was vitally interested in the welfare of the company and his employees. He was also interested in her welfare, yet how like him to give her this news across the expanse of his desk. It was the story of her life. Bitterness burned the back of her throat. She was a very little girl when she first realized that the priority of the company took precedent over her and Mom. He was right, of course. She knew a great deal about Speed King. She learned at a very early age that if she was going to have any kind of relationship with her father it would have to include his business.

Through the years she had spent a lot of time in this office. Both she and Mom knew that Harry was happiest when he was here in this room that looked out over the manufacturing plant. Perhaps that is why she and Mom had been so close and it had been so difficult to deal with him. Now he was dying, but still worried about the company. Harry finished wiping his nose and started to speak once again.

"Dad, stop," she said as she got up from her chair and walked around the desk. She pulled his leather swivel chair around until he was facing her and then she dropped to her knees, put her arms around his thin shoulders, and buried her face in his chest. He stroked her beautiful black hair as she sobbed and hugged him. Tears made furrows down his wrinkled cheeks as he patted her strong shoulder.

The crew sprinted for the van before the Speed King drag racer had even stopped moving. Doug threw himself through the side door, his stomach sick with fear for Loren, as Doc started the van and slammed it into gear. He drove down the access road to the end of the track, with the crowd waving them on along the way. As they slid to a stop, the Safety Safari was putting out the last of the fire. Loren was sitting on the pit wall with two medical workers hovering over her; she looked shaken but unhurt. Her helmet and driver's suit were black with soot, but to Doug's experienced eye there were no burns evident. *At least she's talking and seems coherent,* he thought. He stayed out of the way until the medical people were done assessing her.

Doc walked over and sat down beside her with his hands on his knees. "You okay?" he said.

"Yeah, Doc, I'm okay. Boy, that thing made a move, didn't it? I don't think it blew up until we crossed the line. I hit the kill switch and thought I pulled the chutes, but I don't know what happened," she said in a small voice. "I don't think I ever had one blow up quite like that before."

"Well, you had a great run that put us as top qualifier so far, but I don't know if we got anything left to race with. Looks to me like the bottom came out of the motor and when it did, it took the tire off. We'll look at it after awhile. The main thing is that we can fix it," Doc said. "You gonna be able to drive?"

"Yeah, I'm okay. Probably be a little sore, but I'm fine," Loren said in a stronger voice. She was looking over Doc's shoulder to the media crew waiting to interview her.

After he was sure Loren was okay, Doc walked back to the car and walked around it twice. He smiled inwardly and said to no one in particular, "That was some run. Didn't leave anything on the table after that one."

About that time, the slide truck showed up and the crew got busy winching the broken car up the ramp. A few minutes later the crowd parted like the Red Sea and the wrecked dragster was unceremoniously dumped beside the hauler. The rope with its accompanying signs was hooked back up, and the crowd pressed in, staring as the crew began to go to work stripping the wreckage.

Alphonse stood looking at the car with his hands in his pockets. He could hardly believe his eyes. Less than thirty minutes ago he had been sitting in the cockpit, and the car had been pristine and together as could be. Now it looked to him like a burned, twisted piece of junk. He stared again at the cockpit and then looked over at Loren. *Must have been quite a ride,* he thought.

He watched her giving yet another quick interview from the front seat of the van, assuring everyone that she was okay and just fine. "Oh yes, I'll be ready for tomorrow's qualifying run."

Just like it's a normal everyday thing to strap yourself into a 300-mile-per-hour kamikaze rocket that has a tendency to self destruct, Alphonse thought. And that she did it with a brilliant smile and a toss of her blonde hair made it even more amazing.

"Yeah, I'll be fine. They'll have the car fixed or go to the backup. Whatever Doc decides. Oh sure, I'll climb back into the car. We're running for the championship and every run counts."

"Do you think the car has any more in it?"

"Well, if it does, I'll do my best to find it." She finished the interview and waited for the camera crew to leave before painfully climbing into the hauler.

Alphonse found himself standing next to Paolo and said, "Pally, are they going to put this thing back together?"

"Yeah, I expect so. Doesn't look like the chassis is bent, though they will have to measure it to be sure. I'm sure they got enough spares. I looked in the engine bay in the hauler, and they got four fresh bullets ready to go. They also have a couple of spare rear ends and all sorts of chassis panels. They even got a spare wing, so I think they have enough parts to fix the thing. Dragsters go through parts like crazy, man. I never saw so many cylinder heads and blower parts. They have cases of pistons and rings and bearings and stuff. They must have about sixteen cases of spark plugs. What an inventory. Must be a million dollars worth of parts in there," Paolo said while shaking his head. "Looks like they are top qualifiers so far tonight. The rest of the qualifying sessions will be run in the heat of the day tomorrow, and the track will be slicker and the air not as good, so the numbers will probably stick. Usually the night qualifying session is the quickest. I imagine they will be working on the thing most of the night. The NHRA doesn't run them out of the pits at night like NASCAR does us."

"Paolo, would you want to drive one of these things?" Alphonse asked in a quiet voice while he pondered the wrecked car.

"Who me? Are you nuts? These things are sideways rocket ships with no brakes. No thanks! It takes a special breed to make these suckers go fast. I'll stick to Cup cars, a full roll cage, and a good brake pedal. Orly says 200 miles per hour is plenty. I can't imagine what it's like at 300 miles per hour. I give Loren all the credit in the world. That little girl has got guts, I tell you. When they light that big motor off and I see those big ole flames coming out of the headers, I get nervous. I know you don't know a lot about motors, Alphonse, but I'm telling you these things are stressed to the max. That is why it is so violent when they come apart. Look at that. See there," Paolo said, pointing to the engine sitting in the car. "The whole bottom of the block is gone and when it went, it went so hard it broke the rear wheel and took the tire clean off the rim. Loren is lucky she didn't get on her head, or slammed into the wall, especially when she was traveling over 300 miles per hour when it happened."

"You got that right," Alphonse agreed.

A few minutes later, Loren limped down the stairs out of the hauler with her clothes changed and her face washed. She was pale and looked a little shaky, but her hair was combed and she was wearing fresh makeup. She looked around for a minute and then saw Doug helping one of the crew download the computer tape from the box on the race car. She was favoring her ankle and limping noticeably as she walked over to him and spoke softly. "Doug, could I ask you a favor?"

"Sure," he replied with a smile.

"Would you drive me back to the hotel? My ankle is starting to swell and I have to get an ice pack on it and then get off it. Everybody here is going to be pretty busy trying to put the car back together and Doc suggested I ask you."

"You bet, Loren. I'd be glad to."

"We have two team vans and Doc said you could use one and then bring it back later."

"Okay, no problem." Doug got the keys and helped Loren get into the van. She was grimacing in pain by the time he got her settled in and the door shut. She slid the seat back and put her ankle up on the dash. He went over to the team cooler and grabbed a plastic bag and filled it with ice. "Here, let me put this on it." He wrapped her ankle in a red shop rag.

She thanked him with a weak smile.

He worked the van through the pits and out onto the boulevard in the darkness of the night. When they were headed in the right direction he looked over at her and saw her face in the oncoming headlights and realized that she was even more pale than before. "Hey! You okay?" he said as he reached over with his right hand and patted her shoulder.

"Yeah, I mean no. I'm just a little shook, that's all." She put her face into her hands and cried quietly into a tissue with her shoulders heaving.

Doug didn't say anything and a few minutes later pulled into the hotel parking lot. He stopped the van and said, "Where's your room . . . or if you want I can get a wheelchair out of the lobby? I'm sure they have one."

"No!" Loren said vehemently. "No! I'm okay. No wheelchairs. Just give me a minute, Doug. My ankle will be okay. Actually, I think I hurt it when I climbed out of the car. I don't think it's all that bad." She giggled a tight little laugh. "That's funny, isn't it? Drive the car on one of the fastest runs ever for our team and then hurt my ankle getting out of the car."

"Come on, Loren. You had a pretty good scare. It's okay to be afraid. Orly says the driver who isn't a little afraid sometimes is crazy and not safe to run with." Doug tried to put his arm around her shoulders. "You were pushing that monster as fast as you could and it came apart. Dragsters do that. You better than anybody should know that. Cry if you want to. I won't tell anybody. Maybe I'll cry with you. I was pretty scared for you myself." Doug tried to joke her out of her mood. It didn't work.

Loren shrugged his arm off, then looked down and spoke into the tissue in her hands. "Yeah, I'm scared and I don't know what to do about it, Doug. When I strapped into the car tonight I could hardly breathe I was so scared. This is a new thing for me. I never used to be afraid of anything. Now I'm afraid almost all the time. I'm afraid to say anything to Doc because he will pull my ride. He doesn't have all that much confidence in me anyway. The only reason I'm driving for him is because it makes good PR. Sometimes I wake up in the middle of the night and I'm shaking because I'm so scared." She pounded the dash with both her fists as she clutched the tissue. Then she turned to Doug and looked at him in the darkness.

"Doug, you can't tell anybody I said that. Okay? Promise me you won't say anything. Promise me." Her voice went up an octave as she repeated the words, "Promise me."

"Why don't you quit? You don't have to drive. You're young. You could do a lot of different stuff. I read somewhere that they want you to do some modeling and things. Driving dragsters is dangerous business."

Loren was still looking intently at Doug as he spoke. When he said the word "quit," she turned her head and looked out the window. "My room is on the back of that wing over there. If you just drive around I can get out. I'm on the ground floor so I'll be okay."

"Hey, don't get mad at me. You could quit, you know. There are plenty of people that would love a chance to sit in one of Doc Brewster's cars. Doc would understand."

"No, Doug, you're wrong. Doc wouldn't understand and neither do you. Now just drive me around to my room. I have to elevate this ankle and get some more ice on it. I have to get back in the car tomorrow."

Doug did as he was told and pulled up in front of the double doors leading to the hallway and her room. As soon as he stopped, Loren had her hand on the door handle and was pushing the door open. Doug leaped out of the van and ran around to her side to help her walk but she waved him off.

"I can do it," she said through clenched teeth.

He went ahead of her and opened the door to the hallway.

"Give me your key and I'll open your room."

"No, Doug. You've done enough. Thanks. I'll see you tomorrow." With that, she limped down the hall and disappeared around the corner.

Doug stood looking after her for a minute and then shrugged his shoulders and got back in the van.

She had just told him something, but he wasn't sure what. She was nice as ice cream when he first got here and really seemed glad to see him. It was as if she was waiting for him to get here so she could talk to him, but now he wasn't more than gum on the carpet. She was right. He really didn't understand . . . but that didn't mean he was done listening.

By the time Doug got back to the racetrack at the fairgrounds complex, the crowd was beginning to thin. It looked like things were winding down for the night. In contrast, the activity in the Speed King pits was still going strong. The crowd in front of the rope had shrunk quite a bit, but there were still a number of gawkers hanging around. The pace wasn't exactly frenzied, but there was a constant flow of motion as the crew went about its business in a professional way. These guys were used to working together and there was little talk and an economy of motion. The dragster was the center of attention, much like a queen bee in a busy hive. Now it was stripped to its bare components, with the wheels and all the suspension components pulled off. The blown motor was out of the car and sitting to the side, with its entrails exposed.

🏁🏁

Doc had just completed his assessment of the damage to the chassis and found it was minimal. There would be no need to go to the backup chassis, which was a relief. They could fix this one and in a few hours the car would be good as new. They were still top qualifier and Doc had already decided that they would skip the Saturday morning session and just run the afternoon session. That session would be the last before the eliminations started on Sunday morning, and they would use it purely as a shakedown run. He was pretty much set on what kind of setup they needed to run on Sunday for the first pass. It would be in the early afternoon. If they got through that run with a win, then they would have to make changes as the track got hotter and slicker. Being the fastest car, they would run against the slowest of the sixteen other cars. No telling who that would be. This sport was so competitive it was hard to be a good prophet. Sometimes a crew might not do well during qualifying and then get things right and blow the doors off you and put you on the trailer . . . or in the hauler. They didn't call them elimination runs for nothing. Whoever won went on and whoever didn't . . . went home.

Everybody including Paolo and Alphonse was busy doing something. Paolo was under the car with Doc checking welds, and Alphonse was busy washing parts on the portable workbench. Doug walked over to give him a hand.

"Well, is she okay?" Alphonse asked with a grin.

"No, she isn't okay, and it isn't like you think. Man, she is a complicated lady I got to tell you, Alphonse. I'm not sure I understand what's going on with her. She was real glad to see me and then all of a sudden she is like . . . mad at me. I just had the sense that she was wrestling with something. Like maybe she wanted to tell me something or get something off her chest, but she wouldn't or maybe couldn't. Man, I don't know," Doug said.

"Well, what did you say to her? You musta said something to set her off, man," Alphonse said as he scrubbed out the inside of a valve cover.

"I can't tell you. I promised I wouldn't tell anybody . . . but I'm worried about her safety. She doesn't seem like she's okay."

"Look, Doug, you can trust me. What did she say?"

"Well, basically she said she was scared, and I told her to quit and she got mad."

Alphonse threw the parts he was washing down on the table. "You racin' people, you're all nuts, I tell you. Doug, you haven't got good sense. You about as dumb as that big guy over there when it comes to girls." Alphonse motioned toward Paolo still laying under the car. He went on, "Of course she's scared. Believe me, just being around these ground-shakers makes me nervous. She's scared, but she's proving herself, Doug. She's a warrior. Don't you get it? She got the fright of her life and discovered that she's mortal, and it scared her. As I understand it, she has been doing this for a while, and now it's catching up to her. Then she asks you to help her, not in so many words, and you tell her to quit. No wonder she got mad at you. If she quits, then she gives in to the fear and she's really in trouble. In her eyes she probably thinks that if she starts to run from her fear, then she won't be able to stop. She probably thinks she'll let everybody down and then what?"

"What should I have told her then, smart guy?" Doug asked.

"Let me ask you a question. How do you deal with your fear? 'Cause you know everybody is afraid of something, be it death or dying or the bully in the schoolyard or being poor or homeless. You know that's a fact," Alphonse said.

"I never thought of it before, but I guess the way to deal with fear is to face it head on and then go for it. But then I'm not driving a race car yet," responded Doug.

"Yeah, you're right. But let me ask you another question. How do you deal with your fear head on? Let me answer it for you. You are a Christian, right?"

"Yeah."

"Jesus says a lot of things about fear. The first thing He promises is that He is with us always. No matter the circumstances. He is here right now. We forget that, at least I do. The second thing He tells us is not to worry, because worry has fear at its base. How does that verse go . . . *Do not worry about tomorrow, for tomorrow will worry about itself. Each day has enough trouble of its own."*

"Yeah, but Alphonse, there is a big difference between worry and fear. Besides, Jesus didn't drive any dragster over 300 miles an hour," Doug said.

"Yup, you're right. He didn't. But He did face down the most powerful people in Jerusalem and then hung on the cross for people's sins. Jesus knows a lot about worry and fear. That's why we can trust Him."

The conversation was suddenly interrupted by the arrival of a pizza delivery vehicle driven by a puzzled young man. The track was closed for the night and now there were very few people milling about.

He rolled down the window. "Is this the Speed King pit?" he asked.

He was greeted with a chorus of affirmation from the whole crew.

"Okay, I think I got your supper." He climbed out and started unloading pizzas.

"All right, boys, time to take a little break," yelled Doc. "Let's eat while we discuss a little strategy."

There was another chorus of affirmation as a workbench was cleared for the food and greasy hands were wiped clean.

I will lead the blind by ways they have not known, along unfamiliar paths I will guide them; I will turn the darkness into light before them and make the rough places smooth. These are the things I will do; I will not forsake them.

Isaiah 42:16

"I'm not sure if something broke or not, but it swapped ends so fast there was nothing I could do about it."

Johnny Benson, Winston Cup driver

IT WAS LATE when the guys climbed into Paolo's Chevy and made the short run back to the hotel. They were tired, just like the rest of the Speed King crew. It was nothing new for Doug and Paolo, but for Alphonse it was a stretch.

"You racin' people work too hard," Alphonse muttered from the backseat. "I want some fame and glory to go with all this hard work. Oh yeah, and some money, too."

Doug and Paolo both laughed. "Fame and glory, yeah that's us, right Doug?" Paolo said.

"Oh yes. That's us," Doug said sarcastically. "Bear always says grease-paint and elbow grease don't mix so good. I guess he means . . . well,

I'm too tired to figure out what he means, except I know racing, no matter what kind, takes a lot of work."

"Money helps, too," Paolo echoed.

Alphonse was oblivious as he dozed in the backseat. Paolo eased the Chevy into the parking lot and chose a spot under a bright streetlight. As the guys got out, he popped the trunk and brought out his car cover.

"Yo, Doug, help me put this on."

Satisfied that the car was covered, they headed into the hotel. Doug said to Paolo as they strode through the lobby, "What time is the photo shoot tomorrow and what are we supposed to be doing?"

"The shoot is in the morning about ten, I think, and don't ask me. Helen set it. They want to take pictures of you and me with the Speed King dragster crew. Guess they want some shots of us with Loren and Doc. Hey, it's not my thing. You know that. Seems like a bunch of hype, but it got us a free week here plus some extra pocket change. And we can go play on Monday. Jimmy won't get here with the hauler until Wednesday night, and they won't open the pits up until Thursday. Bear and Orly and them won't get here until late Thursday afternoon, so we got some time to really play. You know, hit the beach, Disneyland, all that. Alicia is going to fly in on Wednesday. Did you get all that?"

"Yeah sure. Tell me again in the morning, okay?" Doug mumbled as he opened the door to the room and flipped on the lights.

All three of them stood in shocked amazement as they surveyed the room. It was totally and completely trashed. Every piece of clothing had been pulled out of their bags and then cut to ribbons. Even their duffel bags were cut in pieces. Shaving cream was all over everything. The beds had been cut up with a knife and the stuffing pulled out and thrown all over the room. Even gouges had been cut out of the carpet on the floor. Personal belongings were tossed all over the room but nothing was intact. If it was breakable, it had been broken. The room reeked of shaving lotion and shampoo, which had been poured over everything. The only things not destroyed were the three Bibles laying on the top of the dresser. They were untouched and stood out like pearls in the midst of the pigpen that was the rest of the room.

Alphonse rubbed his eyes and said, "I don't believe this. This can't be our room. Tell me this isn't our room, you guys. What is going on here?"

Doug stood speechless as Paolo said, "Yeah, it's our room, and I hate to tell you, but it's our stuff. There are our uniforms over there and they're cut to pieces. You gotta be kidding me! Did you ever see such a mess? I wonder why they didn't tear up the Bibles, too?"

Doug pushed his way past Paolo and Alphonse and strode into the room. He picked up a shirt that was one of his favorites. "Look at this. This thing has been shredded, man. Whoever did this took their time."

All three of them jumped when the voice behind them spoke. "Well, boys, have you got an explanation for us?"

They turned to face two police officers standing in the doorway, flanked by the manager of the hotel.

Bear was an early riser, but 5:30 A.M. was just a little too early. Besides, it was Saturday and it wasn't a race weekend. And he was in his own bed instead of the motor home, which was unusual in itself. He really would have liked to sleep in, maybe to 7:30 A.M. or so. Suffice it to say he was not happy when he answered the shrill summons of the telephone by the bed.

"Hellowhoisthat?" he said into the mouthpiece with a sour voice.

"Hey, Bear, sorry to wake you, but we got a situation here and I'm not sure what to do."

When he heard Paolo's voice and the tone in which he spoke, Bear's eyes flew open and he was instantly awake. This could only mean trouble of some sort. Somebody was hurt or in jail or worse. Being a wise man and also being used to dealing with crisis situations, Bear had sense enough not to interrupt Paolo with useless questions until he finished his story.

"Uh-huh," said Bear into the mouthpiece. "So the room is completely trashed. Everything, except the Bibles. Amazing. They had to know somebody to get in, I bet. They think it was the gang that tried to sell Alphonse drugs? Say, Paolo, what did you do to set these guys off?" Bear scratched his stomach as he listened. "So as I understand it, all you guys have is the clothes on your back, the hotel is booked, and you can't stay in your room. The desk clerk says everything is booked for miles around, on account of it being a race weekend. So whatta you guys gonna do? Did you wake Doc up? Oh, he's sleeping out at the track in a motor home with the crew. The only one at the hotel is Loren. Smart man, he's asleep, while I'm talking on the phone three thousand miles away. No, I know that isn't funny and I'm sorry. I know you don't know Doc very well. All right, let me think for a minute. Give me your number there and I'll call you back in a minute."

Bear hung up the phone and scratched some more as he thought about this situation. He muttered out loud. "Lord, please give a little wisdom as I try to sort out this mess involving some of your sheepish children." He chuckled out loud and repeated the expression, "sheepish children . . . yup, that's them all right."

Then he reached for his address book and looked at the clock on the nightstand. *Oh boy, 5:30 A.M. here means it's 2:30 A.M. there. He is not going to be happy.* Then he dialed the phone. "Oh Hildy. Didn't expect to hear your voice. Henry Erickson here. You know, Bear. Sorry to wake you. How you doing? I hate to do this, but I wonder if I could talk to Harry? I have a little problem out there involving some of our folks."

It was an awake bunch that took the Indian Hills exit off the San Bernardino freeway. Indian Hills Drive took them up into the Claremont Hills as they read Bear's directions to Harry's house. They followed the numbers in the darkness until they came to a gated driveway. Paolo eased the Chevy up next to the code box and stopped.

"Read the numbers Bear gave to us, Doug, and I'll punch them in," said Paolo.

Doug did as he was told and Paolo punched the numbers into the keypad, then they waited. At first it seemed like nothing was going to happen. Then the gate swung open in a slow, majestic fashion.

"Man, this is right out of a movie. This is weird," said Alphonse.

When the gate reached its apex, Paolo rolled the Chevy through, doing his best to keep the exhaust quiet.

"What did Bear say? Didn't he say we're supposed to go to the guest house on the right? They would have the lights on for us and we were to just make ourselves at home?" Paolo asked.

"I don't know, Paolo, you talked to him," said Doug.

Doug was irritable and Paolo could tell he was in no mood to make small talk.

The truth was they were all a little shook. The police had put them through an inquisition, which was surprising considering they were the victims and not the perpetrators. Fortunately for them, the lady officer they had seen earlier in the parking lot after the run-in with Ricky and the gang showed up. She verified their story, and that at least gave them some credibility. Even so, the police questioned them separately and then compared their stories. The hard part was when they made them empty their pockets and patted them down. They even took Paolo's keys and searched the Chevy. It seemed like they had answered question after question until the police were convinced they hadn't trashed their own room.

Then they had to deal with the hotel manager. He was less than sympathetic. Paolo had enough and was on the verge of getting in his face big time. They hadn't done anything. The room was locked and here was their key. It was all their stuff that had been destroyed. What kind of place was this and where was hotel security? The room was on the second floor and somebody must have had a key to get inside and tear the place up. At any rate, they were stuck. It was the middle of the night and they had no place to stay. On top of that, they didn't even have any clean underwear, let alone a razor or toothbrush. Everything was trashed or broken. No rooms were available for the weekend within a thirty-mile radius, so what were they going to do?

They did what they had done in the past. They picked up the phone and called Bear. He would know what to do and he could fix anything, one way or another. That is what Winston Cup crew chiefs did for a living. They made stuff work. So Paolo called him and he fixed it. Now they were creeping up the dark driveway of the owner of the Speed King Oil Company, and they were going to spend the night in his guest house.

The guest house was a two-bedroom cottage facing the swimming pool in the beautifully manicured yard. It, of course, had its own bathroom, hot tub, and fully stocked kitchen. Paolo quietly parked the Chevy in the driveway, and they made their way into the place through the ornate front door. There was a note on the hallway table. It read:

Boys, make yourself at home and use whatever you need. Will see you in the morning. Sleep as long as you like. Bear said he will contact Helen and that they will expedite new uniforms and do the photo shoot on Sunday before the race. She will contact you with the details. Enjoy. Relax.

Harry Hornbrook (Phil. 4:6–7)

"Look at that, Paolo," said Doug as he read the note over Paolo's shoulder. "He even put your favorite Bible verse by his name. You know, the one that says, *Be anxious for nothing, but in everything by prayer and supplication, with thanksgiving, let your requests be known to God; and the peace of God, which surpasses all understanding, will guard your hearts and minds through Christ Jesus.*" Doug was really quoting the verse for his own peace of mind. The room-trashing had unnerved all three of them, but they were reluctant to talk about it.

"Yeah, pretty neat," Paolo replied. "Mr. Hornbrook is a big-time evangelical Christian. He heads a lot of ministries and stuff. The pastor at my home church in San Francisco was telling us about him. He does a lot of work for the Lord."

In the meantime, Alphonse was walking through the place and whistling softly to himself. "Man, this place is all right. Check it out. I'm going to cook in that hot tub, cop me a few zzzz's, and then go for a swim in the morning and pretend like this is how I live all the time."

"Yeah. What are you going to swim in, your underwear?" asked Paolo. "Don't forget man, every bit of our stuff was trashed. Dog, that makes me mad."

"Well, you might as well chill, Pally. Nothing we can do about it tonight," Alphonse replied.

Doug had already stripped down to his shorts and was between the sheets in one of the large double beds, with his eyes closed.

Paolo looked at him and said, "I don't know how that guy does it. He can fall asleep quicker than anyone I've ever seen."

Paolo was wrong. Doug really wasn't asleep. He was thinking about Loren. He was worried about her. Obviously she was hurting. He didn't know what to do for her. He also liked her a lot and his concern was maybe just a little selfish. She was so pretty. She was one of those girls that just had natural beauty and gave the impression that she wasn't aware of it. Doug loved the sound of her voice, the way she tossed her hair, and the little mannerisms she used. Why she drove that dragster was beyond his comprehension. He supposed some guys might be intrigued because she was a driver. Doug was a realist and had been around race cars his whole life. There was no illusion of romance connected to what Loren did. Pure and simple, it was dangerous. Doug closed his eyes in the darkness and prayed for her safety once again. Then he prayed that God might use him to help her. Maybe give him the right words to say or something.

Back at the hotel, Loren laid in bed watching TV but not really seeing it. She'd never felt so trapped in her life as she clenched the covers in her hands. She was in the midst of a full-blown anxiety attack again and her heart was racing madly. It had been building ever since the crash. It was like some animal waiting until dark to emerge, then pouncing on her without warning. She felt short of breath and was so pumped full of adrenaline she felt electric, like sparks would jump from her fingers if she touched something. The more she tried to relax, the more anxious she became, until she thought she might scream. She worked desperately to keep from hyperventilating. If her ankle had allowed it, she would have been up walking around the room or gone for a run.

She hated hotel rooms. They were all the same. So impersonal. So public. *I wonder how many people have stayed here before me?* Her thoughts triggered another wave of anxiety. Finally, when she couldn't stand it any more, she flung the covers back, hobbled across the room, and rummaged through her luggage. She found what she was looking for, popped the lid off the bottle, and shook the pills into her hand. She swallowed them without water and hated herself for giving in to the fear. She had to do something about this. She couldn't go on much longer. Maybe it was time to quit . . . not just the driving, but quit . . . everything. She pounded the pillow in frustration. "I CAN'T DO THIS ANYMORE," she yelled at the mirror as another wave of anxiety washed over her.

She grabbed the pill bottle and shook a couple more into her hand, swallowed them down, then hobbled over to the bathroom sink and turned the cold water tap on full blast. Cupping the water in her hands, she splashed her face, then stood looking at her image in the mirror. The image looking back at her looked a little sullen but mostly scared.

"What's wrong with you? What are you afraid of?" she yelled at the image in the mirror. She cupped another handful of water and then threw it at the mirror, where it ran down like flowing tears. She hobbled back to the bed.

She lit a cigarette and sat in the bed, holding her knees with one arm, wondering who she might call. Last week she tried calling her mom back in North Carolina. What a joke. Some strange guy answered the phone. Some guy she'd never met before. His voice opened her up to all the memories of nights her mother had brought strange men home to the trailer in the mobile home park. Nights that she spent alone in the dark, trying not to hear the drunken activity through the thin walls. Nights in which she pushed her dresser in front of the door to her bedroom to protect herself. Nights when she crawled out the little window of her bedroom to sit huddled in the darkness with a blanket wrapped around her despair and loneliness.

Then when her mom got on the phone she was so drunk she could hardly talk, except to ask Loren to send her some money, slurring her words and telling her, "I love you, honey. When are you coming home?"

What a joke. She had hung up the phone without responding. She would never call again. Never!

There was no one. She thought briefly of Doug. She chided herself for spilling her guts to him. She hoped he wouldn't use it against her. *He is a good-looking guy, and maybe in a different time under different circumstances* . . . she killed the thought. She could trust nobody, especially men. She knew no one she could call. She shivered and then felt the coming numbness as the pills began to work. The pills gave her a way to get a grip on herself. She stubbed out the cigarette and stared into the empty room, waiting for the darkness. For now, the anxiety had crept back into its cave. She didn't know how long she could keep it at bay.

All my longings lie open before you, O Lord; my sighing is not hidden from you.

Psalm 38:9

"I believe where we struggled last year, I think we will excel this year. I'm very very optimistic. I'm not dumb, but I'm pretty optimistic."

Darrell Waltrip, Winston Cup driver

ORLY MANN WAS SITTING on the back deck of his modest house in what used to be a small town but was now a suburb of Charlotte. His deck looked out over a medium-sized lake. It gave him pleasure to bask in the early morning sunshine, watching the fishermen and drinking coffee. Orly was a popular, well-known driver, but he wasn't the only one that lived on this lake. Several drivers made their home here because it was a gated community and offered a degree of security. But the lake was open space, and periodically a boatful of folks would go by and wave at him. In this day of media blitz, it was hard to keep a low profile, but Orly took it in stride. He didn't mind folks waving. It was when they pulled up to his boat dock and, despite the no trespassing signs, got out and asked for his autograph, that it got to be a bit much. A Saturday morning at home was a rare treat. He was enjoying it to the fullest as he stretched in the sunshine. *Boy, I think the shoulder is finally beginning to heal up.* But then he changed his mind as he used his right hand to pour another cup of coffee. It was still pretty sore.

The Winston Cup schedule kept him moving. In truth, he spent more time living in his motor home than he did here at the house. Then when he wasn't racing somewhere he was making sponsor appearances for Speed King. *Speaking of Speed King,* he idly wondered, *how is Harry doing?* Then his thoughts turned to Hildy, and he felt a pang of sadness. *If there ever is another woman I can fall in love with . . . but then maybe I am in love with her . . . who knows.* The truth was she wasn't in love with him. Their relationship had started slow and then picked up speed until they spent every moment together they could, considering both their schedules . . . and then it ended. Just that quick—it was over. Orly knew why. So did Hildy. It was an issue that separated them like a twelve-foot barbed wire fence. Maybe someday he would be able to resolve it . . . maybe.

Orly's thoughts were shattered by the ringing of the phone. He picked up the portable off the table and knew that it would be Bear. Orly used the cell phone for calling out, and only a couple of people had the number.

"Yeah, Bear, what's up?"

To Orly's surprise, it wasn't Bear on the phone but Hildy. He was shocked to hear her voice so soon after she had just filled his thoughts. Her voice was just as he remembered it, kind of low and silky. Her attitude seemed the same however.

"No, Orly, it isn't Bear. It's Hildy. Bear gave me the number. Listen, I won't keep you long, but obviously you know what is going on with the takeover attempt of the company. Dad and I were wondering if it was possible for you to come out to California a day early and meet with us next Wednesday. We've asked Doc Brewster to hang around after the NHRA race at Pomona, and we would like to have a meeting with you both. We want Bear here as well." The tone of her voice was impersonal and cold.

Orly tried desperately to mine some warmth out of it, but it wasn't there. Then he berated himself for being a fool. She was professional in every sense of the expression, and she was talking a pure business deal and nothing else.

"Sure, Hildy, Bear and I can arrange that. You want us there Wednesday? Where, at the office? What time?" *Two can play this game,* thought Orly as he made his voice as impersonal and professional as hers.

"Yes, we'd like to see you at the office. One o'clock would be perfect. Oh, and Orly," her voice softened just a fraction. "Dad isn't well and he doesn't look all that good. I just wanted you to know that. See you Wednesday at 1:00. Good-bye." With that, she hung up.

Orly pondered the phone as he shut it off. Then it rang again while he was still holding it.

"Yeah, Bear." This time it was Bear.

"Did she call you?" he asked.

"Yeah, you know she did. She asked us to meet with them at the plant office on Wednesday at 1:00, which means we both have to leave a day early," Orly said.

"Well, that puts a rock in the gearbox. Means my Saturday is shot to pieces and I better head down to the shop. That cuts a full day out of our prep time," Bear said in an irritated voice. "Sponsors. I tell you, Orly. Why can't they just write us a big fat check and then leave us alone?"

Orly laughed. "You know better than that, Bear. I'm sorry it cuts into your prep time on the car, but that's the way it is."

"How did she sound, Orly? Was she sweet to you?"

"No, Bear, she wasn't sweet. She did say Harry wasn't well and for us to be aware that he has been sick. Not sure what that means, but her voice sounded kinda strange when she said it. We'll see. Oh, yeah. Old ornery Doc Brewster is going to be there with us. You know what that can be like."

"Oh, that's just great. If there ever was a guy that knew how to pour five gallons of gas on a lit matchstick, it's Brewster. This ought to be some meeting. By the way, I got a call from the kids at 5:30 this morning and they're staying at Harry's house." Bear went on to tell Orly about the circumstances of the hotel room and the confrontation with the gang in the parking lot.

"Seems odd," Orly said. "That Alphonse is a sharp young man, and I hope he takes care of himself. Must have been an inside job or somebody had a key or something. At least they're safe. Harry will take good care of them and make sure they get fixed up with clothes and things. Those kids. They always got something going on, don't they?"

"Yup, they do. I've already talked to Helen and she'll handle everything. Later, Hoss, I got work to do," said Bear as he hung up.

Orly watched the lake as yet another boatload of tourists waved as they went by, nearly swamping a fisherman. This time he didn't wave back.

The clock radio alarm went off, filling the hotel room with its shrill beeping. Loren's eyes flew open and she awoke with a start, her heart pounding. Her mind was filled with two quick realizations. First, she had made it through the night. It was morning and she could see through the small crack in the blinds that the sun was shining. It was a realization that flooded her with relief. The relief didn't last long as she just as quickly realized that the darkness would come again tonight and she would be alone again. In the meantime, she must get back into the dragster and do what she was getting paid to do. That thought filled her with adrenaline and she clenched her fists, closed her eyes, and groaned out loud.

She threw the covers back and put her feet on the floor. The ankle wasn't bad, hardly even swollen. Secretly she had hoped that maybe it would be broken or sprained so bad she would have a legitimate excuse not to drive. She could hang around the pits on crutches, signing autographs and looking pretty while someone else took the risks.

As she stood up, the residual effects of the pills caused her head to swim. A sudden wave of nausea made her stumble to the bathroom. On her knees, she retched into the toilet, waiting for the stomach spasms to pass. When they finally did, she managed to stand up and turn on the shower. She stuck her head under the stream of water and the coolness brought her momentary respite. *I can do this. It doesn't matter whether I can do it or not. I have to do this. I can't do anything else.*

In contrast, across town, it was the smell of food that brought the young men up from the depths of sleep. That, plus the brilliant California sunshine streaming in the open glass doors.

"Come on, hijos. It's time to wake up. Mr. Hornbrook has asked that you join him and Ms. Hornbrook on the deck for breakfast. Get up now."

The voice was female with a thick Spanish accent and belonged to Yolanda, Harry's longtime cook and housekeeper. She was a rotund lady with four sons of her own at home and knew what it took to roll young men out of bed. Bright sunshine and the smell of food cooking worked every time.

"Come on, muchachos. We got some clean clothes for you and tooth-brushes and a little soap to wash you with. Better get up or I'm coming in to get you." Then she laughed and went back out the double doors to the kitchen in the main house.

A few minutes later, the young men came out of the guest house, blinking in the morning sun, freshly showered, and with growling stomachs.

Harry was delighted to see them. He liked young people and de-spite—or perhaps because of—his illness it invigorated him to have them staying at the house. Harry spoke from his chair at the table on the deck.

"Come on, boys, sit down and make yourselves comfortable. Yolanda has breakfast just about ready. Looks like we guessed pretty good on the sizes of the shirts and shorts. Helen has made a few calls and has you set up with team uniforms. They'll be waiting for you at the track. We set you up with a credit card and you can make a stop at the mall after the qualifying session today and pick up the rest of what you need. I hope you fellows didn't lose too much in the way of personal things."

"Thanks, Mr. Hornbrook, you didn't have to do that. We sure appre-ciate it." The three young men spoke almost at the same time.

"No problem, boys. Glad to help out. This is my daughter, Hildy." Hildy was buttering toast and gave them a wave.

"Hi, Doug, who are your two friends there?" she said.

Hildy looked great in the morning sun as her black hair glistened and her teeth shone white with her smile. She'd already been in for a morn-ing swim and was wearing a terry cloth robe over her suit. Her beauty was fresh, effervescent, and bubbling with health and vitality. The effect was devastating on the young men, and two of them lost the ability to speak in coherent sentences. Finally, Doug managed to put some words together as he looked at her with flaming cheeks.

"This here is Paolo, he works for Orly and Bear . . . well, you know the team, and this here is Alphonse and he's from San Francisco and down here for a week with us. Just kinda hanging out, like a vacation sort of. . . ." Doug's voice trailed off, then he gathered his courage and spoke again. "Uh, how you been, Hildy?"

Doug knew Hildy from when she and Orly were more than friends and had always been a little overawed in her presence. She was far too young and attractive to relate to as a mom, but she was too old to be seen as a peer. Besides, she was very sophisticated and it showed. She always did everything possible to put him at ease, but that just seemed to make matters worse. He knew a lot of famous people in the racing world, but being around Hildy was different. It was much easier for him to talk to someone like Loren or Alicia. Paolo didn't have any history with Hildy at all. He had joined the team after she and Orly broke up. Doug noticed he kept his mouth shut. *Smart guy,* Doug thought, *better than saying anything stupid.*

Hildy spoke in a warm, clear, sophisticated tone. "I've been good, Doug. Been staying busy. It's good to see you. You've filled out some since I saw you."

This comment made Doug's ears flame even more as he looked down in embarrassment.

Alphonse on the other hand was feeling good. This was a new experience for him, and when it came to people, there wasn't much that intimidated him. He could see Doug and Paolo's obvious embarrassment and leaped into the breach.

"Thanks, Mr. Hornbrook, for putting us up and all. You certainly have a wonderful place here. I guess we would have had to sleep in the car if Bear hadn't called you. We're grateful you opened up the guest house for us in the middle of the night." Alphonse spoke easily, as if to say he was used to sleeping in folks' guest houses and having breakfast around the pool. His attitude broke the ice a little, and the ensuing conversation was more relaxed and easygoing.

A minute later Yolanda had breakfast on the table. Harry took charge for the moment and said, "Let me ask the blessing," as everyone bowed their heads. "Lord, we give you thanks for good food, family, friends, and fellowship. May we always remember that we can trust you and that you love us. Amen." Then they dove in. Harry neither said nor ate much as he watched the young people eat. It wasn't long before Hildy's natural charm and gift of conversation had the young men worked out of their nervousness. The laughter was quick and infectious.

Paolo was telling the story about Alphonse threatening to take Ricky and the rest of the gang on and then telling them that what they needed was Jesus. They all laughed.

Alphonse turned to Harry and said, "Mr. Hornbrook, could I ask you a question?"

"Sure, Alphonse, go ahead."

"Are you the same Hornbrook that endowed the foundation that runs those ads on national TV about Jesus and the Bible? Those are really good ads and very well done."

Harry and Hildy exchanged looks. Harry said, "Well, it isn't common knowledge and we would like to keep it that way, but in answer to your question, yes, although we are only a couple of members. A lot of people you would never guess are involved in that project."

"I'm working on my degree at SF State. The program is okay, but I sure wish I could transfer down here and get in the production end of the industry. I understand UCLA has a great program. I would really like to get involved in broadcast ministry and use my talents for the Lord. The stuff your foundation is doing is great—very professional. I bet they're getting a lot of response."

Harry replied, "Thanks, Alphonse, but I want to say again that there are a lot of people involved. We just lent our name to it because it was the best way to put the foundation together."

Paolo looked at his watch. "I hate to say this, guys, but we should get out to the track at Pomona. Old Doc will be looking for us. Besides we have to stop by the police station and see some detective to pick up what is left of our stuff, then go by the hotel to see if we can have a room back for tonight."

Harry had already made a decision. He liked these young people and the life and exuberance that came with them.

"No, Paolo, I would like you fellows to come back here. I want you men to use the guest house and spend your time with us. We aren't that much farther away from the fairgrounds than the hotel, and I think you will be much more comfortable here. Please. I insist," Harry said.

The young men looked at each other and Doug finally spoke. "Thanks, Mr. Hornbrook. That's very nice of you. We'd be glad to accept your offer. Thanks again."

There was a chorus of assent from Paolo and Alphonse.

"Good, I'll see you this evening then."

As the guys got up from the table and headed back to the guest house, Hildy caught Doug by the arm.

"So, Doug, how is he really?" she asked.

Doug knew exactly who Hildy was talking about. "I don't know, Hildy. He's Orly. Sometimes he talks and sometimes he doesn't. You know how he is. He gets real focused before the race and usually doesn't say much to anybody but Bear and Jimmy. Sometimes he talks to my dad, but mostly about the car."

Bud Prescott was Doug's father and worked for the Orly Mann Racing Team. Bear was considered the crew chief and team manager, and Bud was in essence the team foreman. Jimmy drove the hauler and spent a good deal of time on the road, but he was Orly's spotter during a race. Bear, Jimmy, and Bud had all been with Orly for a number of years, and they worked together like a well-oiled machine. The thing that made the team function was that they respected each other's boundaries without being disloyal. Hildy was asking questions that Doug considered personal and out of his domain.

"Do you think he misses me?"

Doug colored again. "Man, Hildy, I do-o-on't know." Doug made three syllables out of the word *don't* and then looked around to see if anyone was looking.

Alphonse and Paolo had disappeared into the guest house. Harry was still at the table reading the morning paper, but he was far enough away not to hear their conversation. Doug swallowed and looked into Hildy's piercing hazel eyes.

"Yeah, Hildy, he still misses you. He misses you bad and it hasn't been the same since you and him stopped seeing each other. He spends too much time around the shop and drives Bear crazy. It's like he . . . well, you know. You brought life to him, I think, and he doesn't smile very much. He's still the best driver in the world. But it's like it doesn't really matter all that much to him anymore. I don't know, Hildy. What do I know anyway?"

Doug broke his gaze and looked down at the ground. "I know this much. It's a shame you and him couldn't make it work. You two looked good together and you made everybody laugh when you were around. I don't know what happened or what caused you to break up and not see each other anymore, but it sure doesn't seem right." Doug stood straighter with his hands in the pockets of his shorts and looked Hildy in the eyes again. "And if you ever say I said any of this, I will deny it till my last breath."

Hildy smiled and ran both hands through her long black hair. "Of course, I wouldn't say anything, Doug. I know the code you men have. I was just curious, that's all. If it's any consolation to you, I want you to know that I miss him too. We had a good thing." Hildy paused as if to say more. "Thanks, Doug." With that, Hildy turned and headed into the house.

Unbeknownst to either Doug or Hildy, Harry had heard every word. He smiled behind his paper. He was not so infirm as to be deaf. His body might be dying, but for right now there certainly wasn't anything wrong with his hearing. He clucked his tongue to himself and shook his head. If there ever was a couple that fit together it was Hildy and Orly Mann. Everyone said it was over, but then maybe God had a different plan.

You, my brothers, were called to be free. But do not use your freedom to indulge the sinful nature; rather, serve one another in love.

Galatians 5:13

"But the reality is, when it comes down to it, it's up to the team to evaluate all the circumstances and make a business decision on what's right for them."

Bill Davis, Winston Cup team owner

DOUG SAT WITH HIS ARMS folded across his chest and a scowl on his face as Paolo carefully maneuvered the Chevy through traffic to the Claremont police station. The more he thought about his conversation with Hildy, the more aggravated he became. She shouldn't have asked him what she did. It wasn't right. Wasn't any of his business, anyway. Then she made him say those things about Orly, and she even got him to say what he thought about the whole thing.

"What's the matter with you?" Paolo said, glancing at Doug.

"Women, that's the matter with me. I don't understand any of them. First Loren and now Hildy," Doug replied, crossing his arms even tighter.

"What are you talking about?"

"Hey, Paolo, just be quiet. You of all people wouldn't understand. When it comes to women, you are about as dense as a brick," Doug snapped.

Paolo closed his mouth with a look like a hurt puppy. Alphonse simply smiled with a blank look of innocence in the backseat.

The Claremont police station was exactly what one would expect of a small, upscale Southern California community. The building had a Spanish red tile roof and was surrounded with perfect lawns and well-manicured trees. Paolo eased the Chevy into a visitor parking slot and shut off the motor.

"What are we supposed to do here anyway?" asked Alphonse.

"You know, Alphonse, I'm not sure. They just told us to drop by this morning because they wanted to talk to us. So here we are. Considering the circumstances and what they put us through last night, it probably is smart to do exactly what they say to do," Paolo said.

Doug was still agitated. "Let's get it over with. I'm starting to get mad all over again. Man, I just had those jeans broke in good. I can't see any reason why someone would cut up all our stuff. Steal it maybe, but just wreck everything—sure doesn't make any sense to me. Come on, you guys. Let's get done so we can get out to the track. I'm kinda worried about Loren," Doug said as he opened the door and headed for the entrance.

A minute later they were standing in front of the counter, waiting for a detective to emerge from the back offices. Pretty soon a heavyset guy with a mustache and bald head walked around the counter and introduced himself as Detective Reynolds.

"Thanks for coming down, guys. Why don't you come back here with me. I need to ask you a few questions."

He walked down the corridor with heavy steps, his heels clicking on the tiles. The young men followed. They turned a corner and entered a small interrogation room. Sitting on a chair was Ricky, an arrogant look on his face. He was minus his black stadium coat and watch cap but still had the flannel shirt buttoned up to the collar. Reynolds stopped and turned to the three young men.

"Is this the punk that allegedly tried to sell you dope the other night?"

Ricky stared at the three—his eyes narrowed and his mouth shut. Both Paolo and Doug turned to Alphonse as if to say it was his call.

Alphonse gave Ricky a careful look and thought, *Ricky is a lot younger than he seemed the other night.* Then he said, "Well, it might be, but then again, it might not be. It was dark and everybody was wearing black you know. I didn't really get a solid look at the dude."

Paolo and Doug exchanged looks but kept their mouths shut.

"So, you're telling me you can't be certain that this guy here is the one you had the confrontation with?" Reynolds said.

"Well, he might be one of the guys, but I can't be a hundred percent certain. Like I said, it was dark and all. Lots of guys look like him, you know. He was just kind of an average looking guy. Real cocky though." Alphonse turned his palms up, belying his uncertainty mixed with innocence.

Reynolds was not happy. His professional acumen told him there was something going on here that was out of place. He knew Ricky was the guy and so did these other two guys, but this one wasn't willing to pin it down. Unless he did, he didn't have anything to go on. He turned to Doug and Paolo, "What about you guys?"

Paolo looked back and said, "Alphonse had the best look. We were a little ahead and came back when we saw him talking. Like he said, it was dark and everybody was wearing black coats and stuff."

"Well, Cardoza, I guess I got to turn you loose. At least this time." He muscled Ricky out of the chair by his flannel shirt and stood him up. "Go on. Get out of here. We'll get you next time. You're too dumb to stay out of trouble for long. I'll be seeing you again—you can bank on that."

Ricky gathered himself and without looking at anybody headed for the door.

As soon as Ricky left the room, Reynolds turned his attention to the three young men.

"What's going on here, you guys? I gotta funny feeling you're not telling me the truth, but then I'm used to dealing with punks that don't know the truth from a pineapple. You guys don't fit that mold. Anybody care to enlighten me?"

The three young men looked back at Reynolds with blank looks. Paolo could feel his heart racing. *What IS Alphonse doing? We know that the guy sitting in the chair is the same guy. How come Alphonse doesn't say so?* Well, at any rate, he wasn't going to say anything. It was Alphonse's call.

Reynolds stared at them and then spoke. "Well, here is where we stand. We got no suspects for who trashed your room. Ricky had an alibi, but it was with a couple of his punk friends so that was suspect. You say you can't be certain it was him you had the altercation with, so I got nothing to go on there. I got no reason to tie him into the vandalizing of your room. So it looks like, unless something breaks, we got nothing. Oh yeah, the hotel manager will probably sue you for the damages. His insurance will cover some, but if he doesn't sue you, then the insurance company probably will." Reynolds wiped his palms together and patted his stomach like he had just finished lunch. "Well, I think that's about it, so thanks for coming in," Reynolds said as he got up.

Doug's face was flushed as he spoke. "Now wait a minute, detective. How come we're getting the pressure? It was us that had all our stuff trashed. Plus, it seems to me the hotel has some responsibility in the security department. Fellow locks his room, he should at least have some sense that it will be the same as when he left it."

"I can't help you with all that, son. My only job is to catch the perps. You will have to talk to your lawyer, I guess. Thanks for coming in." With that, the young men were ushered out of the room.

There was silence until they got into the Chevy. As soon as the doors shut, Paolo turned to face Alphonse sitting in the backseat.

"Okay, buddy, what's going on? You about got us hung. How come you didn't finger him? All three of us know that he was the banger that got in your face."

Alphonse put his hands up as if to ward off the accusation. "I couldn't do it. I saw that kid sitting in that chair with that look on his face and I just couldn't do it. I'm sorry to put you guys in that spot, but I just couldn't make myself finger him. Yeah, he was the one, we all know that, but man . . . I kept thinking about me a few years ago. I was just like him. If it wasn't for the Lord working through people like Pastor Tom, I could be banging myself. I might even be dead, like so many of the guys I grew up with in the hood. You know that, Paolo. God rescued me from all that and I got away from it. If I fingered that kid he would go right into the system and who knows what would happen to him then."

Doug looked out the window and cleared his throat. "Hey, Alphonse, I don't know your circumstances and all that, but when a guy breaks the law, he should do the time. That guy is probably responsible for all of our stuff getting trashed and he needs his attitude adjusted. I'm not sure you did him any favors by letting him get off. Besides that, you really put me and Paolo in a bad spot. I don't like lying to the police. Next time just count me out."

Paolo could see that emotions were getting out of control. The last thing he wanted was for two of his best friends to get into a heated discussion. He also knew both sides. Doug didn't know what it was like growing up without a father and being forced to live in a subsistent housing project where despair was king. To watch his mama work two jobs to make ends meet. He also didn't know what it was like having dark skin and facing all the prejudicial stuff that went with it. Paolo himself wasn't Caucasian; he had a dark olive complexion and dark wavy hair. He got his share of dirty looks and comments, but it wasn't anything like Alphonse had to deal with. When Paolo first met Alphonse, he was an angry young man, but in the last few years he had matured. God had taken that anger and molded it in a way to make it a positive attribute. Alphonse wanted to succeed. Maybe deep down it was the anger that drove him. He studied and worked hard and someday maybe would be in a position to help others in coming out of difficult backgrounds. But the anger wasn't very far below the surface, and Paolo knew from experience it could flare into a white-hot flame given the wrong type of fuel.

"Look, guys, cool it," he said. "Let's let it go. Alphonse did what he thought was right, Doug; let's let it go at that. Come on, we need to get out to the fairgrounds and check in with Doc and the team."

Doug didn't reply and simply stared out the window.

Alphonse reached over the back of the seat to pat Doug's shoulder, "Hey, I'm sorry, Doug. I didn't mean to put you in a spot to violate your integrity. I made a judgment call and maybe it was wrong . . . but I did what I had to do. If I sinned against you, man, I'm sorry."

Doug didn't say anything for a minute, then finally he stuck his hand over his shoulder, palm up. Alphonse slapped it and that was that.

It was close to noon as they fought the traffic into the fairgrounds and parked the Chevy. There had been little conversation the rest of the trip, but Paolo sensed things would calm down between Doug and Alphonse. At least he hoped they would.

As soon as the young men stepped under the rope into the Speed King pit, Doc Brewster was in their face. "Where you guys been? We coulda used you this morning. Your new uniforms are here. Jump in the hauler and get changed and I'll put you to work."

Paolo exchanged looks with Doug. They worked for Orly Mann Racing and not Doc Brewster. They were here strictly for public relations and were more than willing to lend a hand, but Doc didn't really have the power to order them around like his own guys, and it was rude to say the least. Besides, Alphonse didn't work for any racing team at all and was here as a guest.

"Come on, get going. We got to get this thing ready for this afternoon," Doc yelled over his shoulder.

They shrugged at each other and did as they were told, heading up into the hauler to change. Doug spotted Loren sitting in the lounge area of the hauler smoking a cigarette. As soon as she saw him she stubbed it out. She looked a little pale, but she flashed him a smile.

It surprised him to see her smoking. He had never seen her smoke before and never smelled cigarettes around her. "Hey, Loren, how ya doing?" he said.

"Doing okay, Doug. Had a good night's rest and the ankle is much better. I can even walk without too much of a limp. Ready to go today. How about yourself?"

"Doing good. Kind of a short night though. Did you hear what happened to our room and all our stuff?"

"Yeah, Doc was talking about it. I guess when your new uniforms came there was a note with them or something. Strange. Who was it that did it?"

"Don't know, but we think we might have gotten tangled up with some gangbangers."

Doug went on to tell Loren about the events of the night before, but it wasn't long before Doc was yelling his name. The next thing he knew he was downloading computer tapes and comparing power curves in a new software program with Doc looking over his shoulder. Paolo was already under the dragster, bolting up the oil pan as they put the finishing touches on the new engine and gearbox combo.

The morning qualification session was history, and no one had been able to better the Speed King time of last night. After one qualifying session this afternoon, the sixteen qualifying spots would be set. The hot afternoon sun changed the air density, and the track was now slick with a thick coat of rubber that baked in the heat.

Doc was confident that their time would stand, but he wanted one more run under these conditions. "It will probably be the same tomorrow come race time. Setting the clutches on these monsters is tricky business. I want to make sure we have it dialed in," Doc said.

The car was buttoned up. Soon the call came out for the last qualifying session. Loren came out of the hauler, limping only slightly as she zipped up her driver's suit. Doug noticed her hands were shaking as she fought the zipper. Doc walked with her as they pushed the car to the starting line, talking in her ear with his arm around her shoulders.

Alphonse once worked as a busboy at Golden Gate Fields in Berkeley and had seen horse trainers talking to jockeys in much the same fashion just before a race. Alphonse wasn't asked to steer the car today. He didn't volunteer either. Today everybody seemed to be in a different mood. Doc's irritation had everyone on edge and the fun was gone. He noticed the guys on Doc's crew kept exchanging glances with each other, like they knew something everybody else didn't know.

They pushed the car into the line behind the starting area—joining the other top fuel cars. Paolo found himself standing next to Ikey Johnson, one of Doc's crew. He was standing with his arms folded, looking off into nowhere with a tired look on his face.

"Did you guys work all night?" Paolo said.

"No, not all night, but pretty late. That blasted Doc. Man, that guy is bad," Ikey said.

"Yeah, I know. Those crew chiefs can get testy sometimes. Bear gets a little crotchety when things turn a little sour," Paolo said.

"No, Doc is different. You know he tuned that motor so radical yesterday it was either going to blow up like a hand grenade or set top time.

It did both. Didn't tell Loren, either. Man, I watched him do it. That thing could have gone sky high at half track and she could have been hurt bad. But Doc, he don't care. It's all about winning. That guy will do anything or sacrifice anybody. I've had an offer from another team. It don't pay as good as this one, but I think the working conditions will be a lot better," Ikey said. Then looking at Paolo, added, "Hey, don't say anything to Doc, okay? He still owes me money, and if he knows I'm leaving, I'll have to sue him to get it."

"You got it," said Paolo. "I didn't hear anything." Then he spoke again, "Hey, what kind of tune-up does he have in the motor today?"

"Nothing radical. He doesn't want to lose another motor. Besides, there's nothing to gain this afternoon. No way he could better last night's time with the sun and weather like it is."

Paolo was shocked. To think that a crew chief would risk a driver's life just to be top qualifier was beyond belief. He thanked the Lord that he didn't work for Doc and then thanked him that Loren wasn't hurt worse.

The runs started and the cars went off again two by two. Soon it was time for the Speed King fueler to make its run. Loren put on her helmet with its built-in face mask. Then she slithered down into the cockpit of the car, putting her arms over her head as she wriggled into the fitted seat. It seemed like her heart was coming out of her chest, and the blood pounded in her ears. She was afraid. Terrified would be a better word. She felt like she was on the verge of passing out, but no one could see her face behind her helmet. The only thing that showed were her eyes, and they were wide with fear. This was the moment she had feared all night. She had done nothing but think about it all morning. Now, like a very bad dream, it was turning into reality. It was all she could do to control herself. She was on the verge of climbing out of the car when Doc reached in, grabbed her belts, and pulled them tight. Then he reached over and flipped the magneto switches. She heard the starter motor whine as the engine ground over. It started with a rumble. The sound flashed through her body with a charge of adrenaline. Her chin was literally trembling. She felt like she was being electrocuted. Loren let out a groan, but the sound was lost as the exhaust from the huge motor pounded the ground.

She shook her head, trying to clear the fear. *I have to get ahold of myself*, she thought. "Come on, it's only for a few seconds. It'll be over very soon. Come on, come on, you can do this. COME ON!" She yelled at herself inside the confines of her mask and helmet. Bit by bit, like spooning peanut butter into a bottle, she was able to shove the fear down the back of her throat. At least for the moment.

She gritted her teeth and eased the car into the waterbox and punched the throttle. The tires erupted into blue smoke as the rubber was heated by the spinning friction with the pavement. The car crow-hopped down the strip for fifty yards and she brought it to a stop. She eased the lever between her legs into reverse and backed the car up with Doc's directions. A crewman patted her on the helmet and pulled the pin on the blower and punched the computer. The car was ready.

Loren's hands were shaking as she released the brake to stage the car. She had no thought for the dragster next to her and really couldn't see anything but the dragstrip end, a quarter of a mile away. Today the finish line beckoned like some starving shipwrecked sailor looking for relief. *I'm coming*, thought Loren. She rolled forward to break the first light beam and trigger the bottom amber light. Then she crept forward to break the second beam in full stage. The Christmas Tree flashed to green, and the world dissolved into a blue-gray foggy mist of smoke and clutch dust.

The run was a disaster from the beginning. Loren committed the most awful of the cardinal sins for drag racers. She left late. That is to say, her reaction time was so slow she was almost a full second behind the lights. Then the car hazed the tires and, in the language of the sport, "went up in smoke." She lifted her foot from the throttle to pedal the car, and despite Doc's careful instructions not to do so . . . willfully punched it down again. The tires stopped spinning for a split second and then immediately went up in smoke again, throwing the car side-ways as the blower belt flew into the air. The fuel pumps charged the huge barrel valves that poured the volatile nitro-methane fuel into the cylinders and the motor hydrauliked. Fuel pouring into the motor had no place to go and filled the combustion chambers beyond their capac-ity. When the huge pistons came up, they created tremendous pressure for a nanosecond. Then the whole motor exploded in a ball of flame and shrapnel as the car bounced down the strip. Loren felt the heat and the concussion from the explosion just behind her head. Screaming, she pulled the brake lever as hard as she could. She popped the chutes, which filled with flame, and then it was over. The fire was out and the dragster bounced to a stop.

The car came to rest, practically right on the finish line. Trailing plumes of blue smoke testified to the destruction in the engine compartment.

Loren popped the release on her belts and fought her way out of the car. She stood up in the seat and ripped the mask and helmet off her face. She stepped out of the car, dropped to her knees on the asphalt, and vomited in front of one of the largest national TV audiences to watch qualifying for a drag race. She was still on her knees when the Safety Safari medical people rolled up to her.

Doc was livid and hopping up and down on one foot. He saw it coming from the beginning and had grabbed his head with both hands. How many times had he told her not to pedal the car in qualifying? Especially now in the last session. It always blew the motor big time, and they were already set for the race. Now they had to rebuild the thing all over again. He was cursing to himself as he climbed into the van for the run down to the end of the strip.

"That's it," he yelled. "I'm done with her. She's finished. I don't know why I let them talk me into putting her in the car anyway." Then he cursed some more.

Paolo, Doug, and Alphonse didn't even make a move for the van as it headed down the strip. "Did Loren do something wrong, Pally?" Alphonse asked as they both looked down to the end of the strip.

"Yeah, I think so, Alphonse. She left really late. That is to say, she missed the lights. She pedaled the car when it went up in smoke, kinda like taking your foot off the gas pedal, then stomping it down hard. That kicked the blower belt off and probably upset the timing. You could weld with the sparks those magnetos throw out. Then the motor filled itself with fuel and it didn't have any place to go. Then it blew up. That nitro is worse than dynamite. Some explosion. I think there are pieces of piston and block in the next county. At least it was all behind Loren, and the tires stayed on this time. Yeah, judging from the looks of Doc and the way he's running his mouth, I would say that Loren did something wrong."

Doug stood with his hands in his pockets, watching the medical people help Loren out of her suit. His face reflected Loren's pain, and he shook his head as he watched them check her out. She didn't appear to be hurt. She just looked sick.

Fifteen minutes later Doc was in full song as he threw things around the pit stall. The car had been pulled back from the strip, and it was sitting once again up on jackstands. The engine was still leaking lifeblood, but everything else looked pretty much intact. The media was having a great time as Doc ranted and raved. He kept pushing microphones and portable tape recorders out of his face with short bursts of profanity. His temper had gotten the best of him. He was making comments about things like inexperience and how much it cost to race these days and what inexperienced drivers could cost a team. "It wasn't my idea to have a young girl drive, but economics and sponsors collaborated together to force me to put somebody in the car that shouldn't be there," Doc told the media.

A few minutes later the Safety Safari dropped that somebody off in front of the pit area. Loren waved off the media people that were underfoot and didn't look anybody in the eye as she headed for the sanctuary of the hauler. Doc followed her in and a minute later everyone could hear him yelling and carrying on.

Doug looked at Paolo and Alphonse and they nodded. All three of them stepped into the hauler and headed back to the lounge area. Loren was sitting behind the table looking very small with her hands clutched together and head down as Doc shook his finger in her face.

Doug reached out and gently grabbed Doc's shoulder and pulled him around. "Come on, Doc, use your head. That's enough. I thought you were a professional. Get ahold of yourself. Don't beat her up anymore. It's only a race car, and you've been in this business long enough to know that these things happen. Now stop."

Paolo jumped in. "Come on, Doc, you're embarrassing everybody. Take a break for a minute."

Then Doug turned to Loren. "Come on, Loren, get your stuff, we'll take you back to the hotel."

Doc sputtered for a minute, looking old and slightly ridiculous. He clenched his fists and stared at Doug, his jaw tight. Then he looked back at Loren and snarled, "If you go with these guys, you are finished, kid. I'll put somebody else in the car right now and sue you for breach of contract."

Loren said nothing as she slid out of the booth. She was fighting a battle inside herself. Part of her was saying, take your licking. You screwed up. He'll get over it. Don't mess up your chance to make it big. Don't be afraid. Don't be a chicken. Come on.

The other part of her was saying, it's time to quit, Loren. You don't need to torture yourself anymore. Come on, give yourself a break. It's okay to quit. She swallowed, then made a decision and stood up.

She peeled off her driver's suit and carefully folded it on the table. She stood in front of the men in her flameproof long underwear. She gave the driver's suit a final farewell pat, gathered her things, then spoke. "I'm sorry, Doc, but I'm done. I can't do this anymore."

"I mean it, kid. I'll sue you and you won't have two nickels to rub together." Doc's voice rose in volume as Loren pushed passed him and headed to freedom. He started to grab her shoulder again, but this time it was Paolo that stepped in front of him.

Paolo's bulk filled the aisle, effectively blocking the way as Doug and Alphonse followed Loren. Doug stopped long enough to grab a Speed King Oil Company jacket and throw it around her shoulders.

"It's over, Doc. Do what you gotta do," Paolo said, then turned and followed the others out.

The eyes of the LORD are everywhere, keeping watch on the wicked and the good.

Proverbs 15:3

"We went from one extreme to the other. . . . I kept complaining and they would adjust and I would keep complaining. I probably sounded like a cry-baby."

Ward Burton, Winston Cup driver
car #22 Caterpillar Pontiac

THE WORD WAS OUT. Doc had done it again. He was about to can another driver. There was a large, noisy crowd gathered at the entrance to the pit stall, all craning their necks and standing on tip-toes, hoping to see some of the carnage. The yellow restraining tape was stretched and looked like it might break at any moment as folks strained to see what might happen. Six or eight media folks with TV cameras, microphones, and tape recorders were inside the pit stall waiting for Loren to come out of the hauler and make a statement about the lousy run.

Loren started to step down the stairs and then, seeing the crowd, shrunk back. She was trapped. Suddenly all of her resolve melted and she didn't know what to do. Doc was behind her and the mob was in front of her. She started to panic.

Paolo saw the look on her face, turned back to Alphonse and said, "Take her arm and don't let go of her. Then follow me and Doug. Have her hang on to the back of my shirt if you have to."

Then he said to Loren, "Don't say anything to anybody. We'll get you out of this."

She looked at him wide-eyed with pale tight lips and nodded her head.

Paolo and Doug were familiar with this type of scene. It happened often in Winston Cup. Whenever something controversial went down in the pits, which was fairly often, it drew an instant crowd. People liked conflict . . . as long as it didn't involve them. The difference was that in Winston Cup there were ten times the crush of people and media.

Paolo stepped down the stairs and waved the media folks away. "Nothing to say right now, guys. Take all the pictures you want, but no comment right now."

Paolo knew that nobody would be able to get a clean shot of Loren as she walked behind him. He was sixteen inches taller than she, and outweighed her by at least a hundred pounds. His shoulders were twice as broad, so it would be like walking behind a billboard. Considering that she was dressed in her flameproof long johns with an orange-and-yellow Speed King team jacket over her shoulders that came down to her knees, it was probably a good thing.

"Doc will tell you everything you want to know. He's right behind us. Probably be a press conference in a few minutes. Let us by, please." As Paolo was speaking he was quickly working his way through the pit stall and into the crowd.

Doug stayed on his left shoulder, making the same motions but keeping his mouth shut.

Alphonse put Loren's hand on the back of Paolo's shirt and whispered into her ear, "Hang on." He rode drag, snuggled up behind them both. Loren instinctively held on to Paolo's shirt with a death grip and followed along with her eyes on the ground.

The crowd parted, letting them through, and then closed behind them, which effectively slowed the media folks. Paolo and Doug both knew that was how it worked. They had seen Bear and Orly do it a hundred times. The key was to keep moving and stop for nothing. Alphonse maintained a tight grip on Loren, making sure she followed close while protecting her back.

Finally, they cleared the crowd. The security guard at the gate to the VIP parking lot shut down the stragglers. Paolo popped the locks on the Chevy and they clambered inside and shut the doors.

He looked into the backseat at Loren sitting beside Alphonse. She looked very small and frightened, clutching a piece of tissue in her hands with which she occasionally dabbed her eyes.

A few minutes later they were in front of the hotel. Loren took a few deep breaths before getting out of the car. Doug peered intently at her and said, "Hey, girl, what are you going to do? You want to hang with us for a while? It's still early in the evening. We could see a show or something?"

"No, I need to go back to my room," Loren said a little louder and more stridently than she intended.

Alphonse spoke gently from beside her, "We were going to do the chapel service at the track tomorrow morning, but I think that's out."

Doug and Paolo both nodded.

"So I think we're going to church somewhere close to Harry's house. We could pick you up for that and then play the rest of the day."

Loren shook her head, her blonde ponytail fanning over her shoulders.

Doug pulled out a business card and scribbled a number on the back. "Okay, no problem. Listen, here is the number where we're staying. Give us a call if you change your mind. In fact, just call me later and we'll talk. What are you going to do now? You going to head back to North Carolina?"

Loren took the card and said with fresh tears in her eyes, "I don't know what I'm going to do yet. I have to go now. Maybe I'll call you later." With that she was out and disappeared into the lobby of the hotel.

Paolo said to no one in particular, "I'll sure be glad when Alicia gets here. She would know how to handle this situation. At least she could stay with Loren and she wouldn't be alone."

"When are we picking her up?" Alphonse asked.

"She's on an early morning flight Wednesday. I wonder if I should call her and let her know what's happening."

"Probably wouldn't hurt. It would give her a chance to pray at least. Loren looks like she is coming apart at the seams. This has been a stressful time for her."

"You got that right. Can you imagine having to work with that Doc guy?" asked Doug. "That guy is a piece of work."

"You guys don't even know half the story. I was talking to Ikey before the run this afternoon, and he told me that Doc had such a radical tune-up on the car last night it was a wonder it finished the run. It could have blown up at half track and Loren might have been hurt real bad," Paolo said.

"I was wondering about that. That sucker really let go. Can you imagine sacrificing a driver like that? If that guy wasn't so old and prune-looking, I'd smack him around some," Doug said. "Poor Loren. Well, at least she's done with him."

When Loren got to her room the message light was blinking on the phone. She picked up the receiver and punched the code to listen. The voice on the other end told her that Doc Brewster was no longer picking up the tab on her room and she needed to come to the front desk to make arrangements on how to pay.

He didn't waste any time, she thought, throwing the receiver down and turning her purse upside down on the bed. She pawed through the contents, searching through the various bottles of pills until she found the one she wanted. She shook one out, then shook out another, and swallowed them both without water. *I'll feel better in a little while,* she reasoned. *This is just to calm my nerves a little.*

Harry had seen it all from his easy chair. The Sports Network was carrying the last qualifying session in order to do a buildup for the broadcast of the race tomorrow. Harry flipped on the VCR recorder to make a tape and then watched with interest. They showed a tape of last night's spectacular qualifying run and the ensuing crash. Harry shook his head as he watched Loren nail the lights with a perfect start, and the car hook up as it blasted down the strip trailing a blue cloud of clutch dust. They showed the engine exploding in slow motion. Harry could see parts of the block knocking the rear tire off the rim. It was a wonder the car stayed upright.

Then he saw today's race. He saw the car going up in smoke and the motor coming apart again as Loren pedaled the car, and today it was live. The media had a heyday, as Doc made an absolute fool out of himself with his ranting and raving. Doc had made dumb moves in the past and done things that Harry struggled with, but today was the frosting on the cake. Harry shook his head. Even the smartest of men make dumb moves on occasion. He wasn't thinking about Doc but himself. He never should have aligned Speed King with Doc. It created a lot of publicity because Doc was always news of some sort or another, which brought notoriety to Speed King This wasn't all bad, but it was time to sever the ties. Doc was more liability than asset, and it was time to make a change. If they were going to fight this takeover thing, they would need to pull some money from the advertising budget. This latest fiasco gave him the excuse he needed. *It will still be tough,* he thought, *but this makes the meeting this week a little easier.*

"Hildy," he shouted over his shoulder, "would you come in here and watch this with me? I need your advice."

Two hours later the three young men were cavorting in the pool when Hildy came outside on the veranda and yelled, "Doug, Loren is on the phone for you."

Doug streaked out of the pool to take the phone from Hildy's hand. It was like talking to a different person. Loren seemed together and calm as she talked with Doug.

"Yeah, I'm okay. I was wondering if your offer for tomorrow still stands. I don't want to be by myself while the race is going on. I feel pretty strange as it is. I don't know about the church thing. I'm not much of a churchgoer, but I'm willing I guess. I'll buy lunch afterwards."

The next morning Loren felt fresh, if a little subdued, when the guys arrived to pick her up. She was pleasantly surprised at the church service. The place was full of young people, the music was contemporary, and the pastor was upbeat and alive as he presented God's Word. Later that afternoon she found herself humming one song with the phrase, *Holiness, Holiness, is what I long for.*

It just kept repeating itself in her mind. She tried but couldn't remember the rest of the words.

After church they went back to Harry's house in Claremont at his invitation. Hildy was gone. She was headed back to San Diego for a couple of days to wind down some personal business.

Loren found herself liking Harry almost immediately. It was unusual for her to meet somebody and feel comfortable with them from the beginning. Perhaps it was because Harry was genuinely interested in her and yet wanted nothing from her. He didn't try to make her jump through any hoops and simply accepted and appreciated her for who she was. He listened to her when she spoke, and the more he listened, the more freedom she had to talk. It was a new experience for her. He was kind and she responded to his kindness. It was like that with the guys, too. They didn't expect her to be anything other than who she was. She didn't have to be the daredevil driver or the blonde empty-headed model . . . she could just be Loren.

The rest of the day was slow-paced and kick back. The PR shots were a wash with Loren being fired or quitting . . . depending on who was telling the story. They watched the results of the race on the tube that evening with Harry.

Doc's car went up in smoke in the first round and was eliminated. That was that. Drag racing was about reaching the finish line first and then moving on to the next round. The loser went home or, in the language of the sport, was "put on the trailer." They watched as Doc waved his arms in disgust at the start line. Some unfortunate soul was given the task of trying to interview him and had to duck when Doc lost his head and took a swing at him.

Once the car was eliminated, Loren felt as if a huge burden had been lifted off her shoulders. "I told Doc the clutch wasn't right. I told him it wasn't my fault yesterday. That's why it went up in smoke. Once the tires are loose you can't do anything with it. I fought those clutches all weekend, but he wouldn't listen to me," she told the men.

They nodded in response.

The next couple of days were pure heaven for Loren . . . but the nights were agony. They played hard. The guys picked her up early each morning and dropped her back at the hotel late in the evening.

Doug announced that he had never swum in the Pacific Ocean, and Loren said she hadn't either. So they spent Monday at the beach in Venice and not only swam in the ocean but took in the whole wacky Venice beach scene. Paolo just about killed himself when they rented roller blades, but everyone stayed out of his way as he stumbled along the concrete trails.

In the words of Alphonse, "Stepping in front of Paolo on roller blades is the equivalent of stepping in front of a truck on the LA freeway."

They did Disneyland the next day and Loren loved it. After that it was Knotts Berry Farm, and then the whole Hollywood scene. She was the center of attention, with three handsome young men to escort her. They were kind to her and she felt protected and safe with them. They didn't overstep their boundaries and treated her with respect. They included her in their conversations and jokes, and most of all, they made her laugh. They knew how to have fun in a genuine way.

For the first time in her life, Loren was almost having fun, too. But in the back of her mind lurked the thought, *Night is coming, and I will be alone and in the dark.*

Doug was smitten and fell more in love with her each day.

Loren sensed Doug was falling for her and deep inside she wanted to respond, but she couldn't. She noticed Paolo and Alphonse could also see his affection and were careful to give him space. She was trying hard to keep the facade but her world was crumbling.

The nights were long black holes of emptiness and frightened despair. She slept in the chair, with the lights on. The only thing that kept her together was the knowledge that the guys would pick her up in the morning . . . and the various combination of pills. It was all that would allow her to close her eyes and rest.

Alphonse knew what was happening with Loren. He had seen it too many times before. Alphonse thought Doug seemed oblivious. His infatuation made him blind to the stress plaguing Loren. Bit by bit, like a frayed old blanket, she was coming unraveled. Maybe Paolo suspected something wasn't quite right. He could see it but didn't quite understand what was causing it. But Alphonse saw the symptoms. The sudden mood swings that went from despair to nearly hyper-giddiness were indicative of some sort of pharmaceutical enhancement. Loren was doing drugs and doing them big time. All the signs were there to see, plain and simple. But for the moment at least, he kept his mouth shut.

It was Wednesday and Bear was tired, even though they had picked up three hours coming from east to west. He and Orly flew most of the night in the company jet to land at the Ontario airport in the early morning sunshine. They picked up the rental car, then had a long, leisurely breakfast, talking little as they perused the newspapers. After settling in at the hotel, they headed to the Speed King plant.

Bear had worked nonstop the past few days and drove the shop crew hard to get the Cup cars ready for Sunday's race. Actually, he didn't have to push them much. They knew the urgency and time frame as well as he did. It was nothing new.

They finally got the loaded hauler out of the shop late Monday. Jimmy had given them a short blast on the airhorn as he pulled through the gates into traffic. The hauler was nicknamed the "circus wagon" because of its orange-and-yellow paint scheme that matched the colors of the cars. Jimmy sat high up in the Peterbilt cab with his ever-present cowboy hat and coffee cup. Bear knew from experience that the radio would be set on the trucker's country-western station. Jimmy would drive safely but consistently fast. When he couldn't get the radio station, he would reach into his cassette box that contained every tape Willie Nelson and Waylon Jennings ever made. The cab of the truck seldom was devoid of some sort of twanging guitar and country lament. He and Cole, the relief driver, would go turn about in the sleeper as the big rig ate the miles to the West Coast practically nonstop. Lord willing, they would roll into the California Speedway parking lot sometime

Thursday afternoon. The rest of the crew would fly in Thursday night to be ready to go to work at the track on Friday morning.

Bear poured himself another cup of coffee and settled back onto the plush couch of the Speed King Oil Company's waiting room. He and Orly were a few minutes early to meet with Harry. Orly sat relaxed in an overstuffed chair, trying to get his shoulder in a comfortable position. Bear regarded him with a genuine look of concern.

"Still hurting?"

Orly looked up. "Yeah, a little. Just stiff from the flight and all that sitting. It'll be okay."

He was interrupted as the big door to Harry Hornbrook's office flew open and Doc Brewster came storming out.

Doc is mad, but then what's new? thought Bear.

Doc shouted something over his shoulder and then turned to see Orly and Bear sitting there.

"I might have known you guys would have something to do with this. I just can't figure what makes you think you're so high and mighty. You guys with your Christian foundations and the way you spout that religious stuff. You guys are crooks and hypocrites. You make me sick."

"Nice to see you, too, Doc," Bear said.

Orly said nothing. Just watched with raised eyebrows.

"Stuff it, Erickson. You and the horse you rode in on." Doc's voice was going up in volume. "Hey, Orly, killed anybody lately?" With that, Doc made an obscene gesture and was out the door.

Bear was on his feet and two steps behind him when Orly caught him and wrapped his arms around him.

"Let him go, Bear. Come on now. It's not worth it. Let him go. Stop now, you're making my shoulder hurt."

Bear quit struggling and tried to get his breathing under control. He was mad. Not just mad but enraged. Doc had just thrown out the cheapest shot anybody could make. It was common knowledge that Orly was involved in a pit incident a number of years ago in which a crewman from another team was killed. Orly's brakes were red hot and had locked up as he hit a patch of coolant in the pit lane and spun the car. The crewman zigged when he should have zagged and got pinned against another car. He later died from his injuries. It was one of those tragic "racin' deals" as the fraternity would say. It also led to a new rule that mandated slower speeds in the pit lane. Racing is a dangerous sport and, like it or not, occasionally folks got killed.

Bear knew the whole thing still plagued Orly and that for a long time he had considered quitting. Especially after he lost his wife and daughter. Doc's comment was mean-spirited and cheap. Bear could and did put up with a lot, but he couldn't handle that type of meanness. Besides, Doc Brewster was not one of his favorite people. On occasion, they worked together on promo stuff for Speed King—commercials for TV and whatnot. Bear always found Doc to be overbearing and a royal pain.

He calmed himself and pushed Orly's arms away. "That guy is a jerk," Bear said.

"Yeah, he is," Orly said.

About that time, Hildy stepped through Harry's door and stood staring at Orly with her hands on her hips and a half smile on her face. She hadn't heard the exchange between Doc and Bear.

Orly was caught off guard and stared back into her hazel eyes. "Hey, Hildy," he said in a low tone.

"Hey yourself, Orly. 'Lo Bear. Come on in, you guys. Dad is waiting." With that, she turned and went through the door.

Bear smiled inwardly. *Talk about chemistry,* he thought. *It is so thick you could practically spread it on bread.*

Orly and Bear walked through the door to see Harry behind the desk, pale and shrunken. Bear exchanged a quick look with Orly, then they both stepped forward to shake Harry's outstretched hand.

"Thanks, men, for coming in a day early. Good to see you again." Harry's voice was hoarse and sounded weak. "Guess you saw Brewster as he made his exit. He wasn't very happy. He has good reason to be upset. We have just pulled our sponsorship from his team. To be honest with you, I am not certain as to why we were ever affiliated with him. The man is not only obnoxious but a liar and a cheat as well." Harry motioned for Bear and Orly to sit down in the chairs in front of his desk.

Hildy remained standing across the room. She studied Orly, soaking in his image. He looked good with his long legs stretched out in front of him as he listened to Harry. She had missed him and felt a lump in her throat, which she quickly swallowed. Part of her wanted to walk across the room and put her arms around his shoulders and press her cheek against his. She resisted the impulse and jerked her head in anger. "Get ahold of yourself," she muttered under her breath.

"You men know about the hostile takeover bid. What you don't know is that I have cancer. There, I've said it. Takes a little getting used to, I mean, saying it like that."

Bear and Orly exchanged looks yet again. Harry went on, "And not only do I have cancer, but I probably won't live out the year. I'm getting used to that, too. Seems like the Lord has other plans for me, which quite frankly is okay. I'm looking forward to seeing Hilda again soon. So at any rate, I have decided to step down and sell the company."

🏁🏁

Bear said nothing but inwardly groaned. If Harry sold, it meant that most likely Speed King Oil would withdraw their sponsorship from the Orly Mann Racing Team. That would have far-reaching ramifications for the organization. Sponsors with the integrity of Speed King were hard to find. Harry knew the Winston Cup business inside out. He had been with Orly for many years. Oh, yeah, they could find a new sponsor, maybe even get more money, but what a hassle. If history was any indicator, those teams that changed major sponsorship spent a lot of time tooling the image and promoting the products—time that was better spent doing research and development on race cars. After all, the business of Winston Cup was racing, not promotion. But corporations wanted a return off their $3 million to $9 million a year of sponsorship. New sponsorship meant a lot of extra driver appearances and all kinds of special stroking for pet company projects. Working with Speed King was a luxury. All their products were automotive related, and it wasn't like pushing laundry soap or beer or something that wasn't even connected to cars. Besides, Harry bought all the space on the car.

Traditionally, Winston Cup cars were parceled up like a side of beef, with the choice cuts costing the most. The hood, including the nose section and sides of the car, were prime sponsorship territory. A secondary sponsor might purchase space on the quarter panels and decklid. Every square inch of the car, inside and out, was for lease. Sometimes it meant trying to keep a whole bunch of folks happy at the same time. Harry bought all of Orly and Bear's cars. Different products might be featured on different parts of the car, but they were all manufactured by Speed King.

More important, Harry was a friend and a brother in the Lord. Dealing with Harry was as simple as a handshake. His word was his bond. Same with Orly and himself. Oh sure, they signed contracts to keep things legal, but the real business was carried out with integrity. Things were discussed openly and agreements were made. They shook hands and the deal was done. The paperwork came later. Bear groaned inwardly again as he thought through the ramifications of Harry's decision.

Bear realized Orly was on a different track when he asked, "Have they done all they can for you, Harry? I mean with chemo and all that?"

"Yes, they have, Orly. I have prostate cancer and it's starting to show in the bones now. I'm not sure how long I have, but it's all in God's timing."

Orly nodded. "What can we do for you? How can we help you?"

"Well, like I said, men, I have sold my controlling share of the company, but I haven't told you who I sold it to. I would like you to meet the new owner and CEO, and your new boss." Harry swiveled in his chair and motioned to Hildy, who was leaning against the wall with her arms folded.

"Just exactly what this means to the Orly Mann Racing Team is up to her. Now it's her turn to talk."

For everything that was written in the past was written to teach us, so that through endurance and the encouragement of the Scriptures we might have hope.

Romans 15:4

"The motor blew up and dumped oil. There wasn't a whole lot I could do. I was along for the ride then."

Ricky Rudd, Winston Cup driver
car #28 Texaco Ford

ALICIA CAME DOWN THE JETWAY through the gate at the Ontario Airport with quick steps and a smile on her face. Her beautiful long black hair fanned out behind her as she ran the last few steps to throw herself into Paolo's arms. She gave him a quick hug and then hugged Doug and Alphonse.

Loren felt an immediate stab of jealousy. Alicia looked so fresh. So full of life. So . . . together. It made Loren feel immediately like an outsider. Like she was tainted somehow. She could tell by the expressions of the guys that Alicia was special. Paolo's face just lit up when he saw her and he couldn't stop smiling at her. It was apparent that all three of the young men had a history with her and it was good. Somehow it made the last few days that she spent with them inconsequential. Like they didn't count or hadn't happened. Suddenly she felt very much alone, and that feeling made her anxious.

Alicia turned to face her and stuck out her hand. "Hi. I'm Alicia, as you can tell. I'm really glad to meet you. The guys have told me a lot about you, especially Doug. It's fun to finally meet you."

Loren reached madly for her facade, pasted it on, and flashed a brilliant smile. She returned Alicia's handshake and said, "Good to meet you, too. I've heard a lot about you as well."

Alicia turned to face the young men. "Well guys, we've got one day left before we go to work. What are we going to do?"

Loren kept the smile frozen on her face. Alicia's statement brought it all home to her once again. It was like a blow to the pit of her stomach. These folks would be going to work tomorrow when the Orly Mann Racing Team came together for the weekend in preparation for the California 500 on Sunday. *What am I going to do? I could fly back to North Carolina, but there isn't much back there.* When her father died when she was fifteen, her mother got serious about her drinking. No telling who was living with her now—she always had a steady stream of loser boyfriends. That guy that answered the phone the other night might have been replaced three or four times by now.

Loren had been mostly on her own since she was sixteen. By then her mother no longer cared what she did. It was only through a series of circumstances that she got a top fuel ride. One night a friend of a friend introduced her to some guys that crewed for a top fuel team, and she found herself pulled into the racing fraternity. Her good looks and natural intelligence helped. She liked the closeness of the racing family. As soon as she got out of high school, she took a full-time job doing promotional work for one of the teams. The locations might change, but by and large it was the same group of people. It was while she was working there that they asked her to do modeling on the side. She modeled everything from driving gloves to brake pads, and one small job led to another.

She learned quickly to use her natural beauty and charm to open opportunities. She was attractive and knew it. In a sport mostly dominated by men, it helped her to survive. Then came the opportunity to drive. She started in the amateur ranks driving a Super Stock car for an older guy who liked to wrench but no longer wanted to drive. She had natural talent with lightning-fast reflexes, and it wasn't long before she moved to the pro ranks. From there it was a steady upward climb . . . that is, until she lost her nerve.

The ride with Doc Brewster's team was the pinnacle. Driving top fuel was where it was at. If she had done well with him, she would have been set and could have driven for any number of teams. She could have named her own price and made a very decent living and perhaps been a representative for a good sponsor. It would have paid good money and given her the opportunity to settle down someplace. She had been living in a cheap, run-down apartment in North Carolina but gave it up to travel with Doc's team. Everything she owned she carried with her. The sky would have been the limit. Now it was gone.

The truth was she didn't have enough reserve left on her credit card to pay the hotel bill. She felt another little stab of panic at that thought. She wasn't sure what she was going to do or even where she was going. No money left and no direction. The contrast with Alicia and the guys was more than just painful, it was agonizingly painful.

"Excuse me, but I have to hit the Ladies', be back in just a minute." Loren disappeared quickly into the restroom and shut the door of a stall. She fished in her purse for the right pills, popped them in her mouth, and swallowed them without water. *I need to numb the pain to give myself time to think,* she reasoned, then told the voices in her head to shut up.

Later that evening Bear sat in his room at the Claremont Hotel with Orly—the same hotel where Loren was staying. Ordinarily Bear and Orly would stay in the motor homes at the track, but because they were a day early, they were staying here. The motor homes wouldn't come rolling in until tomorrow, probably about the same time as Jimmy with the hauler. A couple of the crew were the designated drivers. They would make sure that they were stocked and ready to go for the weekend.

Bear much preferred staying at the track rather than a hotel. Staying in public venues was getting to be a real bother. For Bear, it was simply a matter of convenience. It meant that he spent less time fighting traffic and could be within walking distance of the garage area.

But Bear knew that for Orly it was more a matter of survival. They had eaten in the hotel dining room but it was a meal filled with constant interruptions. The racing crowd was already starting to gather for the weekend and Orly was spotted early in the dining room. According to Bear's calculations, he'd given at least a dozen autographs and politely declined to sign the seat of a rather tipsy lady's white trousers. She had settled for a picture instead. The constant stream of interruptions made conversation difficult. Bear knew it was time to make a retreat when a tour bus showed up with fifty or sixty boisterous race fans that came boiling into the lobby to hit the registration desk. It wouldn't take them long to find out Orly was in the dining room.

Bear signed the check and said to Orly, "Come on, Hoss, let's get out of here. I don't know how you do it. You are always so patient with the folks. They drive me nuts."

"You know why, Bear; they ultimately pay the bills. Without them there wouldn't be any stock car racing." Orly signed yet another autograph.

Now at least, in the privacy of the room, they had a chance to talk about the day's events. Neither had spoken much after the meeting. Both of them needed a chance to think things through. It had been a major surprise to realize that Hildy was taking over the company. Even more shocking was learning Harry was dying.

"How you feel about the meeting?" Bear asked with his legs crossed and his hands folded over his knee.

"To be quite honest, I feel pretty good. She challenged our socks off. Told us we better start winning because Speed King was going to need the additional exposure. Sounds to me like Hildy is going all out to promote the company and increase the revenue. Firing Doc Brewster was a good move. I don't know why Harry put up with that guy as long as he did. She terminated the contract with him over that clause that says something about being detrimental to the sponsor's interest."

"I don't know if she can make that one stick. You know Doc will fight it."

"Yeah, he might, but that's the lawyer in her, Bear. That plus she doesn't like anybody that won't play fair. The truth is it doesn't change our circumstances at all. At least for this year. It affects me some personally. You heard her say that they're going to do a lot more promo stuff using my image and whatnot. That means more of my time. But hey, if it helps them generate the income they need to fight this takeover thing, I'm game."

Orly got up to walk around a little. Bear wasn't surprised. He had never seen Orly sit still for very long in any circumstance. The two-hour meeting in the Speed King office had been intense. Orly had gotten up several times on one pretense or another.

Orly turned to face Bear. "You sure sputtered when she said she was going to commission a whole new publicity campaign using you as the crew chief poster boy." Orly laughed.

"You know I hate that stuff. I'm no good in front of the camera. Those spots with Doc were really bad."

"Yeah, but she's a sharp lady and has some great ideas. She's going to use you. Then she is going to do some stuff for Speed King with the Thunderfoot Ballet boys. That idea she has about Bud and Doug Prescott as a father-son thing is great, too."

"You still love her, Orly?" Bear asked.

The abruptness of the question made Orly stop his pacing. He wasn't offended. He ran both hands through his hair. "Yeah, I do, but I don't know what to do about it. Ghosts from the past and all that."

Bear was the only person in the whole world who could have asked Orly that question. Not only that, but Bear was the only person in the whole world who would get a straight answer. Bear himself was a bachelor. Never been married. Never even been in love. He liked women, but he had yet to meet one who could get as excited over a new cylinder head as he could. His passion was racing. It took most of his time and virtually all his energy. There was just no opportunity for him to develop any type of a lasting relationship. He lived by himself in a modest home on the edge of a lake, not too far from Orly. He shared the place with an old and rather cantankerous cat that tolerated nobody but Bear. When he wasn't racing, he was generally down at the shop. In the off-season, as short as it was, he went fishing. Usually off the Florida coast and sometimes in Baja, California, or even down in South America, and usually with somebody connected with the racing world.

Bear got up and patted his friend on the shoulder. "You'll figure it out. Just don't give up. That is one mighty fine lady. Excuse me if I chase you out, but I'm going to bed. By my watch it's after one in the morning. See you in the morning. Oh hey, if you try to call me on the cell phone, you'll get Doug instead. Somehow we got them switched at the shop. Musta been when we were charging them up. So if you need me, use his number and I'll answer. I'll swap with him as soon as I can." With that, Bear opened the door and Orly headed back to his own room.

Orly couldn't sleep. He went over to his bag and pulled out the worn Bible and sat down at the table. He opened it to Psalms and began reading. It was something he did when he couldn't sleep, which lately was more often than not. The text of Psalm 37:4 jumped out at him: *Delight yourself in the* LORD *and he will give you the desires of your heart.*

He bowed his head and prayed out loud, "Yes, Lord, I know you will, but Lord, I don't know what it is that I want. I'm so lonely all the time. Why did you have to take them away from me?"

The room was silent. Orly put both elbows on the table and closed his eyes. He could see her in his mind's eye and he ached to touch her. Just to take her in his arms for an instant. Just the touch of her, the smell of her hair, the feel of her arms around him. The joy they shared when the beautiful baby girl came into their lives. A child that was the product of their love for each other. Blonde curly hair and twinkling eyes. She had her mother's smile. Orly smiled to himself as he remembered. The smell and touch of a new baby. The incredibly soft skin and the joy that came with holding a child in your arms, a child that was your own flesh and blood.

Then in a heartbeat it was gone. A drunk driver in the late afternoon, doing over 80 miles per hour on a city street, ran the stoplight and broadsided the minivan. They were both gone instantly.

Orly wasn't even in town. It was the off-season, but he was in Atlanta doing some testing when the news came. The next few days were a blur. The only thing he really remembered was that Bear and Pastor John were by his side almost every minute. He wanted to die, to go and be with them, but he couldn't.

It had happened six years ago, but the pain was still there. Initially, the pain was sharp, like a dagger piercing his heart, and brought him to his knees in agony. A pain so wicked it incapacitated him, took his breath away, and made him want to cease to exist. After a while it turned into a dull ache that never quite went away. He knew that it wouldn't. He knew that it would be with him the rest of his life. That was why he had called it quits with Hildy. She tried and so did he, but the ghosts from the past just kept getting in the way. The residual effects from the pain kept manifesting themselves in his thoughts and his actions. Hildy deserved better. At first she didn't agree, but he finally convinced her and they agreed to part friends.

Orly thought about Hildy and this afternoon. Seeing her after such a long time knocked him off balance. *I really have two legitimate reasons,* he told himself, *never to be connected with anyone again.*

To fall in love with somebody else would somehow tarnish the memory of what I had before. It would be disloyal . . . in a sort of strange way. The love he had for his wife and child was unique. He needed to make a monument of it, to be worshiped and held sacred.

The second reason was more selfish. He wasn't willing to run the risk. God might take them away, and he couldn't go through that again. No way. It would kill him. If he committed to somebody, he might lose them. He would rather be lonely than go through the agony.

But then there was Hildy. She was fresh, full of energy . . . alive. She was so beautiful, so feminine. Just looking at her made him ache to touch her. Whether he wanted to admit it or not, the truth was that he loved her very much. *I want to be with her. I might even be able to make a life with her if I just didn't have so much baggage to bring along.* He turned his head and regarded his own image in the mirror across the hotel room. *I look tired,* he thought. *How ironic that one of the most recognizable stock car drivers in the world is sitting alone in an empty hotel room.* He looked down at the verse once again. *What are you saying to me, God? How can I really trust you, when you took away the desire of my heart?*

The day had gone quickly for Loren. She tried not to like Alicia but found that impossible. Alicia was more alive than anyone she knew and so full of fun that it was impossible not to share her infectious vitality. And Alicia quickly set out to make Loren her friend. It was obvious from the banter that she shared with the guys that she was quick and usually half a step ahead of them. She made every effort to pull Loren into the conversation, and before long they had the guys on the run. When Alicia heard the story about Doc, she was honestly sympathetic. In some respects and perhaps in other circumstances, Loren could have really let her hair down and enjoyed herself. But she was afraid to do that. She couldn't allow herself to get connected to these people. They were great and would be wonderful friends, but she didn't belong. She was on her own. Behind the lovely smile and the tossing blonde hair lay a very scared little girl.

This day they decided to make the short run south to San Diego and do the zoo, Balboa Park, and maybe the beach if the sun came out. Loren was grateful for Doug. Her cash reserves were down to zero. She had been spending money like there was no tomorrow, buying lunch for everybody, and even trying to put gas in Paolo's car. He wouldn't let her, of course. When she was nearly broke, she made a pretense of doing the ATM machine but said her card wasn't working right.

"The magnetic strip has worn off or something," she said.

Doug stepped in and loaned her the cash they needed to play today.

"I'll pay you back as soon as I get home," she promised. She laughed inwardly and thought, *Wherever that is.*

She was more than flat broke. She owed for the hotel and some room service meals. How she was going to get out of that was beyond comprehension at this point. She couldn't even stand to think about it right now. She would deal with it later.

It was late as Paolo threaded the Chevy through the freeway traffic and headed back to the hotel. Loren was in the backseat between Doug and Alphonse. For the most part she had given up smoking for the week, except at night, but now she desperately wanted a cigarette and could feel her anxiety build as they neared the hotel. *Maybe I could trust these folks and just pour out my story to them. I really don't have any place to go, and if I did, I don't have the money to get there, let alone take care of myself.* She pondered the thought for a couple of minutes.

Doug broke into her thoughts. "So you figured out what you gonna do yet?"

The conversation stopped in the car as the rest of the group paused to listen to her answer.

She wanted to cry out to them with all of her heart . . . but she couldn't. It was just too demeaning. Too embarrassing. She faked it with a smile.

"You know, Doug, I think I'll take your advice and head back to North Carolina. I know some of the folks back there, and maybe I could hook on with a team in their PR department. I'm pretty good in that area, you know. I'm sure I could get a job. Things have been slow in the modeling department lately. I probably should check out some new agencies. I'm going to check out of the hotel tomorrow and book a flight back to the East Coast." Her answer seemed to satisfy Doug.

"At any rate, I'm done driving. That's for sure." She followed this last statement with a little hollow laugh.

Paolo pulled up in front of the lobby. "Hey, Alicia, did you know Bear and Orly are staying in this place tonight, same as you and Loren?" he asked.

"Yes, Pally, I knew that. Who do you think made their reservations?" she snapped back at him.

She was irritated and she couldn't quite put her finger on why. Maybe it had to do with Loren and Doug. It was obvious to the rest of them that Doug really cared about the girl. You could tell he would really like to develop a relationship with her, but she would have no part of it. Kind of kept him at arm's length. Oh, she was nice to him. Very friendly in fact, but she wouldn't allow him to get close.

Actually Alicia was irritated because she felt like she was playing Doug's part to Paolo. Paolo wasn't exactly holding her off, like Loren was to Doug. He was simply oblivious that she would have liked to hold hands and at least have him walk beside her. She made a little noise in her throat and opened the car door. "Well, I had fun today, guys. I better get checked in and make sure they haven't given my room away. I'll see you out at the track tomorrow. Loren, you want to meet for breakfast tomorrow morning?"

"Uh, thanks, Alicia, but I'm going to get going and see if I can get an early flight. Thanks for the offer," Loren responded. The thought of having breakfast with Alicia seemed very attractive, but she didn't dare risk eating in the dining room. Who would pay?

Doug jumped out to hold the doors for them as both girls slipped out of the car.

"See you, Loren. Hey, I've got one of the team's cell phones," Doug said. "Give me a call when you figure out what flight you're on. I could maybe give you a ride to the airport or something." He quickly wrote the number down on a scrap of paper and handed it to her.

"Thanks, Doug. I will. I'll call you before I go." She had no intention of calling him, but it was easier to say that she would. On impulse, she gave him a peck on the cheek.

He was surprised and brought his hand up to touch where she kissed him. She studied him for a moment. He sure was handsome. He had that sandy colored hair she really liked and he was so tall. He was kind and gentle, and that she really appreciated. In different circumstances she might have allowed herself to get involved, but right now things were complicated enough. She had to get to her room. She was dying for a smoke and she needed something to calm her nerves so she could sleep. She waved and headed through the doors.

Alicia followed her, then headed to the desk.

Paolo put the Chevy into gear and started to pull out, when Alphonse interrupted.

"Paolo, pull over here in the parking lot. Let's talk a minute."

Paolo pulled the Chevy into an empty space in the far corner of the lot and shut off the motor. He and Doug turned to face Alphonse in the backseat.

Alphonse began, "Have you guys noticed what I've been seeing in Loren?"

"What are you talking about?" Doug said. He was still basking in the afterglow of Loren's kiss on his cheek.

"Doug, you mean you haven't noticed the mood swings and the trip to the ladies' room every so often? The girl is classic, man," Alphonse said.

"I still don't know what you are talking about," Doug replied.

"Doug, the girl has a problem with drugs. She's doing stuff, man, to help her cope. Can't you tell?" There was an irritated, exasperated tone to Alphonse's voice.

"Man, you are out of it. Loren's not doing anything like that. She's just stressed. You are out in left field here, man. There's no way she is doing anything." Doug's voice was now equally exasperated.

Paolo jumped in. "He's right, Doug. Loren is doing drugs of some sort, man. Remember when she dropped her purse at Knotts the other day? I helped her pick it up, and man, she must've had six or seven pill bottles in there. On top of that, she has been acting strange ever since we picked her up at the track at the fairgrounds."

"You guys are both nuts. No way. She isn't doing any of that stuff." Doug was getting hot now.

"Hey, Doug, chill bro. We aren't trying to bust her or anything. What me and Alphonse are asking . . . think with us bro . . . is how we can best help her. It's obvious to me and Alphonse that she hasn't got any money. That thing at the ATM machine was a show, man. Didn't you pick up on that? Alphonse and me have been covering her every way we could. Picking up the tabs for lunch, buying the tickets, and everything. By the way, I'm keeping track of your share, so you owe us." Paolo laughed, trying to lighten the mood. Then he went on, "We want to help her, that's all."

Doug sat with his arms folded. "Okay, I admit that I'm not as 'California' as you guys. I didn't grow up in the big city. Maybe I don't have as much exposure as you guys to drugs and all that." Doug paused, "Yeah, she was acting kind of strange there a couple of times." Then he went on, "I'm not sure what we can do. Maybe we should just go talk to her right now?"

As Doug finished his thought there was an insistent tapping on the window of the left rear door. Alphonse leaned over and looked up.

"Hey, it's that guy Ricky. The guy that tried to sell me dope. You know, the guy at the police station." He opened the door as Ricky stepped out of the darkness and flung himself into the backseat next to Alphonse.

As he dropped into the seat he said, "Does this thing go, man?"

Paolo recovered enough to say, "Yeah, it goes."

"Get it moving, man. They're right behind me. Come on, man, get it moving. I ain't kidding. Let's go," he shouted.

It was too late. The figures came out of the darkness. It was hard to tell how many. They had baseball bats and clubs, along with can openers and screwdrivers. Without warning they went to work on the Chevy. The interior of the car resounded with the thumps and scrapes as they gouged, beat, and battered the bodywork. They were careful not to hit the headlights or taillights but practically every inch of the body was either gouged or dented. In the midst of the melee, Paolo let out a bellow and started to get out. But Ricky yelled in his ear.

"Stay here, man. They will hurt you if you get out. Stay here."

Doug grabbed his arm and Alphonse grabbed his shoulder. He shrugged them off and threw open the door of the Chevy, slamming it into a guy who grunted with pain. Paolo reached for him, but he eluded Paolo's grasp and ducked away, yelling obscenities. Paolo let out another roar and chased two more guys around the car. One guy stopped to take a swing with a baseball bat, but Paolo hit him with his shoulder, knocking him to the ground. The guy was up in a flash and disappeared into the darkness.

The whole thing lasted maybe twenty seconds. Then they were gone, melting into the darkness, leaving the guys in the car stunned. The Chevy—a battered caricature of what it once was.

There was no sign of the vandals, but the sound of a derisive laugh echoed across the parking lot from the darkness. Paolo stood staring into the blackness with his fists bunched and a hungry desire to hurt somebody. He raised both arms and roared back at them like a lion on the African savanna.

Though I walk in the midst of trouble, you preserve my life; you stretch out your hand against the anger of my foes, with your right hand you save me.

Psalm 138:7

"I think we found some answers today that will help us. Unfortunately the motor didn't last."

Derrike Cope, Winston Cup driver
car #30

LOREN SLID HER KEY CARD through the slot and opened the door to her room. The maid had been there and all the lights were off. She hated that. Going into an empty room was bad enough, but going into an empty dark room was even worse. She fumbled for the light switch and blinked as the darkness was dispersed. The message light was blinking on the phone again. She knew it would be the manager. Tomorrow they would come looking for her if she didn't call the desk. She took the receiver off the cradle and put it under a pillow, then played the message to make the light stop blinking.

She looked around the room again. It was impersonal, functional, and incredibly lonely. She thought for a minute of calling Alicia but dismissed the idea quickly. Instead, she sat on the edge of the bed and emptied her purse. She gathered the pill bottles to take inventory. *I am going to be out in a couple of days, and then what will I do without my "friends" to help me?* Her source was one of the guys on Doc's team, but that was out now. Besides, what would she use for money? She lit a cigarette and looked at the pack in her shaking hand. One left. She counted what was left of the money she borrowed from Doug. Twelve bucks and some change.

Suddenly it was all too much. She started to cry and the hot tears rolled down her cheeks. The panic started to rise up from her stomach and her chest got tight as she tried to breathe. She would hyperventilate if she didn't slow herself down. She fought the top off a pill bottle and shook out two, then three, pills. She looked at them in her hand and then shook out the rest of the bottle. There were maybe ten or eleven. Quickly she put them all in her mouth. She ran to the bathroom and washed them down with water cupped from her hand. She held on to the edge of the bathroom sink and got her breathing under control. She felt sick and incredibly tired.

If I'm going to do it, I might as well do it right, she thought as she turned and went back to the bed. She popped the caps off the rest of the bottles and poured the varied assortment of pills into her hand without counting or looking at them. Then it was back to the bathroom for more water to wash them down.

She felt a sudden surge of panic, but she fought it down once again. *I wonder if I have time to write a note?* Then she laughed a short bitter laugh. *To who?* Then a picture of Doug flashed across her mind and she started to cry once again. She slid off the edge of the bed to sit on the floor, waiting to feel the effects of the drugs. Tears rolled down her cheeks and dripped off her chin as she quietly sobbed.

🏁🏁

Paolo couldn't see much in the darkness, but he could see enough. He ran his hands over the body of the car like a trainer would a valuable race horse that had somehow been injured. The pristine body of the Chevy was no longer pristine. The front fenders, hood, and grille were all badly dented and gouged. The deep purple paint was marred and scratched at practically every point. Paolo felt sick.

The other guys got out of the car and stood surveying the damage. Doug was appalled. It had all happened so fast. Ricky spent more time searching the darkness than he did looking at the car. Suddenly Paolo turned and grabbed him by the shirt and slammed him against the side of the car.

"Did you do this, punk?" Paolo said as he held the kid practically off the ground.

Ricky's eyes flashed defiance. "No, I didn't do it. They was waiting for you and I tried to warn you. I owed you guys, man, for not getting me busted. I was trying to help."

"Come on, Paolo, let him down, he didn't do it," Alphonse said.

Paolo reluctantly let him go. His big shoulders were bunched, and he was more mad than he had ever been in his life. He kept pounding his big fist into his open left palm.

"Who was waiting for us? That group of punks you run with?" asked Paolo with a snarl.

"No, man, it was the same guys that trashed your room. They want this turf and they got more guys than us. They been cutting us down. Two of my crew got stabbed last night and they been chopping us one by one." Ricky was shaking with fear and his jaw trembled as he spoke.

"Why did they trash my car and do our room?" Paolo asked. "We don't give a rip about your so-called turf and all that garbage. You guys make me sick. You live in such a fantasy world. You talk about turf like you owned it. You guys don't own zip. Never worked for anything in your whole lives. You're just punks. Cheap, low-down, rotten punks that won't let anyone succeed at anything if they can help it. All you guys do is destroy stuff. You never build anything, just wreck it."

"It may be a fantasy world, Paolo, but it's real, man. They kill each other over it, you know," Alphonse said.

"Yeah, and sometimes they kill innocent people too, with their stupid drive-bys. So why'd they do it? Who are they, punk, and where can we find them?"

While Paolo was talking to Alphonse and Ricky, Doug had stepped away from them and pulled the cell phone out of his pocket. He quickly dialed Bear's number, then realized with a start that he had the wrong phone. He was carrying Bear's phone instead of his own. They must have gotten switched back at the shop. Well, no matter. Bear was probably carrying his. He dialed his own number. The phone rang twice.

A groggy voice answered, "Yeah."

"Bear?"

"Yeah, it's me."

"Are you in the hotel?"

"No, Doug, I'm on an airplane to Singapore. Yes, I'm in the hotel, in my bed asleep. Whatta you want?"

"Bear, we got a situation and I was wondering if you could come and help us?"

"Doug, you guys aren't in jail again are you? What am I going to do with you folks? This isn't like Daytona is it?" Bear had a note of irritation in his voice. "All right. Where do I hafta go and how much money do I hafta bring?"

"Actually, Bear, we are in the north parking lot of the hotel, and I don't think money is going to fix this one. At least not right away. We need your help, Bear. I've never seen Paolo like this. I'm afraid he's going to hurt somebody. Could you come right away?"

"Yeah, all right, let me get my pants on. I'll be there in a minute."

"Hey, who you talking to? You're not talking to the cops are you?" Ricky asked as he saw Doug on the phone. Paolo and Alphonse turned to look as well.

"No, I just called Bear. That's all."

Paolo ignored Doug and grabbed Ricky by the shirt again and shoved him up against the car. "Answer me, punk. Why did they trash our stuff and why did they trash my car?" Paolo drew back his fist.

Ricky cowered and tried to protect his face with both hands. The words poured out of him in short bursts. "Don't hit me, man, please don't hit me. I been hit enough. I'll tell you, okay? Look, they saw us with you guys the other night and they caught me when I ran. I told them that you guys were rollers from San Francisco and you brought a load of dope to sell at the races. One of the janitors at the hotel is married to somebody's sister or something. He got a key to let them in your room. They was looking for dope, man, and when they didn't find any, they trashed all your stuff. They been watching you since then and decided they was gonna trash your car to teach you a lesson. They are tough guys, man." Ricky's voice trailed off.

Paolo still had his fist cocked like a loaded gun. He tightened his grip on Ricky's shirt. His face was twisted in anger and the muscles in his arm bunched as he shifted his weight. Doug and Alphonse exchanged scared looks and tried to decide whether to grab Paolo or not.

Bear's voice came out of the darkness. "Paolo, are you sure that's what you want to do? If it is, I'll hold him and you punch him. Looks like a tough hombre. Might take all four of us to beat him up good. Maybe we ought to pray first and ask the Lord for extra strength."

Everybody jumped at the sound of Bear's voice. Paolo visibly relaxed and some of the tenseness went out of his body.

Bear's tone changed. "Let him go, Paolo. It's not worth it, my friend. Turn him loose. He's just a kid. Come on now, let him go."

Paolo uncocked his fist and grabbed the front of Ricky's shirt with both hands. He pulled him close and put his face an inch from Ricky's. "I will, but I don't want to." With that, he shoved him back against the car and turned to face Bear.

"They trashed my car, Bear."

"I can see that, Paolo. That's a lovely color but you been around race cars and such long enough to know that it is just a car. It can be fixed. It's just a machine and we can make it right again. Hurting this young man is not so easily fixed. Things is things, Paolo, and people is people. Jesus didn't die for things. You know that. He died for people." Bear said this as he walked up to Paolo and put his arm around his shoulders. "I know you put a lot of sweat and money in this thing, but it is still a thing. God has put a lot of work into this young man here and put him in amongst you guys for a reason. I don't think that reason is to rearrange his physical appearance, so to speak."

Then he turned to the other guys and said, "Now, will somebody explain to me what the Sam Hill is going on!"

🏁🏁

Loren fought her way off the bottom of consciousness and struggled toward the surface. It was like paddling through jello in slow motion. She was still sitting on the floor with her back against the bed. She tried to get up, but her arms and legs would not move. She fell over sideways and retched on the carpet as waves of dizziness overcame her. Her stomach cramped and she retched again. She gathered her resources and mumbled to herself, "I need to sleep." A quiet but insistent voice spoke in her head.

"Loren Janine, get up. Go to the phone. Do it now, Loren Janine."

"No," she answered back, "I can't. I can't do it. I need to sleep. Leave me alone."

The voice repeated itself over and over again, forcing her by the sheer will of its incessant chanting to move. Inch by slow inch, she pulled her arms under her body and fought to push herself up. She reached for the phone and pulled the whole thing down onto the floor next to her body. Her eyes refused to focus and she retched again. A piece of paper fluttered off the bed to land beside the phone. She looked at the numbers, not comprehending who or what they meant. Slowly . . . painfully . . . she punched them into the keypad of the phone.

🏁

Bear had just slipped his pants off and slid between the covers when the phone rang. He had finally gotten Paolo settled down and the guys headed over to Harry's with a promise that they would assess the damage to the car in the morning. Ricky was with them, which was a little strange considering he got this mess started. Alphonse insisted that he go with them. It was too dangerous for Ricky to be roaming the streets, especially with his own guys and the other guys looking for him. Ricky seemed very relieved not to be on his own. It took Paolo a while, but he finally got control of himself and settled into a major sulk. In truth, Bear couldn't blame him. Being a car guy himself, he knew the work it took to make something look as sharp as the Chevy. At least how it used to look. *Ah, it's just a car and they can fix it,* he thought.

He picked up the room phone, wondering who would be calling him now. Then he realized it wasn't the house phone ringing but Doug's cell phone instead. He punched it on and said, "Yeah, what is it?"

For a long minute there was nothing but labored breathing. Then a wheezy voice groaned, "Heeeelp meeee."

Bear sat up in bed with his full attention on the phone, "Who is this please?" Then he listened intently. Again there was nothing but labored breathing, then finally in one stretched out word, "LooorrrrenJaaaaa-nine."

Bear heard the connection break, and the line went dead. He stared at the phone, his mind racing. It took him but a minute to realize that it was Doug's cell phone, so this person, whoever it was, was trying to get ahold of Doug. He could sort of make out the name. It was Lawrence James or something like that. He thought at first it might be a prank, but then it just didn't sound right. Quickly he punched in the number to his own cell phone and waited impatiently for Doug to answer.

This time it was Alphonse that had Ricky up against the wall. "Look, man, this is a class place we are staying at. I don't want you messing with anything. Okay? You got it?"

"Yeah, I got it. I know how to be cool," Ricky replied.

"Well, you showed us that, didn't you. Look what you did. You got our stuff trashed and Paolo's car messed up. If I was you, I would stay away from him." Alphonse motioned toward Paolo, who was going through the door of the guest house.

Ricky looked at Paolo and then back to Alphonse. "Yeah, yeah, I will. That dude is mad."

The cell phone went off in Doug's pocket like an alarm clock, making him jump. He fished it out and answered it.

"Doug, this is Bear. Do you know somebody named Lawrence or Larry or something like that? Somebody that might call you on your phone?"

"No, nobody I can think of, Bear. Why?"

"Well, I just got a call on your phone from somebody saying, 'help me,' and then when I asked them their name, they kind of slurred their words . . . the best I could get was Law . . . or Lerr or something like that, then the line went dead."

Doug swallowed fast, then recognition hit him like a two-by-four in the stomach. "Bear, could it have been Loren? Did it sound like a girl? Could it have been Loren Janine?"

"Yeah, it coulda been. Why? Do you know somebody with that name? Oh wait, that's the little girl that drove for Doc. The one he fired. The one from North Carolina, right?" said Bear.

"Yes, that's her. Bear, now listen to me. She's staying in the same hotel as you. You got to check her out and make sure she's all right. Promise me, Bear. You are right there. Please do it for me."

"You know what room she's in?"

"No, I don't. You'll have to find out at the desk."

"You know better than that, Doug. They won't give me her room number. It's against hotel policy. Guys like Orly would never get any sleep."

"Well, call her anyway. At least they will connect you with her room. In the meantime, I'll call Alicia; she might know. I'll call you back." Doug hung up.

Bear wiped his bleary eyes and picked up the house phone. "Hi there, could you connect me with Loren Janine? Yes, she's a guest." Bear held the phone and waited. After six rings the desk clerk came back on.

"Sorry sir, no answer. You could leave a message on her voice mail if you like."

"No, I'll call back. Say, you don't know what room she is in, do you? Oh, it's against policy. Well that makes sense, don't it." Bear hung up the phone, thinking to himself that it was worth a try.

In the meantime, Alicia answered the phone, half asleep.

"Alicia, it's Doug. Do you know what room Loren is staying in?"

"Uh-uh. Why? Oh wait. I think she is on the north wing. There are four hundred rooms in this place, you know."

"Well, we think she might be, well, not okay, if you know what I mean."

Alicia was fully awake now. "What do you mean, Doug, not okay? What's that mean?"

"Alicia, I'd rather not say. I was just wondering if you knew where her room was."

"Doug Prescott, this is me, Alicia, you're talking to. Now tell me, what is going on?" Alicia was insistent and the tone of her voice brooked no argument.

Doug told her what they suspected. Alicia frowned as she pulled her clothes on with one hand and held the phone with the other.

"Doug, do this. Call Bear and tell him I'll call him in a minute with Loren's room number." Alicia threw down the phone and ran a quick comb through her long black hair. She put just a hint of lipstick on and then literally ran out of the room.

A couple of minutes later she was at the front desk. There was a young Hispanic girl behind the counter sorting mail. Alicia surveyed her quickly as the girl turned to face her.

"Hi, can I help you?" she said.

"Yes, you can. I left my purse in my girlfriend's room along with my room key thing. You know, that card thing." Then Alicia lapsed into perfect Spanish. "Oh, I like the color of your fingernails. What color is that?"

The girl smiled broadly and replied in Spanish, "It is called blush rose and I have the lipstick to go with it. It is pretty, isn't it?" She held her nails out for Alicia to inspect closer.

Alicia was dutifully impressed and they chatted for a minute about nails, lipstick, and hairstyles. Then Alicia said again in Spanish, "I need to pick up my purse, but I forgot her room number. I tried to find it, but they all look the same. I didn't want to knock on the wrong door." She giggled. "It's pretty late, you know."

The girl giggled herself. "What's her name and I'll tell you?"

Two minutes later, Alicia was on the house phone talking to Bear. "Room 437, Bear. I'll meet you there."

Alicia arrived first and looked down the hallway to see Bear with Orly walking quickly toward her. She knocked on Loren's door.

No answer. She knocked insistently again. Still no answer.

Bear and Orly stood behind her, "How we going to get in? Do you think we ought to get the manager?" Bear said.

Alicia looked down the hall. "No, let me handle this. You guys just walk away and wait until I call you."

Bear looked puzzled for a minute. Then Orly pulled his arm and they walked down the hall past a waiter pushing a cart for room service. Bear looked back over his shoulder to see Alicia talking with him. A minute later he opened the door with a pass key and Alicia stepped inside the room, waving back at the waiter as she shut the door. Twenty seconds later the door flew open and she beckoned frantically to Orly and Bear.

"Hurry!"

Orly sensed the urgency in her motion and sprinted past Bear. He entered the room to see Loren lying on her side on the floor beside the bed, her blonde hair matted around her face. The room smelled of vomit.

"Is she breathing?" Bear asked.

"Barely." Orly ran his finger around the inside of Loren's mouth to clear her airway.

"Bear, call 911 and tell them to hurry. Looks like an overdose of pills or something. Tell them to hurry but go easy on the sirens."

Bear already had the phone cradled next to his ear.

"Alicia, get me a wet towel, and some cold water. Let's make sure her airway is clear. It's a good thing she was on her side. If she was on her back, she would have choked to death."

Loren's breathing was shallow and slow but she was still pushing air in and out. Orly watched carefully as he wiped her face and neck with the towel, prepared at any moment to jump in with CPR. The cold water on Loren's skin made her groan. Her eyelids fluttered but her eyes remained unfocused and glazed.

A few minutes later the rescue squad showed up with the hotel manager right behind them.

Then the eyes of those who see will no longer be closed, and the ears of those who hear will listen. The mind of the rash will know and understand, and the stammering tongue will be fluent and clear.

Isaiah 32:3–4

"If I don't feel I can provide him the equipment he needs to win, I'll tell him. And I'm sure that if he feels he can't get the job done for me, he'll tell me."

Richard Childress, owner of the
Richard Childress Racing Winston Cup team
that fields Chevrolets for Dale Earnhardt

ORLY STOOD LOOKING OUT the window of the Claremont Hospital waiting room. The sky was just beginning to lighten with the early morning sun. It was overcast and the sun looked red as it broke over the horizon. Orly was shaken. Looking into the window, he could see the reflection of Bear, Doug, Paolo, and Alicia in various states of uncomfortable slumber in the waiting area.

The paramedics were good. They had Loren stabilized and to the hospital in what seemed like a very short time. The ER crew, led by a young doctor, pumped her stomach and administered the proper medications through an IV. He said that probably another ten minutes and it would have been hopeless. As it was, they had to wait for the effects of what she had metabolized to wear off before they could assess what, if any, damage had been done. That's what they were all waiting for now. The doctor said he would come out and let them know how it was going in a little while.

Doug managed to get Loren's mother on the phone in North Carolina, but she was so drunk she couldn't make sense. They would call her back sometime today. The hotel manager was in a snit. He was complaining that Loren had ripped them off for four nights plus some room service. Now she had upset the guests, and they were going to have to clean the carpet in the room. Orly listened to him for a few minutes, then told him to put her bill on the Orly Mann Racing Team tab. That made the guy happy, or at least it shut him up. Then Orly made a mental note to remind Helen and Alicia that they wouldn't be staying in this place again. He was glad he had Alicia gather up Loren's things and put them in her room before they left. No telling where her stuff would have wound up.

He took a breath and blew condensation on the glass. It would be nice to get out to the racetrack and move into the motor homes. Maybe things would settle down a bit. After all, they did come here to run a race.

He'd been sitting in his hotel room thinking about death, his loss, and generally feeling sorry for himself when Bear banged on his door, and the next thing he knew, they were all involved in saving someone's life. Why would a young vivacious girl like Loren, who had so much to live for, try to take her own life? Somehow his memories seemed worn and well used. Still precious, no doubt about that, but maybe God was telling him it was time to move on. Maybe it was time to stop feeling sorry for himself and put a little focus on other people. Maybe, just maybe, *that* was the true desire of his heart. When it was all said and done, life was pretty short anyway. Look at Harry dealing with the fact that his life was just about finished. Harry looked wistful when he shared the thought with Bear that it seemed like his life had gone by pretty fast. Then there was Hildy trying to carry on Harry's legacy, at least for a while.

Hildy. Orly's thoughts lingered on Hildy. The color of her hair, the beautiful eyes that looked right into your soul. The feel of her hand, so cool and feminine, when she touched him briefly in Harry's office. Orly put both hands in his back pockets and breathed some more warm air on the cold glass. Hildy. The words *desires of your heart* echoed in his mind.

Twenty minutes later the doctor stuck his head in the waiting room. Everyone sat up as he spoke. "I think she's going to be okay. We cleaned her system out pretty good, and she's groggy and sick. Obviously we're going to keep her a day or two just to make sure she's okay. You can come in and see her before we take her upstairs if you want."

They followed him through the swinging doors to the cubicle where Loren was laying on a gurney. She looked pale and small, her lips waxy, the blonde hair tangled and sweat-soaked. Her eyes were closed, but she opened them as the group gathered around her. She looked up at the faces, not recognizing Orly and Bear, but acknowledging Doug, Paolo, and Alicia.

"Who found me?" she said in a very tired, tiny voice.

No one spoke for a minute and then Doug said, "Well, I guess we all did. Alicia was the one that got in your room, and Bear and Orly here gave you first aid. Seems like everyone had a hand in it."

Loren blinked her eyes, then nodded her head just a little. "Thank you," she said with an effort, then went on. "I didn't really want to die. I just didn't know what to do." These last words exhausted her. "Thanks," she said again in a barely audible voice.

Loren couldn't tell whether she was dreaming or not, but the words of that song she heard in church with the guys kept repeating themselves in her mind.

> *Holiness, holiness, is what I long for.*
> *Holiness is what I need.*
> *Holiness, holiness is what you want from me . . .*

🏁

"Everyone put a hand on her and let's pray before we go," said Bear.

The five friends gently touched Loren as Bear led them in a prayer of thanksgiving and healing. Then they slipped out and left her sleeping.

"What happens now?" Orly stopped to talk to the doctor who was watching from the doorway.

"Well, because it was a suicide attempt she will have to be interviewed by somebody from Social Services. Then if she is well enough, we will release her. If it looks like she might do herself harm again, they might want to hold her for a few days and maybe put her in a program. From my medical perspective, this wasn't a genuine attempt to end her life. I think it was more a cry for help. I could be wrong, but that's my hunch. My understanding is that she doesn't have any family here or anything, but she isn't going to feel much like traveling for a few days. Personally, I would feel much better about her if there was somebody to keep an eye on her for a while."

"Yeah, makes sense," Orly said. "Tell you what, Doc, let me get back to you today. We might have a spot for her and somebody to keep an eye on her."

"Sure, Mr. Mann. I'll be here until this evening." The young doctor changed his tone. "Say, Orly, you got anything for them this weekend?"

Orly smiled. He was used to this. Racing fans came from all walks of life. "Well, I don't know. I hope so. To tell you the truth, I'll feel much better when we get out to the track and get some practice time in. Bear tells me that we might have a shot at the pole . . . but then he always says that." Orly laughed and so did the doctor.

"Take good care of our young friend there."

"Yes, we certainly will. I hope you have a good weekend. Hope I don't see you. I'm working the infield care hospital."

Orly frowned. "I hope you don't see me either. Last thing I need is to get hurt again."

"I'll let you go, but while we're talking, how's the shoulder?"

"I think this California sunshine is helping some. My doctor in Carolina said it would just take a while to heal. So I have to live with it, I guess. Thanks for asking."

Orly headed out the doors of the hospital into the gray overcast morning. He walked down to join the group gathered around Paolo's Chevy in the parking lot. Bear had the hood up and was checking out the engine compartment as Paolo explained to him what he had done and the modifications made to the motor. The dents and scrapes in the bodywork looked even worse in the daylight. Orly walked up and ran a hand over the front fender.

"There's good metal in these old cars, Paolo. I think the body will clean up nice. Boy, that is a nice color. Is that one of those new DuPont formulas? It changes as you walk around it."

"Yeah, it is, Orly. Thanks. It was nice till they trashed it last night," Paolo said.

"It was odd they didn't knock the lights out or break any glass. Wonder how come?" Bear said.

Doug responded, "Ricky said it was because they want you to drive around in the car. That way everybody can see what they did to you. Kind of like an object lesson, I guess."

Bear grunted, then asked, "You guys going to do a police report?"

"I don't know, Bear. Seems kind of pointless. I think I just want to drive it out to the Speedway and cover it up. Then when and if I get it back home, I can take my time to have it fixed."

"Well, we can talk about it over breakfast. Come on you guys, I'm buying. Let's go eat," Bear said.

Alicia was standing next to Paolo, shivering in the early morning cold. "You men. How can you think of eating a big meal after staying up all night? Can you drop me at the hotel? I'm going to go back to bed for a while. We don't have to be out to the track until this afternoon."

Alicia wanted time to think. She had been with Loren all day and never realized the girl was hurting so bad. Then to see her lying on the floor so near to death was sobering. She and Loren were nearly the same age and it was scary. For the guys, it was okay to go out and eat. They had done their part in saving her. At least that was what Alicia supposed. For her, as a woman, it was different. She needed some time to sort out her feelings.

"You bet, Alicia. Why don't you guys take her back to the hotel, and me and Orly will meet you in the dining room in a little while," Bear said.

A few minutes later, he and Orly were in the rental car. "So what are you thinking, Hoss?"

"I'm thinking that I might ask Harry and Hildy to take the kid under their wing for a little while. They could put her up in the house. Wouldn't hurt for her to have a chance to talk to Harry some. Maybe give her the opportunity to get herself straightened out."

"Yup. I was thinking the same thing. We can give Hildy a call later. We can do the usual thing we've done in the past. You know, stake Loren with a no-interest loan until she gets on her feet. That would take that pressure off of her. I know she doesn't have insurance, because I talked to the business people while you were talking to the doctor. I gave them the shop address and told them to send the bill there. We'll cover it until she gets in a position to pay it back."

"You know we're taking a risk, Bear. Doug told me the girl is probably hooked on drugs. She might just disappear."

"Yeah, there is always that possibility. Somehow I don't think so. Kid has a lot of character to push one of them big fire-breathing dragsters to over 300 miles per hour."

"Got that right. More courage than what I have," Orly said.

Yeah right, thought Bear, but said nothing. This was Orly Mann speaking here. The same guy that could bring a stock car off a corner at Daytona or Talledega an inch off the wall at nearly 200 miles per hour. Not only that, but he could do it consistently for 500 miles in close proximity with forty-some-odd other stock cars.

"At any rate, Bear, it's worth the risk."

"That it is, Orly. Not our money anyway, belongs to the Lord. Hey, not to change the subject, but did you see the weather report?"

"No, what'd it say?" Orly said as he craned his head to look up at the sky through the windshield.

"Well, you're not going to believe this, Hoss, but they're predicting rain for the next three days, heavy at times. Saw it on the TV in the waiting room."

Orly groaned. "Rain? How can that be, here in sunny Southern California?"

At the knock on the guest house door, Alphonse leaped out of bed and struggled into his new pants. He mentally complained that practically everything he owned was now brand new. Took a while to get stuff broke in.

He opened the door and greeted Hildy.

"Alphonse, I thought you would like to know that Loren is going to be okay. They pumped her stomach in time. Orly and everyone talked with her and had a chance to pray with her. Doug and Paolo will be here to get you in a while so you guys can head out to the track."

"Thanks, Hildy. That's great news. Praise the Lord! He answered our prayers."

"That he did, Alphonse."

After Hildy left, Alphonse turned to see Ricky regarding him from a chair. "Hey, man, didn't you go to bed?"

"No. I was afraid I might get in the wrong bed. I might get in that big guy's bed. He's still pretty mad at me and I didn't want to make any more trouble," Ricky said.

"So what did you do? Just sleep in the chair?"

"Yeah. I'm used to it. We got a lot of people living in our house most of the time, so I just sleep wherever I can." Ricky shrugged his shoulders like it wasn't any big thing.

"Hey, Alphonse, could I ask you something?" Ricky didn't wait for an answer. "Before them two guys left last night to go to the hospital, the three of you kinda stood there and you, like, prayed. Is that what you was doing?"

"Yes, Ricky, that's exactly what we were doing. We were praying and asking God to take care of Loren and for wisdom for the doctors and stuff."

Alphonse could tell by the look on Ricky's face and the tone of his voice that he was thinking through some things.

"Did you used to be a banger?" Ricky asked.

"You bet I was. I was running with a gang in Hunter's Point in the projects in San Francisco. Had a street name and everything."

"Well, how come you ain't running with them no more?"

"It's pretty simple, Ricky. I realized that running with those guys wasn't going to take me anywhere. Then a church group came into the hood one day and was doing some stuff, mostly for the little kids. I met a guy named Tom, a white guy if you can believe it. He told me about Jesus and who he was and why they were doing what they were doing there in our neighborhood. But the biggest thing was that he not only told me about Jesus, he acted like him, too. Then one day I nearly got shot and it scared me real bad. So I called Tom and he came and picked me up, and later on we prayed together and I put my faith in Jesus. I got to tell you, Ricky, my life hasn't been the same."

"Was it real hard to give up banging? I mean, like the only thing I got is my crew. They're my family. I dropped out of school last year. My mama don't even know what day it is most of the time. I got so many brothers and sisters. I'm not even sure who my dad is. I been on my own pretty much since I was a little kid."

Alphonse flashed on what Doug had told him about Loren. *Same story, just different circumstances,* he thought.

"Yo, Ricky, let me ask you a question. How old are you? What kind of future do you see for yourself? What are you going to do with your life? I looked at banging and I realized that there wasn't nothing happening, man. If I stayed in the gang, I would end up one of three ways: I would be a big-time doper, or I would be in jail, or I would be dead. God delivered me from that. I'm going to school and I want to do something with my life. I got a future and I can see God using me. I'm in college, Ricky. You see what God can do?"

"I'm sixteen. My birthday's next Tuesday and I'll be seventeen. I don't think too much about the future. Me and the crew we just do it one day at a time." Then his eyes brightened and he looked at Alphonse with hope. "But you know what? I am a great artist. I can draw. My mama told me I should go to art school sometime because I have real talent. That's what she told me. I can draw pretty good."

The conversation went on. Alphonse was careful. Ricky might have been a punk, but underneath that layer of bravado was a scared teenager. A kid with hopes and dreams just like anybody else.

"Alphonse, can I tell you something? I mean, can I trust you, man?" Ricky asked sincerely.

"Yes, you can trust me, Ricky."

Ricky nodded, then took a big breath. "Alphonse, I got no place to go and my own crew is after me because they think I ratted them out to the cops. When I jumped in the big guy's car I was just trying to stay alive. It was really my crew that did his car and it was really my crew that did you guys' room. I was there, Alphonse. I helped trash your stuff. I'm sorry, man. I'll go now if you want. You been so nice to me, protecting me and everything, but I'll go now." Ricky put his hands in his pockets and stared at the ground.

About that time Yolanda yelled from the deck. "Boys. Breakfast is ready. Come and eat."

135

"No, Ricky, I don't want you to go. You stay here with us. Let's go eat, but I want you to think about something. Why did you guys leave our Bibles? Why didn't you trash them, too? You trashed everything else."

Ricky started to reply, but Alphonse cut him off. "Save it until after breakfast."

Ricky looked like he had just been given a hot brick and didn't have any place to lay it down.

They headed out to the veranda. Yolanda motioned them inside the house. "We will eat in the house this morning. It looks like it's going to rain." Then she said to Ricky in Spanish under her breath, "Don't steal anything from these people. They are nice people."

Ricky frowned and replied in Spanish, "I wouldn't do that. I got respect, Señora." He looked around the well-furnished house, his cap in his hand.

Hildy overheard the conversation but said nothing. Yolanda looked at her and winked. She knew Hildy spoke fluent Spanish because it was she herself who taught her.

Hildy pulled out a chair and said to Ricky in Spanish, "Please sit here, young man. Our house is your house and you are most welcome here. My father, Mr. Hornbrook, will be down in a few minutes."

An hour later Doug and Paolo came into the guest house shaking the rain off their jackets.

"Yo, Alphonse, what's up, my man?" Paolo said as he threw himself into a chair that groaned in protest.

"So how is she doing really?"

"Actually, she isn't bad. She's tired and sick from the drugs and them pumping her stomach and all. I guess when you try to commit suicide with pills, they aren't too gentle pumping your stomach," Doug said with a glum look. "You know, guys, I feel pretty stupid. I should have done something sooner or said something to her. I can't believe I didn't pick up on the whole scene as quick as you guys did."

Alphonse shrugged. "Truth is you did okay, Doug. She is alive and she got a major wake-up call. Maybe she can get herself straightened out now."

"Maybe. I wonder what's going to happen to her when she gets out. I saw Bear and Orly talking but I don't know if they got a plan or not," Doug said.

"Come on, Doug, when is the last time you saw Bear without a plan? They got something working I bet," Paolo spoke from the chair.

"Hope so," Doug replied in a small voice.

Ricky was standing in the far corner of the room trying to look invisible when Paolo's voice cracked out.

"Ricky! Get your you-know-what over here. I want to talk to you."

Ricky jumped when Paolo raised his voice. He looked around the room for an easy exit and seeing none, put his hands in his pockets and walked over to Paolo with small steps. Paolo sat in the chair like some oversized monarch passing judgment. Ricky stood in front of him, looking at the floor.

"Ricky, my little gangbanger buddy, I want to apologize to you."

Ricky looked up, disbelief on his face.

Paolo put an arm on each side of the chair, looking even more like a king. "No, I'm serious. I lost my cool last night. You were trying to warn us and I overreacted. I blamed you for what those guys did to my car. I'm sorry. I get mad real fast but I get over it really quick. I have a real bad temper sometimes and I can act like a real jerk. Just ask these guys." He motioned to Doug and Alphonse.

Alphonse spoke, "Uh." He cleared his throat. "Uh, maybe before you say too much more, Paolo, you ought to listen to what Ricky has to say."

Just then there was a knock on the guest house door and Hildy entered the room.

Ricky looked up and said to her in Spanish, "Do you have any rope here, Miss Hildy?"

Hildy responded in Spanish, "Rope, what on earth do you need with rope?"

"Well, I'm going to make a confession of a terrible sin to this macho big hombre here and I think it would be better to tie him in the chair first. I think he's going to be very angry with me when I tell him what I have to tell him," Ricky replied.

Hildy laughed. "No, I don't think Paolo will hurt you. How about if I stand right here while you tell him what you need to tell him. Okay? Maybe I can protect you."

"Yes, that would be very good I think," Ricky said, again in Spanish. Then he turned to Paolo and began to speak, this time in English.

"My friend, Alphonse, has introduced me to a very special person this morning. A person named Jesus and I have asked him to forgive my sins, the bad things in my life, and to be my Lord and Savior. I want him to change my life like he has changed Alphonse. Alphonse told me and showed me in the Bible that I should tell another brother or even two or three brothers if I have done something bad that caused them a lot of trouble. I have caused you guys a lot of trouble and I have to tell you about it. I know you are going to be real mad at me, but I got to tell you anyway."

Ricky went on to tell Doug and Paolo that it was him and his fellow gang members that trashed their room and that it was his gang that smashed up Paolo's car. In the midst of Ricky's disclosure, Doug got up to stand beside Paolo's chair, his arms folded like a chamberlain supporting a king. Neither he nor Paolo said anything, they simply listened to Ricky talk.

Finally Ricky wound down and finished his confession. No one said anything for a minute or two.

Hildy broke the silence. "I'll leave you guys alone to settle this. Don't forget who you are and, more important, what you are." With that, she was out the door and gone.

Hildy was no sooner back in the house than the phone rang. Yolanda answered it and then spoke to Hildy, "It is Mr. Mann and he wishes to speak to you. Do you wish to speak to him?"

Hildy took a breath and then reached for the phone, "Hildy here."

The sound of her voice took Orly by surprise. It wasn't that he didn't expect her to answer, it was just that he had forgotten how warm and responsive she could be. "Hi there. It's me, Orly. Guess you know that, don't you."

Hildy smiled. He sounded about sixteen years old, calling a girl for a date. She decided to put him at ease. "Yes, I knew it was you. What's up?"

"Listen, I know you have the press conference with your dad tomorrow morning and I wondered if you wanted me to sit in with you. I could answer questions about the racing program, and it would probably be good for the PR and the stockholders. I'll be at the track anyway . . ." his voice trailed off, then he regained momentum. "Well, I thought it couldn't hurt."

"I'll check with Dad, but I'm certain he would appreciate that. He is going public with his cancer. It's a big step for him."

"Yes, I know it is, but what does the new CEO think of the idea?"

"You're asking me what I think?"

"Yes, Hildy, I'm asking you what you think. You're the boss, and you know I have the utmost respect for what you think."

"I guess I'll have to think about it some before I make up my mind."

"Would you mind thinking about it over dinner with me tonight?"

There was silence on the other end of the line. Hildy's thoughts were mixed. *Am I up for this?* she wondered. Part of her panicked and she screamed to herself, *No! I won't go through this again.* Part of her rejoiced at the thought of spending time with him.

"I was thinking we could head for the coast and get away from the racing crowd before the weekend picks up speed. There's that little place over in Laguna Beach."

It sounded wonderful, so tantalizing. Hildy swallowed, bit her lip and then reluctantly said, "Orly, I'm not sure that's a good idea. I don't want to do this all over again."

There was a different tone in his voice. One that elicited a peculiar sympathetic response from her.

"I know you don't, Hildy. Let me take you to dinner and we'll talk about it. If you don't want to take the time to go over to the coast, we could eat here in town. I just thought it would be nice to be together again. Just the two of us. Please Hildy, take a chance. It will be okay, I promise," he pleaded.

Oh brother, she thought, *I'm such a pushover.* "All right, Orly, pick me up at six and we can eat downtown at the Sizzler. I don't have time to go to the coast. Besides, I don't want to leave Dad that long." The Sizzler was the least romantic place she could think of on short notice. It would help her keep her feelings in check.

"See you at six. The Sizzler is fine, Hildy. Any place is fine . . . but Hildy . . . oh never mind. I'll take what I can get." Then Orly went on, "Oh yeah, I have something else I want to talk to you about. I got another wounded duck that needs someplace to land."

"We'll talk about it. See you this evening." Hildy hung up the phone.

After Hildy left the guest house, the guys sat and stared at each other in silence. All, that is, except Ricky. He stood with his hands in his pockets and his head down.

Finally Doug spoke, "Well, what do you think we ought to do with this guy, Paolo?"

"I don't know. I been sitting here thinking of all kinds of things. The best I can come up with so far is to strip him down, tie him up, cut up all his clothes, and then leave him in the lobby of the police station."

Ricky said nothing, just hunched his shoulders a little more. Alphonse started to say something, but Paolo put up a hand in a gesture that said, "Hold it, I know what I'm doing."

Paolo went on. "But then after I thought about it and after talking to Bear earlier, and now finding out that Ricky has become a Christian, I guess that isn't an option."

"I don't know. Still sounds pretty good to me," Doug said, "but on the other hand, I guess it probably isn't the right thing to do."

Alphonse cleared his throat, "Uh, guys, maybe you might ask Ricky what he thinks should happen?"

Ricky raised his head. He had tears running down his face. "I told Alphonse that I wanted to pay you guys back, but I don't got any money right now. I don't even got a place to live and now I don't even got any friends because my crew is going to be looking to hurt me. So I don't got anything right now, but I could get a job and then I could pay you back. Sometimes I work at the car wash. They pay six bucks an hour."

Alphonse spoke again. "Ricky, I didn't say this to you before, but I have a better idea. I'm willing to take a chance on you. You do have friends. We are your friends. We want to help you out. Right guys?"

Paolo stood up from the chair, his mind made up. He towered over Ricky, who continued to look at the floor. "Is that right, my man? Did you really put your faith in the Lord Jesus?"

Ricky looked up, "Yes, I did, and I meant it, too."

Paolo extended his hand, "That makes us brothers then, and God's Word says that brothers are to live together in harmony." Paolo took Ricky's hand and held it tightly. "I forgive you, Ricky."

Doug waited until Paolo was done, then he took Ricky's hand. "That goes for me, too. I forgive you, Ricky."

"Okay, everybody, listen to my plan," Alphonse said.

Hildy knocked on the door of the guest house again and then came in.

"I just remembered why I came out here the first time. Bear called and said for you to check the battery on your cell phone. Also, there is no reason to go out to the track because it is raining. But he wants everybody in the garage tomorrow morning ready to go at 7:00 A.M. He also said Alicia would have everybody's credentials. He is buying dinner at Buca de Beppo tonight at 6:00."

For this is what the Sovereign LORD says: I myself will search for my sheep and look after them.

Ezekiel 34:11

"Qualifying is a race in itself, so we haven't lost anything there, but I sure wish I could have shown what we had."

Ward Burton, Winston Cup driver

ALPHONSE HAD A PLAN all right. He called San Francisco and talked to Pastor Tom at the church.

"Yeah, we can find a place for him to live," Tom said, after hearing Alphonse's request. "There are several folks in the church that would be willing to take a chance and put him up."

"I know a couple teachers at the Industrial School of the Arts in the city. They might be able to get Ricky into some sort of program. It's looking pretty good." Alphonse hung up and turned to Ricky.

He could see Ricky was getting excited about the prospect of making changes and maybe getting his life together.

They hung together all day, just chilling out. They even braved the rain and horsed around in the pool, and took in a movie in the afternoon. Later that evening they met Bear at the restaurant. Buca de Beppo was a world-famous restaurant chain known for its family-style Italian food and boisterous atmosphere. It was a fun place and everybody was having a great time.

When the meal was about over and everybody but Alicia was so stuffed they could hardly move, Ricky told Alphonse he was going to hit the restroom. Then he never came back. He didn't say good-bye or see you later or anything, he was just gone. Alphonse waited, then did a few laps around the restaurant, but Ricky was history.

Deep down in his gut, Alphonse wasn't surprised that Ricky had split. Even though Ricky was just a kid, he was pretty independent. But Alphonse was hurt. He was hoping they had something working that would give them the foundation for a real friendship. Doug and Paolo were puzzled as well. On the ride back to Harry's guest house, Alphonse found himself scanning the sidewalks and the street corners.

"Hey, guys, maybe he might show up at the guest house later or something," said Alphonse with a note of hope in his voice.

"Yeah, maybe," said Paolo. He didn't sound convinced. "Yo Doug, what time we got to be at the track in the morning?"

"Bear wants us there at 7 A.M. I think."

Paolo groaned. "The party is ovvvver. Time to go to work."

Alphonse said nothing. He was still scanning the sidewalks.

When Paolo and Doug woke up to the alarm at the crack of dawn the next morning, Alphonse was gone. No note, no nothing, just gone. His stuff was still there in the room, but he was not there. Alphonse knew how to take care of himself, but Paolo still worried. He didn't have a whole lot of time to dwell on the situation, however, because he had to get out to the track and get set for qualifying.

No racetrack looks good in the rain, especially this one, thought Bear as he stood in the doorway of the garage slot assigned to the team. *It's a lot like watching a beautiful woman getting a facial and her hair done at the beauty parlor. Some things are better left unseen.*

This track was built for the warm California sunshine. It wasn't a place designed to accommodate a liquid deluge. There weren't a lot of places for folks to take shelter, and those out in it were trying to hold themselves together for dear life. It wasn't just raining, it was pouring.

The rain was racing down the front straight in sheets driven by the wind in the morning grayness. The eleven-degree banking on the corners of the two-mile track added impetus to the water that ran down to the infield to create an ever-growing small lake.

The California Speedway was barely three years old and despite the bath it was receiving just now, was state of the art. It sat on a 530-acre site forty miles east of the Los Angeles basin. It was built on the ashes of the old Kaiser Steel Mill and rose up out of the desert sand like some medieval but ultramodern circus grounds. The only part of the steel mill left was the concrete water tower rising 128 feet from the center of the infield. Right at this moment the rail around the top of the tower was dripping water, which was whipped by the wind in broad arcs across the infield. The palm trees surrounding the parking areas were bowing and scraping as they threw their fronds up in unorganized frenzy. It didn't rain very much in this southern part of the Golden State, but when it did, it went all out.

Everything about the place was fresh and new. The garage area was pristine and on a race weekend would be a veritable beehive bustling with activity. Not today. The cars and gear had been pulled from the haulers as each garage stall was meticulously set up . . . but that was it. The multicolored race cars, usually the center of everyone's attention, sat alone and unattended. Some had their hoods up, while others were on jackstands with wheels and tires off. But for the most part, they sat mute in silent uselessness.

Oval track racing doesn't happen in the rain. Stock cars run slick racing tires that get more grip as the rubber builds heat. Slick tires and wet pavement don't mix.

Bear stood inside the garage with his hands in his back pockets, watching the rain sweep across the pit compound. His view of the track was limited by the luxury suites built just behind pit lane. He could see the grandstand on the outside of the front straight. The flagpoles lining the top edge were bending as the wind tore at the flags. On a regular Friday, there would be several thousand folks sitting up there watching practice and, later on, qualifying.

Bear pulled the schedule out of his shirt pocket and looked it over for the third time this morning. This was a full weekend. The Winston West cars were supposed to practice first, then the Busch cars, and then the

Cup cars. From the looks of things, nobody would be on the track anytime soon. They had already lost half the morning. Not one car had turned a wheel. Even if it stopped raining right now, it would still take at least an hour, maybe two, to get the track in shape to run. The Cup cars were scheduled for two one-hour practice sessions before the first qualifying session this afternoon. The fastest twenty-five cars would be guaranteed a starting spot for Sunday's race. Those that didn't make it today would have another shot at it tomorrow.

Every Winston Cup team wanted to be one of those first twenty-five qualifiers. Once a car was in the race, all the effort could be put toward making the car competitive for the race. Preparing a car setup for a one-lap qualifying run was a lot different than setting it up for the race. In qualifying, the cars ran one at a time with special motors and chassis setups that were designed to get as much speed as possible out of the car.

The fastest car sat on the pole and picked up a bucket of extra prize money. Bear quite honestly thought that the Speed King Chevrolet had a shot at it. He was disappointed at the loss of practice time.

He turned back to face the crew sitting in various postures of relaxation around the garage area. Paolo was sitting on a stack of tires with his back against the wall, trying to catch a little sleep. Even though they went to bed relatively early last night, Paolo still looked tired. He looked like he was thinking deeply about something, too. He had been really quiet all morning. He jumped as Bear yelled.

"Hey guys, let's put those other shocks back on the car and change the track bar."

There was a chorus of groans as a handful of shop rags came flying his way. "Come on, Bear, we just did that. Now you want to go back to the old setup."

"Just funnin', guys. Just funnin'," Bear laughed. The truth was that the car was as ready as it was going to get. They were at the stage where if they did anything more to the car it would probably be wrong. Bear checked his watch, then said to Bud Prescott, "I'm going to walk over to the media center and check out Harry's press conference. Tell the boys to be ready. You know as soon as it's over, the media folks will be by to ask us what we think. Tell the guys not to say anything."

"Got it, Bear, no problem. Everybody knows," Bud said.

Bear grabbed a raincoat and headed out into the wind.

In contrast to the weather outside, the media center was warm as toast. There was a large group of journalists sitting in the rows of plush chairs surrounding the raised platform. Harry was sitting behind a table with several microphones in front of him and Hildy was at his side. Occasionally the room would light up with a camera flash as folks took pictures. Harry looked tired and in pain. The cold, rainy weather was taking its toll on him, but he still managed to convey a level of charm and confidence. Orly stood off to the side with his arms folded, leaning against the wall. His face was impassive and unreadable. Harry had finished reading a prepared statement and was ready to take questions.

Bear slipped into the back of the room. He was close enough to overhear one reporter talking into a microphone.

"There you have it, folks. Harry Hornbrook, the owner and CEO of Speed King Oil Company and a fixture around racing for thirty-five years, has just announced that he is stepping down and turning control of his company over to his daughter, Ms. Hildy Hornbrook. He has also disclosed that he is under treatment for cancer and is optimistic about the future."

"Optimistic!" Bear snorted to himself. Then he looked over at Orly and saw the look on his face. Bear knew that look and he didn't like it. *When Orly closes his face off like that it means he is upset about something.* Bear frowned.

One reporter raised his hand. "Mr. Hornbrook, rumor has it that you are facing a hostile takeover by a large corporation that has targeted you as a potential acquisition. Is this true?"

"As the new CEO, I would like to respond to that question if I might," Hildy said. "Any time a company is as successful as Speed King has been and is today, you face opposition. It is true that a certain conglomerate is trying to take control of us. We have been in contact with our minority stockholders, and we feel certain that we can still be the viable, independent profitable company that we are today."

Bear smiled to himself. "That's the way, Hildy." Certain words like successful, viable, independent, and profitable have positive impact. Just like words like opposition and conglomerate have negative impact. *This lady knows what she's doing.*

"Ms. Hornbrook, aren't you a little young and inexperienced to handle a company like Speed King? After all . . ." the question came from the back row.

The whole room waited to hear Hildy's response. She laughed an easy, confident laugh that struck a responsive chord in every man in the room.

"Yes, that is a legitimate question. But don't forget who I am. I'm Harry Hornbrook's daughter. I have been involved with Speed King practically my whole life. What I know about business I learned from my dad. We have a solid board of directors with a tremendous amount of experience. I plan to listen to them very carefully, and I might add that they have given me a unanimous vote of confidence. Next question please."

"Doc Brewster has said that he's no longer affiliated with Speed King. Is this true? He has also said he's contemplating litigation against the company as well. Have you cut off sponsorship of his NHRA program?"

"Yes, that's true. We felt it was in the best interest of the company to sever relations with Mr. Brewster at this time. This doesn't mean we're getting out of the drag racing business. Currently, we're negotiating with two other teams to carry the Speed King logo," Hildy responded.

"What about Winston Cup?"

"Our current contract with the Orly Mann Racing Team runs through the end of this year, and as the season progresses we will continue to evaluate on both sides," Hildy responded again.

"Hildy, I mean Ms. Hornbrook, Speed King has been a sponsor of the Orly Mann Racing Team since its inception. Does this mean that you are considering not sponsoring them? Are you thinking of sponsoring another team or getting out of Winston Cup entirely?"

"I stand by my original statement."

Bear swallowed. This was news to him. He thought their relationship with Speed King was solid. At least it seemed that way after the meeting in Harry's office the other day. Bear looked over at Orly, who was still standing against the wall with that impassive look on his face.

"Maybe we could have a response from Orly Mann. Orly, how would you define your relationship with Speed King?"

Orly spoke without unfolding his arms. "Well, folks, don't misunderstand. Speed King is still our sponsor. Every racing team and sponsor go through a period of evaluation at the end of the year to try to figure how they might do things different or better. I think a lot of it hinges on how well we do this year. Racing is all about winning, and a winning team has a better opportunity to sell product. That's what it's about." Orly smiled and went on. "Now don't misunderstand me or misquote me. We have been affiliated with Speed King for a long time and we would like to be for a long time to come."

Finally the press conference was over. Harry and Hildy headed out one door and Orly went out the other. Bear hustled to catch up with him.

He finally caught up and tried to match Orly's long-legged strides. Orly looked over at Bear and said nothing.

"I take it the date didn't go well last night," Bear said.

Orly still said nothing, just looked straight ahead.

"Uh, Hoss, do you mind telling me what's going on? I am your partner, you know."

Orly looked at Bear. "You know, Bear, I'll be very glad to get back in the race car. At least there I know what I'm doing."

Bear mumbled, "Well, of course you do, Orly. You always know what you're doing. Every move is carefully planned and . . ."

Orly interrupted, "Here's the deal. She acted mad the whole evening. She accused me of taking her out just to keep our business relationship solid. She insisted we stay in town and we ended up at the Sizzler, which was a disaster. She should have known better. You know I can't go into a place like that. It was just one interruption after another. Before it was over, folks were lined up two-deep for autographs. We finally got out of there with our dinners half-eaten. I tried to talk to her in the car, but it wasn't happening. So I just gave up. She is done with me, Bear, and I think it is for the best. Especially if she is going to be the boss of our primary sponsor. I just have to keep it on a business level." With that, Orly walked off into the rain toward the motor home compound. He yelled back over his shoulder, "Call me when this rain stops and we can get back to something we know."

148

Doug took a breath, squared his shoulders, and knocked on Orly's door. When it opened, Doug noted the sour expression on Orly's face. It surprised him. Orly seldom looked upset, even in the most difficult of circumstances.

"Hey, Doug, what's up?" Orly looked around Doug. "I see the rain's still coming down in sheets."

"Orly, I'm sorry to bother you, but did you have a chance to talk to Hildy about Loren?" Doug asked, wiping rain off his face.

"Doug, I'm sorry, but I just didn't have the opportunity. Bear and I have taken care of her hospital bill. We're having it sent to the shop and she can pay us back when she's able. We also set her up with some cash so she can get on her feet. She doesn't know it yet, but when they release her, the doctor will make sure she gets it. Other than that, I don't know what else we can do."

Doug shrugged. "Yeah, I know, Orly. I was just wondering. Well hey, you and Bear have done a lot for her. She'll be okay." With that, Doug left.

A few minutes later Doug popped into the garage, looking for Bear. He found him talking with a couple other crew chiefs in a corner. "Hey Bear, I'm going to take off for a while. Nothing happening here. Looks like it's going to rain the rest of the day. Mind if I take a rental car for a few minutes?"

Bear hardly paid attention. Just waved an okay to him.

It took him a while to get across town in the rain. He stopped in front of the gate, debated a minute, then keyed in the code. Doug eased up the driveway of the Hornbrook house and parked the car in the driveway. Then he made a dash through the rain and knocked on the door. A surprised Yolanda took his wet jacket and ushered him into the living room. Harry was ensconced in his overstuffed chair in the corner by the big picture window overlooking the yard and pool. He had already changed into pajamas and bathrobe. He looked very tired. This morning's conference had worn him out. Hildy came into the room, still dressed in the dark business suit she'd worn to the track. She seemed agitated.

"Doug, what brings you over here? Did you leave something in the guest house? I thought you guys moved out to the track yesterday," she said, removing her small diamond earrings as she spoke.

"No, Hildy, I didn't leave anything. I, uh, I wanted to talk to you about something, actually about somebody," Doug stammered. She still had that effect on him. She was so beautiful and seemed so confident. Watching her remove the earrings unnerved him. It also made him mad. He needed to be able to say what he had to say. "Hildy, could you just not talk to me for a minute? I need to ask you and Mr. Hornbrook something and I can't think so good when you, uh, you know."

Hildy frowned. "Sure, Doug. Whatever you want."

Harry watched him from the chair, saying nothing.

Doug plunged in. "Orly was going to talk to you about this last night, but I guess it didn't happen. You folks know Loren is in the hospital. She is due to be released tomorrow. Well, she doesn't have anyplace to go or anyone to look after her until she gets well. I visited her this morning and she doesn't even have any money. I mean she doesn't have any money at all. When she quit Doc, she didn't even have enough to pay for her hotel room. But money isn't her biggest problem." Seeing that Harry and Hildy were both listening to him intently, he continued.

"You see, Loren is really all alone and she is very scared. She needs somebody to be her friend, but she doesn't know how to ask. She's been on her own practically her whole life and everybody she knows just wants to use her. Doc is the best example. When she didn't work out the way he wanted, he threw her away like an old shop rag. She needs help. I don't know how to help her, but you guys do. I really care about her a lot. I was wondering if you would maybe let her come and stay here for a while until she gets well?" Doug blew out a big breath.

"When is she due to be released from the hospital?" Harry asked.

"Tomorrow morning, the doctor said."

Harry folded his hands and rubbed his nose with his thumbs, thinking. "Doug, let's do this," Harry said after a minute. "Why don't you let Hildy and me talk about this. After we've made a decision we'll call you and let you know. We need a little time to think this through and figure out what the Lord would have us do."

"She isn't a Christian you know, Mr. Hornbrook."

"That is not important, Doug. At least not right now. Hildy and I need to talk first. We'll let you know."

"Well, thanks for listening. At first I felt bad about asking you folks, but it seems the logical thing to me. Anyway, thanks. I'll be going now," he added, as he headed for the door.

Doug started the engine of the rental car and headed down the driveway, praying silently, "Lord, please take care of Loren. You know what's best for her."

Inside the house the battle lines were being drawn. Having learned from past experience, Yolanda retreated to the kitchen and closed the door.

"Hildy, I think we should do this. I would like to ask the girl to come and live with us. We have plenty of room. We could nurture her for a while and help restore her health."

"No, Dad, it is out of the question. Your health is fragile enough. We don't need someone here that might upset you. It is a big enough adjustment to have me move back in the house."

Harry was silent for a minute. Then he said, "Hildy, you know you don't have to move back here. You could very easily get your own place, have your own life. You don't have to take care of me twenty-four hours a day. Running the company is going to take all your energy. Why don't you get your own place?"

It was the final straw. The events of the past few days were piled on top of each other. Hildy was mad. She was willing to give up her job and life in San Diego to come and keep Speed King Oil Company functioning. She was even beginning to get a little excited about leading the company into the new millennium. But she expected her father to be more grateful, more appreciative.

She turned on him, with eyes flashing. "I don't understand you. I am sacrificing my life for your sake, for the sake of your company, and you don't even appreciate it. I'm doing my best to take care of you and make your last days on earth comfortable and free from stress, and you don't even care. What do you want from me?" she said with her fists clenched on her thighs.

Harry ran one hand over his nearly bald head and rubbed the back of his neck. "I'm sorry, Hildy, I've made a mistake. I was afraid of this.

Let's back up a little. I'll call the lawyers tomorrow and we can begin the sale process."

"What are you talking about? I've made a commitment and I thought we had a deal."

"It's obvious to me this isn't what you really want to do. You asked me what I wanted from you? Well, I suppose I'm asking too much. I wanted you to have a heart for the company and the employees. I wanted you to understand the company like I do. I wanted you to share my vision of what the company could be . . . the future of the company. It's too much to ask. You have your own life and you aren't me." Harry laboriously pulled himself out of the chair. "I'm going to go lie down for a while." He started for the bedroom but stopped. "One other thing. I don't know if you are too stubborn, or you are just blind, or maybe you just don't want to see it, but Orly is very much in love with you. It has taken him a while to work through his grief, but I think he has come to a point where he wants to start over with you. Ordinarily I wouldn't dream of meddling with your personal life, Hildy . . . but you could do a lot worse than Orly. He loves the Lord and I think he loves you. He has for a long time, he just didn't know how to make it work."

Harry staggered a little as he headed down the hall. He braced himself against the wall and turned to Hildy once again. "Speaking of grief, I wonder if maybe that isn't the root of your anger. I miss your mother more than you can possibly imagine and I know that you miss her yourself. I'm going to take a nap. Then I'm going to have Yolanda drive me to the hospital to see Loren. I'm going to give her the opportunity to come and live here for a period of time. No, make that as long as she wants. This is still my house."

Hildy watched, speechless, as Harry worked his way down the hall and turned the corner into the master bedroom.

A few minutes later she stepped out into the rain in her bathing suit, walked down the stairs to the pool, and dove off the end and began swimming laps as fast as she could.

Bear was frustrated and bored. The rain kept coming and he had talked to everyone he possibly could. He had drunk too much coffee and his stomach was upset. He had sat around with the boys and swapped racing stories until the garage was so full of imaginary tire smoke it was hard to breathe. He had fended off the inevitable questions from practically everybody about their relationship with Speed King. He had given two television interviews about the race on Sunday and what they expected. The truth was he didn't know what to expect, but he didn't say that in front of the cameras. He had even signed a handful of autographs as folks tried to find something to do to while away the long afternoon hours. It was obvious there wasn't going to be any practice today nor any qualifying either. Bear was thinking about the alternative when the NASCAR official came around to tell him there was a meeting scheduled in half an hour to revamp the schedule.

In the meantime the Speed King Chevrolet sat in the middle of the garage, ignored like some miscreant stepchild.

The NASCAR official stood behind the podium and spoke over his fat belly into the microphone. "Today is a washout. The forecast is for clear weather tomorrow and Sunday. We don't have enough time to let you practice and then run qualifying tomorrow. As you know, the Busch race is being televised live on ABC at 11 A.M. and is followed by the Kentucky Derby, which is live, too, so we can't move the schedule on that. The bottom line is, folks, we are going to cancel qualifying entirely.

"That's not the only bad news. Because the schedule is cramped, we can only give you a little over an hour of practice tomorrow to set your cars up for the race. Sorry, but that's the way it has to be. Qualifying for the race will be determined as follows. Starting positions 1–35 will be determined by points in the championship standings and positions 36–43 will be determined by postmarks. If we have two entries with the same postmark, then the order will revert to points earned so far in the season. This means that the current points leader will sit on the pole and collect the prize money. We will post the starting grid in a few minutes. Pit stalls will be awarded with the same procedure."

There was a chorus of groans and whistles that greeted this announcement, but everybody knew it had to be this way. In reality it wasn't entirely fair, but the system worked.

Bear grunted. He figured as much. *That's not too bad for us,* he thought. They got knocked down to twelfth in the standings after the crash at Talledega. But it would be okay. Twelfth wasn't bad. Pit stalls were awarded by qualifying position. So at least they would have a decent pit for the race. He'd better get the book out and study what they did last year in terms of setting up the car. The book on this track wasn't too thick just yet. They had run here only twice before. But this was a new chassis this year and it hadn't been dialed in yet. An hour practice session wasn't much. Barely give them time to make shock adjustments and set the suspension. Bear's mind spiraled off into gear ratios and jet settings for the carb. Fuel mileage might play a big part in this race.

"Let's see, the track might be a little green with all this rain, so we'll have to take that in consideration for practice. Then by race time it will have a lot of rubber built up from the other races before us." Bear was speaking out loud to himself as he hustled back to the garage. He looked up at the sky again. The rain was gradually letting up, but it was too late now. In just a few minutes the Winston Cup garage area looked like it was supposed to as the team managers and crew chiefs came back from the meeting. Qualifying wasn't going to happen and everybody was trying to get a jump on practice tomorrow. Virtually every race car in the garage was now the center of attention as crews started changing motors and pulling suspension packages. The place looked like a kicked-over anthill, and Bear was happy to be doing something. The level of excitement and intensity took a dramatic jump as the teams started getting serious about the race on Sunday. As if to add emphasis, the rain stopped completely as the clouds started breaking up in the clearing sky.

Alphonse was okay. He was relatively dry and he had found Ricky. He hadn't talked to him yet, but it was as he expected. Ricky had gone back to his gang, his "crew," as he called it. If they ran true to form, they would give Ricky a good beating and then welcome him back with open arms. Probably tell him that if he left again, they would kill him. Disloyalty wasn't tolerated in any gang. Alphonse knew all about it from firsthand experience.

He had tried to go to bed that night, but he couldn't sleep. Finally he grabbed his coat and headed out to find Ricky. He had an idea where Ricky might be. Maybe he could track him down and talk him into coming back with him. He caught the bus and headed down Indian Hills Drive to the downtown area and the hotel. That was where he first had contact with Ricky. The cop said it was their home turf. He spent most of the day checking out the neighborhoods and looking for gang signs. It took him a while, but he finally discerned the gang graffiti on fences and door fronts that marked the Ranger territory. Once he had the territory marked out in his mind, it was just a question of waiting and watching.

Alphonse spotted Ricky early that evening. He was following a group of about six guys and was limping badly. Alphonse stayed hidden. He would wait for just the right opportunity to reach out to the kid. Alphonse stood in a bus shelter and prayed as the rain turned to a light drizzle.

Bear's cell phone was laying in the top of the toolbox in the garage area. It went off with a shrill whistle. One of the crewmen picked it up and turned and tossed it to Bear.

"Hello," he answered. He listened for a minute, then said, "How bad is it? Not expected to make it! Sorry to hear that. Me? Are you sure? Why me I wonder? Okay. As soon as I can."

"Bud, lock it up for me. I got an emergency. I got to get to the hospital. I'll see you later at the motor home, but I don't know when." With that he was running again, except this time he was heading for the parking lot to grab the rental car. He yelled back over his shoulder, "I want everybody, and I mean everybody, at the motor home a half hour before the garage opens tomorrow morning. We got a lot to do and not much time to do it and I need to talk to everybody."

Bud Prescott responded, "No problem, Bear. I'll have them all there."

It is for freedom that Christ has set us free. Stand firm, then, and do not let yourselves be burdened again by a yoke of slavery.

Galatians 5:1

"We ran good here last year so I'm not too worried about the lack of practice and qualifying . . . I guess we're in pretty good hands at this point."
Dale Earnhardt Jr., former Busch driver,
now Winston Cup car #8 Budweiser Chevrolet

IT WAS 2:30 A.M. when Alphonse looked at his watch and yawned. He was in the older section of town, and despite the late hour, there was still a lot of activity going on. Several of the bars had closed down for the mandatory 2 A.M. closing, and the street was full of noisy drunks that had been shoved out the doors.

He was sitting in such a way that he could see the front window reflected in the mirror that hung on the wall above the pie case. The gang, including Ricky, were hanging in an alley across the street from the diner, smoking dope. His trained eye told him they were doing the occasional drug deal with the after-hours bar crowd.

Alphonse was tired. This was his second night without sleep, but he was reluctant to give up. He was still waiting for an opportunity to approach Ricky alone, but so far no dice. He debated whether to call it quits, but the voice inside him told him to hang on. *Maybe God will give me an opportunity. I'm sure praying one will come.*

The counter man came along with the coffeepot. "Refill there?"

"Yeah, one more time," Alphonse said as he watched the mirror.

Ten minutes later, three squad cars suddenly surrounded the alley. The police jumped out with guns drawn. In just a few minutes, they had several guys up against the wall and started going through their pockets.

Alphonse quickly paid for his coffee and stepped into the street to get a better view of what was happening. He saw the cops cuff several guys and put them in the back of the police cars. It looked like a lot of guys were going for a ride, but so far no Ricky. Alphonse moved around several times to get a better view and make sure he didn't miss him. No, he was certain Ricky wasn't arrested.

Pretty soon it was over. The cops drove off and the street was empty. Even the drunks had run, not wanting to get caught up in the sweep. Alphonse stepped across the street just in time to see Ricky limping out of the alley like a rat out of a hole.

"Yo, Ricky!"

Ricky jumped like he had been shot. He looked like he was about to run. Then it appeared he thought better of it, deciding to brave it out instead.

"Who's calling, man?"

"Yo, it's me, Alphonse."

Ricky visibly relaxed. "Hey, Alphonse, how you doing?"

Alphonse looked at him under the dim streetlight and could tell by the look on his face and the way he was talking that he was stoned.

"What are you doing? You look ripped," Alphonse said.

"Yeah, maybe. My crew turned on me a little and I needed something for the pain. You know, man."

"You mean they beat you, so you got high. How come you didn't get busted when everybody else did?" Alphonse said.

Ricky laughed. "That's 'cause we be smarter than them dumb cops. We hang in this alley 'cause there's a crack in the side of the building that only a guy like me can get through. It goes into a closet, so I just went in there and put a board against the door. They never even look for me."

"Come on, Ricky, let's go. Come with me and I'll get you straightened out."

"No can do, bro. Can't do it, Alphonse, my brother. I got to go and reach out to some people so my crew can get out of jail. Can't leave 'em, it goes against the code. If I did they would hunt me down again and probably waste me next time."

"Hey Ricky, we already talked about this. We can get you set up in the city. Pastor Tom said he would help. I would be there. We could protect you. You know you put your faith in Jesus. God would protect you, man. You belong to him now." Alphonse found himself pleading with Ricky.

"Nah, I can't do that, Alphonse. My crew is my family. I can't leave them. It wouldn't be right. Yeah, I prayed with you guys, but it didn't mean anything. See? Nothing changed in my life. All that happened was I got another beating."

"Ricky, be realistic. They are the ones that beat you and hurt you. You went back to them and look how they treated you. What kind of family is that?"

"It's okay. I had it coming. They explained that to me before they turned on me. They was right. I shouldn't have left them, and I shouldn't have told you what they done to your room and all. I had it coming, man."

Alphonse reached out to take Ricky's arm. "Come on, Ricky, come with me. We'll get you straightened out."

Ricky yanked his arm away. "Don't touch me. I don't want nobody touching me. The next guy that touches me I'm gonna hurt 'em real bad." Ricky staggered a little as he said this.

Alphonse was about to grab him again when two guys came out of the shadows.

"Yo, Ricky, is this brother hassling you?" The guy made the term "brother" sound like the lowest scum on the earth.

Ricky looked at Alphonse. "You better get out of here, Alphonse. They could do you real bad."

"You sure that's what you want? I'll stand up for you if you want me to."

"No, get outta here. Go man, before it's too late."

Alphonse looked at the two guys. They were a different type than Ricky. They were older, more serious, and they looked capable of doing whatever was necessary. They also looked like they might enjoy it. It was dark and there wasn't anybody else around. Besides, nobody would interfere if they saw two Hispanic guys beating up a black guy this time of night in this neighborhood.

"Okay, I'm going. Hey, Ricky, I'm going to be praying for you for the rest of my life, or at least until I know you are walking with the Lord. I think your prayer was real and I know Jesus won't let you go. Remember that."

With that parting shot Alphonse spun on his heel and headed back up the sidewalk. He didn't look back until he was half a block away. Then when he did there wasn't anybody there. Ricky was gone.

Alphonse had a lump in his throat as he walked in the darkness. The kid had had a chance and he didn't take it. But then God wasn't finished with him yet. Who knew what would happen? Only God. Alphonse raised his head and breathed in the cool night air. The rain was done and the air smelled clean and fresh. He wished he felt the same. Now if he could only find a cab. He had enough money to get a ride back up the hill to Harry's place. Then he laughed to himself. "Yeah, that's going to happen. A young black man is going to get a cab to stop for him at 3:00 A.M. Yeah right." Then he resigned himself to a long trek up Indian Hills Drive to the different world at the top.

A scant two hours later Bear opened his eyes in the predawn darkness to the beeping sound of the alarm. He snaked an arm from under the covers and finally found the thing on the night table to shut it off. It took him a second or two to orient himself. He was in his bunk in the motor home at the racetrack. *Let's see,* he thought, *this is Saturday morning and I have just a little over an hour's worth of practice this morning to get the car ready for tomorrow's race.*

His mind shifted into overdrive as he started thinking of setup options like gear ratios and such . . . and then with a jerk he came back to the reality of last night. He was still tired and hadn't been in bed all that long. He spent most of last night at yet another hospital. The call yesterday was from the emergency room of the Pomona Hospital, informing him that Doc Brewster had a heart attack and was in bad shape. Bear's name was the only one on his "next of kin list," which was news to Bear. They asked Bear to come to the hospital and so he went.

When he got there, Doc was unconscious, and the doctor came out to the waiting room to tell him Doc was in rough shape and the prognosis was not good. Even in this modern day there was only so much that could be done with hearts, and they had done all they could. The doctor was guarded but he doubted if Doc was going to make it through the night. Bear was trying to sort that out and at the same time figure out why he was on Doc's list. *Doesn't Doc have any family?* No one could give him any answers.

Apparently Doc was supervising work being done on some cylinder heads at a local machine shop when he collapsed. The guys there were sharp enough to do CPR and call 911. So far Doc hadn't regained consciousness and here he was.

Bear was at a loss, so he waited . . . and prayed. He must have dozed off, because he was sitting in a chair in the waiting room with his head on his hand when the nurse gently shook him awake.

"Mr. Brewster is awake and is asking for you. I think you better hurry," she said.

Bear followed her into the elevator and upstairs to the ICU area. She took him through the double doors marked "No Admittance" and into Doc's room. He was lying on the bed, with tubes and wires going every direction. His eyes were open and even though he was in pain it was obvious he knew what was going on.

"See you got here," said Doc in a low, raspy voice.

"Yes, I'm here, Doc." Bear's mind was full of questions but, considering the circumstances, he decided to let Doc speak. Maybe, Doc wanted to know about the Lord. Maybe God would use this opportunity to draw Doc into his kingdom. "Do you want me to pray with you, Doc?"

"No! Too late for that. That's not why I had your name down." Even though he was weak, Doc was adamant and forceful in his speech. "Want you to just listen to me and do what I say. You're one of the few honest men I know. Can I trust you?" Doc looked up into Bear's eyes.

Bear looked back. "Yes, you can trust me, Doc."

"Am I dying?"

"Well, Doc, I only know what the doctor said, and it don't look so good right now. Doc, I would really like to pray with you."

Doc ignored the last part of Bear's response. "Yeah, I'm dying. I can feel it." He looked up again at Bear. "Now listen to me. There is a little address book in my wallet. On the 'O' page is the name of a bank in Ontario, close to here. On the 'P' page down at the bottom is a number. It is a safety deposit box number at that bank. The key is on my key ring. It has an 'R' stamped on it for a 'rainy day.'" Doc laughed a little wheezy laugh. Then he went on. "Your name is on the list at the bank to get into the box. I set that up with them, too. All you have to do is go there and get it. Do you understand me?" Doc reached out and grabbed Bear's arm with his left hand in a surprisingly strong grip.

"Yes, Doc. 'O' page is the bank, 'P' page is the box number, and the key is on your ring marked with an 'R'. Doc, are you sure you don't want me to pray with you?" Bear was almost pleading in his tone.

"Told you no, Erickson. Too late for that. Now listen to me. I want you to take care of that Loren girl. I didn't treat her right and she done the best she could for me. She wasn't a bad driver. Will you do it?" Doc shook Bear's arm with his clenched fingers.

Bear's mind raced. *This is turning into a bad movie. A safe deposit box in Ontario. Man, who ever heard of such a thing? Everybody knows Doc is a little eccentric, but this goes beyond eccentric to the realm of really strange.*

"Yes, Doc, we're taking care of Loren. Me and Orly."

Doc coughed and lost his breath for a minute. He released his grip on Bear's arm. He finally breathed a big breath and sucked in precious oxygen from the tubes in his nose. He seemed to regain his strength and looked up at Bear again. "Promise me you will do this, Erickson. Promise me you will go to the bank and get in that box. Promise me in the name of that God you are always talking about . . . promise me now."

"Okay, Doc, I promise," Bear said in a quiet voice. "Doc, is there anybody else we can call? Do you have family somewhere? Anybody?"

"Got no one. Don't want no one. Been a gypsy all my life. You promised. Tell Hornbrook I hope he loses the whole blasted company. I never liked him much. Another one of those Bible thumpers. Just like you, Erickson, except you understand motors." Then suddenly Doc went stiff and died. Just breathed out a final breath and that was it.

Bear stepped back and the nurse stepped in. A minute later the doctor came in, pronounced him dead, and that was that. Doc was gone.

Bear swung his legs over the edge of the bed. He sat up and looked at the stuff on the little table next to the window. Sure enough, there was the address book and the key. He looked at the alarm clock ticking away on the same table. It was time to get up and get going. He would think about last night and sort through it when he had time. In the meantime, there were other fish to fry. Bear raised his voice to bellow.

"All right you beauties, time to rock and roll. Let's get them sweet patooties out of them warm beds. We got to get busy." Then he raised it an octave higher. "Come on, time to *get up!*"

He was greeted with a chorus of groans and assorted mumbling as the Orly Mann Racing Team greeted the new day.

Meanwhile, in another hospital across the valley, Loren opened her eyes in the early morning to greet the same new day. She couldn't see outside from her hospital bed, but a big clock in her room counted the minutes and hours. She was getting out today and she was scared. She wasn't sure what was going to happen or even what she was going to do, but one thing was certain. She wasn't staying here in this place.

The nurse came in to check her vitals. "Everything is looking good. The doctor will be in around ten and then you can go home."

Loren smiled a fake smile and nodded her head. "Home." That was a strange word for her. She wasn't sure where that might be. She thought of Doug. He had been to see her twice. The first time she was still out of it and didn't remember much, but the second time he hung around and acted like a cute little puppy. He kept telling her not to worry, that everything would be okay. She smiled and agreed with him, but inside she knew better. Things didn't get better by themselves. He didn't know that she had no place to go and no money to get there. A wave of anxiety washed over her. *I'd better come up with some sort of plan and soon. Maybe I should just throw myself on the mercy of the hospital and doctor. Just tell them I can't leave because I don't have anyplace to go.* She

162

had a vision of herself living underneath a freeway overpass, pushing a shopping cart around like a bag lady. It was too close to reality to make her laugh.

At least Doug brought some of her stuff so she could clean up. He told her Alicia had the rest of it and would get it to her. Loren didn't have the courage to ask about the hotel. They would probably be tracking her down as soon as she got out of here.

Two hours later, Hildy swept into the hospital room with quick strides and greeted Loren. Loren had managed to wash her hair and make herself somewhat presentable, but Hildy's elegance coupled with her confidence intimidated Loren and made her feel like she needed a shower and complete makeover.

"Hi, Loren, how are you feeling?" Hildy asked as she extended her hand in a graceful motion.

Loren took the proffered hand and shook it briefly. "I'm okay, Ms. Hornbrook. Actually, I'm feeling pretty good. Still weak, but I'm okay, I think."

"Call me Hildy, Loren. My father wanted to be here but he couldn't. He's ill and doesn't have the strength to come. But I am here speaking as his representative. I've been doing that a lot lately."

Hildy kept talking. "We want you to come to our place and stay with us until you get back on your feet. My father has the greatest respect for you and he thinks that we might help you. We have a large place with several spare rooms and you would be very comfortable. We want you to come and live with us. The doctor should be in shortly, and when he releases you, we will have a car waiting."

Loren was taken aback. She wasn't quite sure how to respond. Loren quickly put on her own facade of confidence and sophistication. She bridled at the thought of someone taking over her life. "Thank you for your offer, Ms. Hornbrook, but I couldn't possibly accept. I have made other plans."

Hildy cut her off and her tone changed, "Loren, let's look at the facts. I'll not play games with you. You attempted suicide, which is a very serious thing. You need help. You need to have time to think that through. You have no money and you have no place to go. The only family you have is back in North Carolina, and I doubt if they would be much help to you. We have the resources and the willingness to help you. Don't be foolish. Take what is offered to you."

In her weakened state, Loren did not have the strength to maintain her facade for long. Finally it broke apart and fell into pieces on the bed. She bowed her head and started to cry into her hands. She mumbled between her fingers, "I can't do this anymore. I just can't do it. I don't know what to do and I don't have any place to go and I don't have any money left and I don't know who to trust." She sobbed with her shoulders heaving.

Hildy gently patted her shoulder. "Yes, I know, Loren. Why not trust us? The lady driving the car is named Yolanda and she will take care of getting you settled. You'll be out of this place shortly. The sun is shining and it is a beautiful day. The room we have for you has a wonderful bathroom with a nice Jacuzzi bathtub. Come home, get a good soak, and relax. I'm on my way out to the racetrack, but I'll be back later this afternoon. Bear and the guys are coming for dinner tonight. Alicia is coming, too, and she has the rest of your stuff from the hotel. You can either join us or stay in your room. Whatever you prefer. You can do what you like. Now stop worrying. Things are going to be fine. Better than fine, things are going to be good. I'll see you then." With that Hildy turned on her heel and walked out of the room.

Loren stared at the empty doorway, not certain that it hadn't been a dream.

The nurse bustled in and said, "Was that a friend of yours?"

"I don't know yet," Loren responded.

Like some hibernating metropolis, the California Speedway had finally come alive. The desert sun was brilliant in the early morning, and the crisp air was scrubbed clean by the rain of the preceding days. There was a light breeze blowing with just enough force to make the flags atop the immense grandstands wave gaily in the morning air. The San Gabriel Mountains stood in majestic splendor in the background, with a light dusting of snow adding a dimension of grandeur to the morning.

It was still twenty minutes until the garage area would be opened by NASCAR. Bear had the team gathered together at the motor home compound. His long experience taught him that it was much easier to talk to everybody here rather than trying to get them together in the garage area. There was just too much going on over there. Throw in the media folks and it sometimes got impossible.

"Okay, everybody listen up. We have to be sharp this morning if we want any chance at winning this race. We only have one hour of practice and I have several things that have to be checked. The car has to be ready as soon as we can get it ready. I want to be one of the first teams through inspection. We want to give Orly as much track time as we possibly can. We are going to run ten laps maximum and then come in to make changes. I want everybody to be sharp." Bear was waving his arms like a circus ringmaster as he spoke. Bear eyed the sleepy-looking folks on the team, including Alicia and Doug, to make sure they were all listening intently.

"Tomorrow everybody in the whole field will be making adjustments on every pit stop. You guys know that. Practically everybody is guessing on setup, so we have to be extra sharp. Everything that we can determine today will make a big difference for the race. Now get yourself an extra cup of coffee and let's go to work. Oh yeah. Bud and Paolo, I need to talk to you guys for a minute. Jimmy, you stick around, too."

Bud Prescott waited with Paolo until the rest of the team was gone. Bear pulled them aside and said, "We're flying the rest of the Thunderfoot Ballet team in early this afternoon and I want to run some practice sessions with them. You guys know as well as I do that we're going to be adjusting on the car all day tomorrow, a lot more than usual. I want to practice the drill on pulling spring rubbers and doing track bar adjustments. Bud, you are going to have to be real sharp on the right rear tire, and I want you to make sure your tire carrier goes the right way with his track bar adjustments."

Bud nodded. "Yeah I know, Bear. I think it's a good idea to bring the rest of the guys in early. This weekend is going to be different."

The Thunderfoot Ballet Company were the guys that serviced the car during pit stops. All of them were athletes and they were handpicked by Bear for their ability to work fast under extreme pressure and stay calm in difficult situations. Some of them worked at the shop, and a couple had other jobs that allowed them the time off to get to the races. Bud and Paolo were the only two members of the Ballet Company that traveled with the regular mechanics and fabricators to the various racetracks for the whole race weekend. The job of the regular guys was to set the car up for the race by doing the engine swaps, gear changes, and assorted other tasks to get the car ready for the race. Once the race began, they stayed behind the pit wall and let the Thunderfoot boys do their job. Those guys usually flew in on a special charter flight from North Carolina with guys from other teams that did the same thing. They generally got to the racetrack early on Sunday morning. They worked over the wall doing the fueling and tire changing. As soon as the race was over, they hopped back on the charter and headed home.

But this weekend was going to be different. Every Cup car needed adjustments to the handling during the course of a race. The cars were very sensitive to things like track temperature and weather conditions. Usually the changes were minor, like air pressure in the tires and maybe a track bar adjustment, depending on track conditions. Bear knew the practice time allotted was not going to be enough to get the car dialed in. He also knew the track conditions during practice and the actual race time would be much different. They were practicing in the relative cool of the morning on a "green" track with little tire rubber. The race would be run in the afternoon heat, and by then the track would be pretty slicked up. Plus, things could radically change in the three hours it would take to run the 500 miles, and those things would affect how fast Orly could go.

"Yeah, I want to be certain the Ballet Company knows exactly what they have to do to make the adjustments. It might cost a little more in terms of time and transportation, but hopefully it will pay off come race time."

Paolo nodded in agreement. "Things are gonna change a lot in the three hours it takes to run this 500. I guess I'd better be extra sharp with the jack myself. Especially if we need to pull rubbers and make other changes. Everybody better be on their toes and not tripping over each other's feet, especially mine."

Bear turned to Jimmy. "Jimmy, when you are spotting up there today, I want you to keep close track of how Orly is getting off the corner. That's the key to getting around this place. Remember to remind him about the brakes. Brakes are important here 'cause the corners are so flat.

We'll talk some more just before he goes out, but I wanted to remind you in case I forgot."

Jimmy nodded, then took off his cowboy hat and wiped his brow. "You got it, Bear. We'll take care of him." Jimmy knew that if they were going to be successful it would take a team effort.

Doug and Alicia walked up beside Paolo as they headed for the pits and the garage area. Paolo looked over at Doug.

"So that's all he said? He found Ricky, but Ricky isn't coming back?"

"Yeah, that was pretty much it. Said he was going to hole up at the guest house and sleep today. Said he was going to watch the race from the Speed King suite at the track tomorrow. Hildy asked him to help with Harry and keep an eye on him if he got too tired or anything. I guess they are entertaining folks from the plant and some new accounts and stuff. Said we could hear all about it when we go to the house for dinner tonight. That's all he said," Doug said.

"How did he sound, really?" Alicia said.

"Uh, I don't know. He sounded kinda down. I'm not sure. Maybe depressed would be a better word," Doug said, then went on. "Let's put it this way. He didn't sound good."

"Well, we need to pray for him today and we especially need to pray for Ricky. Poor Alphonse. He really wanted to save that kid," said Alicia. "Hey Doug, I guess Loren is moving in with Harry, huh?"

"Yup, that's what it looks like. I think Hildy talked her into it. She should be over there pretty soon. They are releasing her from the hospital this morning."

"Be the best thing," said Paolo. Then he went on, "Hey guys, just one practice session to get through. Then if Orly keeps it off the wall, I can get the Chevy back home to big NC."

Doug replied, "Yeah, Pally, I almost forgot. They got the backup chassis sold. I hope it works out. Maybe we can find a shop as good as the one you had in San Francisco to fix it."

"I don't know, but I'll tell you one thing. I sure would like to get it fixed. I am sick of looking at it all wounded and beat-up like it is."

Those who sow in tears will reap with songs of joy. He who goes out weeping, carrying seed to sow, will return with songs of joy, carrying sheaves with him.

Psalm 126:5–6

"I ran out of talent before I ran out of nerve."

Mark Martin, Winston Cup driver
(After brushing the wall at Rockingham)
car #6 Valvoline Ford

BEAR LOVED THE EXCITEMENT and sense of urgency. They had been sitting on their hands around this place long enough. It was time to go to work and see just exactly what they had . . . and of course, what everybody else had.

The garage area was complete and utter chaos, which was normal just before a practice session. The garages looked a lot like airplane hangars. Each team was allotted only enough space to conveniently walk around the race car, which put them practically on top of each other. It was standard and nobody complained, but it sure heightened the excitement level when everybody was working at once. The noise was deafening. What made it even worse were the number of media people getting underfoot.

He finished setting the float levels on the carburetor and gave it to Bud to bolt back on the engine. He could see Orly standing against the wall, trapped by a couple of journalists trying to get an interview amidst the confusion. As he was talking, a third guy walked up and stuck a tape recorder under his chin to pick up what he was saying. Bear shook his head. He was glad he wasn't Orly and didn't have to put up with all that bother. They had sometimes been known to follow Orly into the restroom to get an interview. He needed to talk to Orly about Doc, but there hadn't been time. Best to just stay focused on the task at hand. Racing required everybody's full concentration.

Bear looked over Bud's shoulder and, when he was almost done, spoke in his ear, "Let's button it up. They will be opening the track in about ten minutes, and I want Orly to be one of the first in line."

In the noise, Bud didn't try to answer, just nodded his head. Paolo rolled out from underneath the car with a rag in his hand. He was checking nuts and bolts and making sure nothing was leaking. Bear looked down at him and Paolo gave him a thumbs-up from the creeper. Bear looked at his watch again . . . it was time.

He walked over to the corner and took Orly by the arm. "Excuse me, folks, but I really need my driver if you don't mind." He steered Orly toward the car and spoke into his ear. "Get in the car and I'll talk to you on the radio, be easier I think."

Orly nodded.

It'd been two weeks since Orly tried to climb into a race car. Cup cars obviously don't have doors. The classic way to get in is to step through the window with the right leg, put your rear on the window sill, and then slide the rest of your body inside while holding on to the roof. Orly wasn't sure whether his shoulder would take the strain, but he was going to try. Bear could see Orly struggling and motioned to Bud and Paolo.

Paolo stepped up behind Orly and supported him around the waist while he wriggled into the car. Once he was inside, he was fine. He took his custom-fitted radio earpieces off the mirror and inserted them into his ears. The mouthpiece was built into his helmet. He wouldn't be able to speak until he put it on, but he could hear.

Bear put on his own unit, as did the rest of the crew. "Hey, Hoss, let's get you pushed out and in the line. I think we got this thing geared pretty good and you should be able to get off the corners. I'm a little worried about it being loose going in with this shock setup, but I'm thinking that as the tires wear maybe it will balance out."

Orly finished buckling the chin strap on his helmet and then pushed the send button on the steering wheel twice—meaning he understood.

Bear spoke again, "Jimmy, you up there?"

"Yeah Bear, I'm here." Jimmy spoke from his perch high atop the grandstands. "I don't believe I have ever seen such a clear morning here in sunny Southern California," Jimmy said in his soft Texas accent.

"Do your best, Jimmy, to keep him out of trouble, will you?"

"Now Bear, don't you go fretting over me. You know I been spotting for Orly for five years. I know what I'm doing up here," Jimmy replied.

It was a fact and Bear knew it. Jimmy was one of the best spotters in the business. Orly trusted him, which was essential. He was unflappable in the midst of even the most dire circumstances. The truth was Bear trusted him too, but he was just nervous.

"Yeah, Jimmy, I know."

Bear heard the mike click twice in his earphones, which meant that Orly was listening and could copy everybody.

The crew pushed Orly backwards until he was clear of the garage. He reached over and flipped the toggles that would energize the systems in the car. Then he flipped up the red cover and lifted the toggle to start the engine. The starter ground half a second or so, then the Chevrolet motor rumbled into life. Orly watched the gauges, then eased the car into first gear. The crew stopped pushing as Orly idled toward the tunnel under the luxury suites that took him out to the pit lane. As he went through, it was like coming into a whole new world. He could see the grandstands across the track. Already there were several thousand people getting settled to watch practice. He idled up to the front of the pit line, the car bouncing some on the cold tires. He pulled in behind a couple of cars and shut off the motor.

Orly was content. He was exactly where he wanted to be. He looked around the inside of the race car. It was all painted light gray and was done so on purpose. The only thing that set it off was the black padding around the roll bars that surrounded his seat. The crew wanted to be able to spot any potential fluid leaks or any anomalies. It was spartan and functional. No frills, no extraneous additions of any kind except the hook welded to the roll cage to hold his helmet. He liked this part of racing. Actually, he liked all parts of racing. He liked sitting here quiet, knowing that in a few minutes he would be doing something that very few men could do, and that was make a stock car go faster than most anybody else. He liked putting his total focus on the job at hand. To put his whole concentration on one thing—making this car as good as he could for the race tomorrow. In the midst of his self-congratulatory reverie his mind wandered and an image of Hildy appeared. He could see her cool elegance. The beautiful hair and the long-fingered, delicate, yet strong hands. Her wonderful hazel eyes, so deep you could almost swim in them. His daydream was interrupted as the car behind him gently gave him a shove as if to say, "You going or not?" The official was waving the cars out onto the track.

Orly snapped into reality and started the engine. He mentally chastised himself for letting his mind wander. He shoved the car into gear, grinding the transmission in the process. He shook his head with a quick snap, regaining his focus.

All race cars have a feel to them. A driver, a good driver, can tell right from the beginning how good a car is going to be. Orly worked the car through the gears, staying low on the racetrack and watching the gauges as things warmed up. He gradually picked up speed. The car was unhappy running this low groove at this speed. That was okay. It wasn't designed to run this speed in this place on the racetrack. It was designed to run flat out. Then Orly would find which groove suited it best. He came off the fourth turn and rolled into the throttle.

"You there, Jimmy?"

"Yeah, Bear."

"He's moving now."

"I got eyes, Bear."

"Doug, you got him on the clock?"

"I got him, Bear," Doug said.

171

They were all used to Bear's anxiety during practice. Bear was trying to keep track of everything, and think of everything, and do everything all at the same time. He was worse than an old sow bear with three cubs.

Bear looked over at Alicia, who was sitting in a folding chair with a portable computer on her lap. She didn't even look up from the screen, just gave Bear a thumbs-up. He nodded. Alicia was hooked into NASCAR scoring and she was keeping track of everybody on the racetrack, including Orly. Paolo was standing behind Bear, looking over his shoulder as he watched Orly. The rest of the crew was back in the garage waiting. Orly was going to run a few laps, then he would take the car to the garage where the crew, under Bear's direction, would make a few changes.

Hildy stood in front of the tinted glass in the luxury suite. Speed King leased it for the weekend to entertain suppliers, their own employees, and the sales reps. She watched as Orly rocketed down the front straight. Hildy knew Winston Cup racing. She could tell by Orly's aggressive moves in the car that he was serious this time around. She had mixed feelings as she watched him go by two cars on the inside and pick off another on the outside before he braked for the wide number one corner. The competitive side of her, which was never far from the surface, wanted him to go fast and beat the socks off everybody. It was that side of her that wanted Speed King to succeed and was genuinely looking forward to the challenge of running the company.

The other side of her feared for him. She grew up with Cup racing. Harry had always been a fan, even before Speed King became so much a part of the sport. Hildy had seen Orly bang the wall so hard that he was pulled unconscious from the car. She had seen him go end-for-end in a series of flips that made the highlight reels for days in the sports news. She had watched as he climbed from the wreckage in which the only thing left intact was the roll cage. Watched as he waved to the crowd then collapsed in agony with broken ribs. When they had been dating, she tried to attend as many races as she could. Through that process, she celebrated with the team when they won and commiserated when things didn't go right. She understood the highs and lows of racing. Now she was learning to understand men.

Harry was a prime example. She truly misunderstood the circumstances of what he was asking her to do. She thought he was asking her to come and take care of him, to nurture him through the illness, and in the process run Speed King Oil. It wasn't what he was asking her to do at all.

He is really asking me to catch his vision for his company. To see how they could develop the market, employ good people, and make a contribution to the world in which they lived. He didn't want her to hang over him and wipe his chin. He had too much pride for that. As long as he had breath he would wipe his own chin. It was a big step for him to give up control of the company to her, but he understood her abilities better than she did herself. He wanted her to make it work.

The house was another example. It wasn't that he didn't want her to live there with him. He wanted her to live there with him as an equal and not relegate him to an invalid's chair just because he was dying. He didn't want to be smothered, and this was hard for her because that's exactly what she wanted to do every time she thought about him dying and leaving her. *I want to grab him and hold him tight and refuse to let him go. To somehow infuse him with my own vitality . . . but I can't.* She knew that now. They had talked at length, and finally came to an agreement. She would be CEO of Speed King and she would live in the house . . . but so long as Harry was able, he would make his own decisions. Speaking of his own decisions, she hoped bringing Loren into the house was a wise idea.

Orly went screaming by again and she could see him hunkered down in the driver's seat, sitting relaxed at 185 miles per hour.

Doug's voice rattled in Orly's ear, "Forty point four, Orly."

Orly clicked the mike twice. *About 178 miles per hour average,* he thought.

"Two laps, Orly, then bring it in and we'll get a tire temp and plug check. How about that right rear shock? You want to make a change?

Is it pushing at all going in? Be sure and reset the telltale. I want to see what kinda 'r's you are pulling down the back chute," Bear said.

Orly clicked the mike twice.

The practice session went by quickly. Orly, like everybody else on the track, was in and out of the garage a couple of times, making adjustments. Each time Bear changed something, they went a little quicker. Orly was getting a sense of what this car wanted. He could tell it was going to be more than just average when they got it dialed in.

The California Speedway was built with almost flat wide corners and the straights gave a lot of room to pass. The car had a good combination of horsepower and handling, and Bear was doing an excellent job of fine-tuning it. But then, just before they were quite ready, the practice session ended. Orly coasted down the back chute with the engine dead to get a final plug read. He coasted into the garage for the last time before the race. He unsnapped the window net and undid his belts as Bear stuck his head in the window.

"Well, we're third quickest today. We're only off by a couple of hundredths, so I think we could be in the hunt tomorrow. What you think?"

"Yeah, I think you're right. This thing really comes off the corners. This motor is heck for stout, Bear, and I think we got the rear end gear just right. It's pushing just a little going in, but I think we can fix it through the race with tire pressure maybe. I think we're going to be okay. You done good there, buddy."

Bear smiled. *When Orly says it is good . . . why then it's good, no doubt about it.*

"Bear, get Paolo over here to help me get out of this thing. I don't want to pull anything and mess myself up for tomorrow."

Bear turned and waved Paolo over, and he helped Orly get out of the car.

"I'll see you guys after a while. I got to go over to the Speed King box and greet folks and sign some autographs and things."

"Sure, Orly," said Bear. "But when you come back I have to talk to you about something. Doc Brewster died last night."

Orly stopped and turned to Bear. "Doc died? How'd he die?"

"Had a heart attack while he was working on some heads down at old Bill's shop. He died in the hospital about 1 A.M."

"Sorry to hear that, Bear."

"Yeah, at any rate, I need to talk to you when you get back. Catch me here or at the motor home. Hey, Orly, say hi to our new boss while you're up there. Don't do nothing to upset the applecart."

Orly frowned, then smiled. "Yeah right." He walked out of the garage with long-legged strides.

Bear turned to Paolo. "Pellegrini, you and Notebook over there go get that beat-up old Chevy you're driving and get it loaded in the transporter. Orly has managed to keep this here race car off the wall and out of everybody's way, so the backup is sold. I'm tired of seeing you moping around here like you done lost your best friend. Let's get that wreck back to Charlotte where we can get it fixed," Bear said as he slapped Paolo on the back. "Then get back here. The Thunderfoot boys will be in shortly and I want to go over some stuff and get to practicing."

Paolo grinned. "Cool." He turned and yelled at Doug, "Hey, Notes, come on and give me a hand."

When Orly entered the luxury suite, the conversation stopped. The twenty or so folks turned to greet him and a round of applause broke out. Hildy took over.

"Well, folks, we are sure glad to have world-famous Speed King Oil Company's own Orly Mann here to sign autographs. Please feel free to visit with him and ask anything you would like." Then Hildy turned and shook Orly's hand. In the process, she slipped him a piece of paper with a note written on it.

Orly settled himself behind a table and picked up a marker to sign autographs. While he was getting settled, he quickly read the note. It said simply, "Will you come to dinner when the rest of the crew comes tonight? I would very much like to talk to you." It was signed "Hildy." He looked up at her, but she refused to meet his glance, choosing instead to busy herself with the guests in the box. Orly folded the note and put it in his pocket.

Loren was sitting in a deck chair on the veranda of Harry's house. She had her eyes closed and was basking in the afternoon sunshine. It felt good and she was glad to be alive. She opened her eyes when Harry came shuffling out. He was wearing a yellow-and-orange Speed King sweatsuit but still had his old terry cloth bathrobe around his shoulders.

He said to Loren, "Do you mind if I join you? You look so comfortable, I hate to disturb you."

"No, Mr. Hornbrook, it's your house, I don't mind."

"Well, I imagine both of us would rather be somewhere else today, don't you think?" said Harry, ignoring her flippancy.

Loren looked over at Harry. He looked old and tired, but his eyes still had a twinkle. He smiled at her.

"I know you would rather be out at the Speedway, Mr. Hornbrook. Rumor has it that you practically helped Roger Penske build the thing."

Harry laughed out loud. "Not hardly, but I do have to admit I encouraged Roger to build the place. If I had had a fraction of his money, I would have tried it myself. But I didn't, so I didn't, if you get what I mean."

It was Loren's turn to smile. She didn't know this old man very well, but already she liked him.

"How are you feeling, Mr. Hornbrook?"

"Well, Loren, do you want the patent answer or do you want honesty?" His directness caught her a little off guard. "Being that it is only the two of us out here, I'll answer that for you. I feel tired, very tired, and I am in moderate pain. I expect that I will die soon. And by the way, call me Harry if you don't mind."

Loren paused for a minute, thinking, then she said in a small, tight voice, "Are you afraid of dying, Harry?"

Harry looked out across the yard and into the trees that surrounded the pool. "I'm not sure 'afraid' is the right word. I suppose I am apprehensive about the process. I am certainly not afraid of the end result. God has given me a strong faith, and I long to see the Lord Jesus and my loved ones. I'm especially hungry to see Hilda, my wife. She died a few years ago." Harry paused, then continued to speak, "What of you, Loren? Are you afraid to die?"

Once again his direct honesty made her pause. "You were honest with me, Harry, now I'll be honest with you. I didn't really want to die when

I took those pills. I guess I was just tired of living." Loren stopped. "No, that isn't right. Tired isn't the right word. Afraid would be more like it."

"How old are you, Loren?"

"I'll be twenty-two tomorrow, in fact, Mr. Hornbrook, I mean Harry."

"And why would a beautiful young lady like yourself, with everything to live for and all the potential in the world, be afraid to live and not be afraid to die?"

Loren got up out of the chair. She was wearing jeans and a baggy sweatshirt and had her hair up in a ponytail. She walked back and forth as she pushed the sleeves of her sweatshirt up her arms. Harry watched—envying her youth and vitality. Even though Loren had been beat up, she was still young and fresh.

Loren turned to face him, speaking to herself as well as to Harry. "I don't know. I've been thinking about that a lot lately. I never used to be afraid of anything. I was tough and hard. I'll be honest with you. I fought off so many drunk advances from the creeps that came home with my mother, I decided that I would never get connected to anybody. Some people said my attitude of toughness made me a good driver, but then one night I woke up out of a dead sleep with this sick feeling inside of me." Loren wrapped her arms around her body and hugged herself as she reflected.

"I never felt such fear in my life. It was a new feeling for me. Then one day I realized that it wasn't new at all. I had been feeling that way for a long time, and I just didn't want to remember it. It was like I was just squeezing it down tight. Then it got to the point I couldn't hold it down anymore. I never had much of a family and I always had to take care of myself and I did a pretty good job. Then it was like I couldn't control it anymore, and all of sudden these terrible bad feelings of fear would wash over me. I was so anxious all the time, that pretty soon I got scared and anxious about being anxious. I could hardly even get back in the car. I have to tell you, Harry, just between you and me. It took all the courage I could find to just sit down in a dragster. That's when I started taking the pills. You know, just to sort of cope." Harry listened as Loren paced back and forth.

"Then that day, when Alicia came and we had such a good time . . . well, that was the night I took the overdose. I took the pills because I finally found out what scared me the most, and I just couldn't handle it." Loren turned to face Harry with tears running down her cheeks. "I can't believe I did that to myself. It was so scary and it scares me right now to think I would do that."

"What was it that you were afraid of, Loren? No, let me tell you what it was. You were afraid of being alone, weren't you? That old goblin of loneliness ate you up. It gets hard after a while because you think that the only reason people want to be with you is to get something out of you. Sometimes you hunger for folks to just appreciate you for who you are rather than what you can give them."

Loren beat on her thighs with her fists and sobbed, nodding her head.

"Am I so bad, Harry, that nobody can like me or love me just because I'm Loren and nobody else?"

"No, Loren, you aren't. You just haven't given the right people a chance. Come here." Harry raised his arms and beckoned her to come. She didn't hesitate, and much like his daughter a few days earlier, she fell to her knees and put her head on Harry's bony chest and sobbed out her grief, her body shaking. Harry put his thin arms around her shoulders and stroked her hair as she sobbed.

"There, there, child, you'll be okay. You've had a rough time and it's okay. Just let it out. You aren't alone now. God loves you, Loren, and we love you, too. Just let it out. You're safe here."

Yolanda quietly walked out and placed a box of tissues next to Harry. He looked up and winked at her and she smiled back.

The conversation around the big table in Harry's dining room was quiet. Paolo and Doug, never ones to miss an opportunity, were packing the food away. Alicia was sticking to vegetables and salad. Alphonse was just sort of picking at his plate. Hildy wasn't eating much either. Perhaps the thing that made the meal subdued was the two empty places at the table. Neither Loren nor Orly had shown up.

Then when the meal was just about over, Loren came quietly into the dining room. She looked spectacular in a yellow sundress that set off her hair and brought color to her still-pale cheeks. She refused to look anybody in the eye and sat demurely down at the empty place between Doug and Alicia, with her hands folded shyly in her lap. No one said a word. Finally, Harry reached over and sent the salad bowl around to her and the rest of the folks picked up the cue. Loren took a piece of garlic bread and placed it on her plate and then looked up. She looked at the faces around the table and realized that these folks were very much her friends. They were giving her all the space she needed right now to help her get through this difficult time. Her eyes filled with tears and they coursed down her cheeks. She tried to wipe them away with the back of her hand until Doug reached over and gave her a napkin. She dabbed a little. Then she spoke in a soft voice.

"I wonder if I could say something to you all?" Everyone looked up at her. "I don't know quite how to say it. So please let me get it out if I can." She laughed a shy nervous laugh. "This is hard for me." Loren looked again at the faces around the table.

They all returned her look with open and sympathetic faces. Alicia was sitting beside her and reached up and patted Loren on her shoulder in encouragement.

"I want to say to all of you, thank you for saving my life. I did a very stupid thing, and I promise you that I won't ever do anything so foolish again. If it wasn't for you people I probably would be dead, and I am grateful you did what you did to take care of me." The words came out in a rush as Loren looked down with tears dripping into her lap.

"I'm sorry to cry. I've been crying all day and I didn't think I had that many tears in me." She laughed another nervous little laugh. She looked around the table and realized that her eyes weren't the only ones wet. Practically everyone had tears of sympathy in their eyes. It had been a scary time. "Anyway, I just wanted to thank you all."

Harry broke the silence. "I think it would be very appropriate if we took a minute to pray and thank God for what he has done in our midst. I will start and Bear maybe you could close."

The time of prayer was heartfelt and intimate as they bowed their heads and gave thanks to God. They prayed specifically for Loren and her return to health, asking God to give her direction and take care of her needs. Alphonse prayed for Ricky and asked God to protect Ricky and draw him close. They all silently prayed for Harry. After a few minutes Bear closed the prayer with a gentle "Amen."

Loren spoke again. "I do need to say one more thing. You know when we went to church last Sunday and we sang that song? I don't even know what the name of it is." She sang the words in a beautiful clear voice, *Holiness, holiness, is what I long for. Holiness is what I need.*

"I couldn't remember the rest of the words, but it kept going over and over in my mind while I was in the hospital, and I think I remembered it even when I was lying on the floor in the hotel room. Well, Hildy told me how the rest of it goes." Loren sang the words once again,

> *Take my heart and form it.*
> *Take my mind, transform it.*
> *Take my will conform it . . . to yours, to yours, oh Lord.*

"Hildy and Harry are teaching me how to let God take me . . . it is through Jesus, and I want you to know that tonight for the first time in I don't know how long, I feel real peace in my heart. I'm so glad to be alive . . . and I'm glad to be here with you all."

No one looked up as Orly stood silently in the doorway. Then Hildy looked across the room and saw him. She smiled and then frowned in consternation. Bear saw her staring and turned in his chair to look as well . . . and then nearly fell off it. He grabbed his heart with one hand and stammered out, "What happened to you?"

Orly was standing with his right arm in a sling and a look of pain on his face. Then everyone turned to look and waited for Orly's answer.

Orly laughed out loud. "I wish I had a camera. I've never seen so many different looks all at the same time before. Settle down, Bear, I'm okay I think. I got run over and knocked down, that's all. The doctor said to rest it tonight and not move it. Said it would be a little stiff, but I will be okay for tomorrow."

"Run over? How'd you get run over?" said Bear.

"I was in the garage next to ours and I got buttonholed by a radio guy and we were standing there talking. One of the crew guys started to back the #3 car out of the garage and he hit a stack of tires. Just nudged it really. Anyway it fell over and hit me in the back right on my bad shoulder and knocked me down. Boy, it sure hurt."

"The #3 car? Wait till I get ahold of them guys. Knocking my driver down in the garage," Bear sputtered.

"It's okay, Bear. They were mortified. I thought we were going to have to call an ambulance for the guy steering the car. He was so upset. It was just one of those racin' deals I guess." Orly laughed again and so did everybody else around the table, especially Loren. "Racin' deals" was just another way of saying that stuff happens, but it was a term usually reserved for accidents on the track.

Orly looked at the dirty dishes on the table and said, "Well, I'm starved. When is supper?"

There was enough left for Orly. When he was done, the younger group headed for the kitchen to tackle the dishes. Bear was taking the opportunity to talk to Harry about the situation with Doc last night and the promise he made Bear make about going to the bank.

"Well, I'm sorry to hear he died. But you know, Bear, Doc has had heart trouble for years. He's been on borrowed time for a while. You know, he and I used to be very good friends some forty-odd years ago, but when I became a Christian that all changed. I'm sorry to hear that he's gone. I wonder what he's got in that box?"

"Don't know, Harry, but I promised him I would go open it up, so I guess I will, come Monday morning. Puts me behind getting back to the shop and getting set up for next week. But at least we're only going to Richmond, which is a little closer than here," Bear said. "I'll give you a call and let you know what I find. Orly said he would stay with me, so we'll let you know."

"Have you made any arrangements for the disposition of his body?"

"I just had the local mortuary pick him up and I figured . . . well, I don't know what I figured. Be honest with you, Harry, I hadn't thought that far ahead."

"I'll tell you what, Bear, let me handle those arrangements. I can make a couple of calls and we'll take care of it."

Bear looked immensely relieved. "Would you do that, Harry? That would be great. I wasn't sure how I was going to fit all this in." Bear remembered Doc's last words about Harry and thought how ironic it was that Harry would be the one to bury him.

Orly and Hildy had walked out on the veranda. Alicia and Paolo were watching them out the kitchen window while they washed the dishes.

"What do you suppose they're talking about, Pally?" Alicia asked.

"I don't know Alicia, but it looks serious."

"Don't you think they look good together, Pally? They're both tall and good looking. I think she loves him. Don't you?"

"I don't know what she thinks. And since when does a couple have to be the same size to look good?" said Paolo, looking down at Alicia. She blushed and said nothing.

The conversation on the deck was indeed serious and Hildy was doing most of the talking. Hildy was leaning on the railing, looking down at the pool below. Orly stood looking at her with his back against the top rail.

"I'm glad you came over. I wanted to apologize for the other night," Hildy said.

Orly started to interrupt but she motioned for him to be quiet. He was intuitive enough to realize that this wasn't easy for her, so he didn't try to speak. As he listened to her, he studied her face in the darkness. There was just enough light to clearly see her profile. *She looks so lovely,* he thought.

"I was angry with you that night and I let my anger get the best of me. We shouldn't have gone to that dumb restaurant and I'm sorry I put you through that embarrassment with the race fans," Hildy said in measured, even tones, as if she had rehearsed it many times. "I guess what I'm trying to say is that I didn't want to believe you when you said you were sorry for the way things worked out between us. I wanted to stay mad at you. You hurt me very much last time, Orly, and I was afraid to trust you."

"*Was,* Hildy? Does that mean you are willing to trust me now?"

"I don't know what I feel, Orly, if you want the honest truth. I thought I had things worked out in my mind. I thought I understood Dad, too, but I found out I didn't." Hildy turned and faced him. The light from the kitchen shone on her face and he could see her eyes . . . those beautiful hazel eyes.

"Orly, there hasn't been anybody in my life like you, ever. I thought we could build a relationship last time, but then all of a sudden, you dropped me. I knew why. At least I thought I did. I told myself I was willing to wait for you to come around. To give you time to sort out your own feelings, but I don't know if I want to do that anymore."

"What do you want, Hildy? Tell me."

"I don't want to have ghosts come between us. I know they will always be there. They were such a part of your life and I respect that. One of the reasons I love you so much is because of them. I want to be cherished and loved by you like you loved them. But, Orly, they are gone. Just like my mom is gone and soon my dad, too. You and me— we are here. We are alive! You know what I want? I want us to see if we can build something out of that. If we can be alive . . . together." Hildy paused and looked down. Then she looked up into his face. "That's what I want, Orly."

"That's what I want, too, Hildy. I tried to tell you that night, but it didn't come out right. It is what I want more than anything else in the world."

Hildy reached out her arms and embraced him. He wrapped his good arm around her as she tilted her head and her lips met his.

Doug looked out the window and said over his shoulder, "Hey, guys, check this out. I think we got a thing going." There was a chorus of cheers and whistles from the kitchen as everyone crowded around the window to see.

It was getting late and Bear was starting to herd the group to the track and the motor homes. Orly and Hildy were still out on the porch, sitting in the lawn swing talking. *Their mood seems to be contagious,*

thought Bear as he looked at Loren and Doug sitting at the table in conversation.

"So what do you think you want to do?" asked Doug. "Do you want to go back to racing?"

"No. I can't do that anymore. I think the fire that drove me is burned out, Doug. I don't have anything to prove anymore." Loren wrapped her arms around her waist. "Hildy has offered me a job working for Speed King doing PR and stuff. I would be good at that. I need a job, that's for sure. They said I could live here as long as I want, but I don't want to take advantage of them."

"What would you do if you could do anything you wanted to?" said Doug.

"Yeah, that old question. But I do have an answer, Doug; I've just never told anyone before. When I was little, there was a horse ranch behind the trailer park and I used to go over there. Pretty soon I got to know the people that ran it and they let me ride the horses. It was kind of a safe place for me. The people were very sweet. I loved it and I really loved horses. I've been to Montana a couple of times, and I always thought that if I made it big I would buy a small place there and raise horses. That's my dream."

"That's cool, Loren. Who knows what God will do?"

Let us throw off everything that hinders and the sin that so easily entangles, and let us run with perseverance the race marked out for us.

Hebrews 12:1

"All a race car driver wants is just a chance to win."

Benny Parsons, former Winston Cup Champion
and now media broadcaster

ORLY SAT PATIENTLY in the Speed King Chevrolet in the pit lane waiting for the command to "start your engines." The cars were lined up two by two, and he could see bits and pieces of the eleven cars ahead of him. He could also see the wind whipping the flags on the back of the main grandstand and wondered: *Is the wind going to be a problem down the back chute? No matter; I'll deal with it if it is.* The shoulder was stiff this morning, but he wasn't even going to acknowledge it. He had put it out of his mind. Later on it would probably hurt so much he would be grinding his teeth, but not now. He had already made up his mind that he was going to the front as soon as he could. They needed the five bonus points for leading a race. Maybe while the tires were fresh they might be able pull it off. Then, if they could lead for a lap or two, he would give it up and lay back some and see what happened.

The preliminaries were done. During introductions, the drivers had gone around the track in the backs of convertibles, waving at the crowd. The governor made a long-winded speech, which was mostly lost in the excitement of the moment. The F–16s made the traditional low-level pass over the crowd with their tailpipes flaming red, trailing thunder that made everyone duck. All the dignitaries had been introduced then shuffled out of the way, so things were pretty much good to go.

Orly was happy. Happier than he had been in a long, long time. *It used to be,* he thought, *that the only place I felt alive and truly in control was right here in a race car. Not anymore. There is another place that I feel alive . . . and that is when I'm with Hildy.*

He was in love, that was for sure, and he liked the feeling. He yawned behind the face mask of his helmet. It was late when he'd left Harry's last night. Then when he got back to the motor home, he couldn't sleep because he couldn't get her out of his mind. She told him this morning at the chapel service that she couldn't sleep last night, either. Later when they went to the drivers' meeting, she sat beside him and held his hand. She was up in the luxury suite right now watching him.

Bear stuck his head inside the car for the tenth time, looked at the gauges, and then around the inside of the car. He looked into Orly's eyes with concern and worry marking his face. "Shoulder okay? You want I should line up a relief driver? You look nervous. You okay?"

Orly met his glance. His muffled voice came out of the helmet. "Leave me alone Bear, I'm fine. You're worse than a long-tailed cat in a roomful of rocking chairs."

Bear nodded his head. "Yeah, you're nervous. I can tell."

It was a joke, because there was nobody in the world more calm than Orly Mann before a race; Bear, on the other hand, always started a race with an upset stomach and an anxious furrow on his forehead.

Paolo leaned against the war wagon and stretched his legs. He looked up at Doug and Alicia sitting on top in the special captain's chairs so they could see the track. Doug stood up and adjusted the big umbrella that shaded them from the warm, early-afternoon sun. The chairs were built with little desktops off the side that curved around the front. Doug

186

had his clipboard on his and Alicia was dialed in on the computer in front of her.

The war wagon (some called it a pit box) was unique. It was a combination toolbox and communication center about eight feet long and nearly four feet wide. It was painted in exactly the same paint scheme as the Speed King Chevrolet. On the backside, it had built-in television monitors that picked up the satellite feeds of the race. The whole crew could see what was happening all around the racetrack. It also had a built-in video feed so that every pit stop could be recorded and later reviewed for critique. Nearly every pit stall had a high pole that stretched out over the pit with a built-in video camera. The front side of the wagon held the gas bottles that powered the high efficiency air guns for the tire changers. Plus it contained all sorts of spare odds and ends that might be needed in the course of a 500-mile race.

Alicia kept track of scoring and made sure Orly knew exactly where he was during a race. Doug kept track of the competition and in general kept an eye on the front-runners. Bear usually started the race sitting on top of the war wagon, but he seldom stayed there very long. Bear would be all over the pit stall at least twenty times before the race was over, keeping track of everything.

"Hey, Doug, is Loren going to make it today?" yelled Paolo.

"Yeah, she's coming with Harry and Alphonse. She said she was feeling almost back to normal." Doug waved for Paolo to come a little closer.

Paolo kicked a tire over and stood on it so he could hear Doug a little easier.

"We had a great talk last night. Man, I tell you, Paolo, she is some girl. You know, Orly is going to be coming out here to the West Coast a lot, and I'm hoping maybe I'll get to see more of her. She's so cool."

Paolo reached up and patted Doug's arm. "Way to go, bro," he said.

The Thunderfoot Ballet Company was rested, practiced up, and ready to go. Paolo looked over his thirty-five-pound jack for the tenth time. In a few minutes, he would be over the wall, cradling the thing with both hands and it better work perfect. Bud was oiling up his air gun and checking it over for the fifth time this morning. The backup gun was lying in easy reach on a coiled hose in case there was some sort of malfunction. Matt, the front tire changer, was doing exactly the same thing with his guns. The tire carriers were making sure the tires were laid out in the proper order and that all the lugs were glued on properly. Everything that could be checked was checked, double checked, and then checked again. In the heat of battle there was no room for error. Paolo had already been over the wall and swept every square inch of the pit box with meticulous precision.

Each team was given a carefully measured space in front of the pit wall to service the car on the pit lane. Each box was marked out with white lines and no work could be done on the car unless it was stopped within those boundaries. But inside those boundaries was the team's territory, and Paolo made sure that every rock or piece of gravel was picked up. They wanted nothing to get in the way of a perfect stop.

Finally, after what seemed like days of anticipation, the words came over the sound system, "Gentlemen, start your engines."

Bear watched as Orly flipped the switches and pressed the starter toggle. He looked up at Bear with a stricken look in his eyes as nothing happened. Bear nearly had heart failure. Then Orly flipped the toggle for real and the motor rumbled to life.

Bear pressed the send button on his radio and said, "Orly Mann, you are bad. You nearly killed me."

Orly keyed his mike and laughed, "I was just seeing if you were paying attention, Bear." Then Orly chuckled some more as he eased the car into gear.

Bear snapped the window net into place and smacked the roof of the car with a double thump.

Hildy stood at the window of the suite watching Orly and the rest of the field head onto the track. The suite was crowded with some twenty or thirty invited guests. Harry was sitting in the back in an elevated chair so he could see over the top of the people. There were two TV monitors on the front wall above the picture window. One carried the satellite feed of the broadcast network showing the race. The other monitor was connected to Orly's in-car camera. The suite was also wired to carry all the radio transmissions between Orly and the crew. It crackled with Bear's voice.

"This here is the final radio check. Everybody got a copy?"

"Gotcha, Bear," said Jimmy from his perch high atop the grandstands.

"Good, Bear," said Bud.

"You Thunderfoot boys got a copy? Give me a wave." Paolo and the rest of the Ballet Company gave Bear a wave. They could hear him through their headsets but wouldn't transmit unless there was trouble of some sort.

"You got it, Orly?" said Bear. Orly's mike clicked twice.

Alphonse was standing beside Harry's chair on one side and Loren was standing on the other. "How you doing there, Mr. Hornbrook? Can you see okay?"

"Yes, Alphonse, I can see just fine. Thanks for asking, and call me Harry."

"Well, I know I'm supposed to, Mr. Hornbrook, but I didn't want to disrespect you in front of all your guests here," Alphonse said in a quiet voice.

"I appreciate you saying that but you forget, Alphonse, I'm no longer the CEO of Speed King. I'm just a guest here in the box like everybody else . . . except her," Harry said as he pointed to Hildy.

"I think you will always be Speed King Oil, Mr. Hornbrook," said Loren as she patted Harry on the shoulder.

"The green is coming out this lap, Orly," said Bear.

Orly's mike clicked twice.

The long line of double-filed cars came off the second corner, bunched up behind the pace car. The driver of the pace car picked up momentum down the back chute and then ducked for the safety of the pits. The pole sitter brought them off the fourth corner as the starter studied them from his perch over the track. Satisfied that all was as it should be, he pulled the green flag from behind his back and waved it frantically. The California 500 was underway.

Orly rolled into the throttle and shifted from third to fourth gear. Cold tires or not, he ducked to the inside going into turn one and dragged the brake with his left foot. The car stuck going in low, and Orly held the line through the second corner. He came off the corner in tenth as Jimmy calmly said, "Clear" in his ear.

Orly didn't bother to acknowledge. The Speed King Chevrolet came off the corner like a rocket ship. He passed two cars down the back chute before they knew he was serious. He picked off another going into three, and another coming off four, and bingo, he was in sixth place at the end of the first lap.

Three laps later he was in fourth. Then with a daring move to the outside, he passed both the second- and third-place cars.

"Clear," sang Jimmy's voice in his ear.

The leader was about six car lengths ahead. Orly chilled for a couple of laps to give his tires a chance to cool, then he clicked the hammer and whittled down the distance between himself and the leader. Three laps later he was hanging off the guy's bumper so close he could see through his windshield. The leader went low. Orly went high, and just that quick he was leading the race.

"Not bad, Orly. Twelfth to first in ten laps," Bear said.

Orly's mike clicked twice. Orly set the pace for the next thirty laps, letting the car dictate to him where it wanted to run on the racetrack. They had guessed right on the setup. The car was working extremely well. Others were not so lucky as the field was constantly shuffled. Some drivers, like Orly, were carving their way up through the pack toward the front, but others found themselves falling back just as quickly.

Orly could feel the tires starting to go away as the car began pushing just a tad going into the corners. He dropped his line to the inside a little, taking some of the wedge off the car to compensate.

On the next lap, one of the guys back in the pack cursed as his car pushed up into the corner and kissed the wall. He didn't hit it hard, but enough to put him sideways and collect another car on the way to the infield.

"Yellow flag, Orly, yellow flag! Got a lot of debris in turn two, stay low, you'll be okay." Jimmy's voice cracked in his ear. Orly clicked the mike twice. "The pace car will pick you up in one. Pits will be open in a minute."

"Bring it in, Orly. We'll get you some new rubber and get you fueled up. All right, you guys, let's go to work. Yellow flag stop. Let's be smooth and don't mess up," said Bear.

"What do you want, Orly?" Bear asked, referring to what Orly might need in terms of an adjustment.

"It's just starting to push a little, Bear. I think the track is tightening up some. You know what to do," said Orly. He was right.

Orly brought the car off the corner and drove down pit lane at the mandated speed. He carefully watched the tach to control his speed. Violate that rule and it would cost him at least a lap; besides it was dangerous. He slid the car to a perfect stop on the yellow line inside the pit box, and the Ballet Company was over the wall in a flash.

Paolo was moving before Orly stopped. In two giant steps, he leaped around the front of the car to the right side. Then in one fluid motion, he slid the jack under the body at the spot marked with a yellow piece of tape. His body didn't even come to a full stop before he leaped in the air and brought his weight down on the handle. A quick long pump and then another short for good measure and the car was off the ground.

In the meantime, Bud and Matt, trailing their airhoses, dropped to their knee pads and fired their air guns in five short bursts. The screaming sound could be heard over the sound of Orly's exhaust. The lugs flew off the wheels and scattered on the ground. As soon as the car was in the air, the wheels were yanked off. The tire carriers who were right behind them both slammed the new rubber on the car.

Paolo bent from the waist to reach the rear tire that was jerked off and carefully laid it on the ground beside the car. He checked to make sure the wheels were on and, in another fluid motion, dropped the jack. He yanked it out and cradled it in his hands as he sprinted back around the front of the car. He cut right behind Matt, now working on the left front wheel, and slid the jack under the car again. A big pump coupled with another short one, and the car was up. He then shifted his attention to Ed Grudem, the gas man, who was dumping the second can of fuel into the car. Each can held eleven gallons. It was the gas man's job to hold the can upright and fit it over the self-sealing nozzle to the gas tank. Tim, the catch man, had his can hooked over the gas tank vent so the air could rush out as the fuel went in. His job was to make sure the tank was as full as it could get and also to see that no fuel spilled on the ground. Both he and Ed wore flameproof aprons.

Ed gave Paolo a quick nod. The tires were on. Paolo dropped the car and stepped back with the jack. Orly threw the water bottle through the window netting and it bounced on the ground. Then under Jimmy's guidance, he accelerated out of the pit box, laying down black strips of rubber.

"Not bad, boys. Fifteen nine," said Bear. In the shuffle of the pit stops, Orly was at the front of the lead group as they hustled down the pit lane to catch the pace car.

Up in the suite they watched the action in awe, and then a series of cheers broke out. Someone said to Hildy, "What did they mean fifteen nine?"

She replied, "That was Bear congratulating the crew for changing four tires and fueling the car in 15.9 seconds. That's a very good time but it was under the yellow flag. When they have to do it under green flag conditions is when it really counts."

Loren watched the race with mixed emotions. She knew what it was to be in the heat of battle with pressure on all sides, and maybe there was a part of her that was envious of those involved. Most of her, however, was glad to be watching instead.

She could tell by Hildy's body language as she stood in front of the window that she was tense. She was supposed to be greeting folks and generally schmoozing them for the company, but she couldn't tear herself away from the race. No wonder. She was in love with Orly. Every time she talked about him, her eyes sparkled. Racing was dangerous and Hildy obviously knew that . . . but it was what Orly did. *I don't envy her,* thought Loren as Orly came down the front straight with the thundering pack six inches off each other's bumpers to take the green flag for the restart. *Loving a race car driver comes with a certain amount of anxiety.*

Orly led a couple more laps and then let the car slide up almost to the wall to let the second-place car take over the lead. This race was 250 laps long on the two-mile oval and they were barely started. Let somebody else lead for a while, and he would do his best to save wear on the tires and conserve the car. He gradually let himself fall back to fifth and tucked in behind the first four cars to ride a little.

The average distance between pit stops was fifty laps. Yellow flags changed that, of course. If a guy could pit under the yellow, he didn't have to worry too much about losing a lap. The pace car led the field around the track at a leisurely pace, and it gave the crew a cushion if things didn't go right. The only thing at stake was track position, which was, of course, important, but staying on the lead lap was essential.

Bear had his nose in the air and he could smell it coming. These next pit stops were going to be under the green, which meant that any mistake could be costly. He waved the Ballet Company over to him and climbed down off the war wagon.

"Be sharp, boys. This one is going to count. We want him to still be up front after this next series. No mistakes, okay?" Bear looked over their shoulders to see at least three media camera teams getting ready to film the stop.

Someone stuck a microphone under his chin and asked, "When's he coming in, Bear?"

Bear just waved and pretended he couldn't hear. He climbed back up on the wagon so he wouldn't be bothered.

"Orly, how's the tires?" Bear asked.

"Getting there, Bear. What you want to do?" Bear could hear the engine screaming as Orly sailed into the fourth corner.

Jimmy interrupted. "Watch that #2 car you're coming up on. I think he's leaking something."

Orly's mike clicked twice.

"We can pit with the leaders or not. What's your flavor?" asked Bear. What he meant was that Orly could come in when the leaders did, which would be in five or six laps at the most. Or he could pit sooner and come back out with fresh tires, and a load of fuel, and maybe get a good run. Everybody else would have to pit too, but it would be after him, and the pressure would be on them and their crews to make it perfect to catch him. That is, if the Thunderfoot Ballet Company did what they were capable of . . . and the yellow flag didn't come out while Orly was in the pits or something.

Well, racing is a risky business, thought Bear. *This one will be Orly's call.*

Orly's mike clicked three times. . . .

Bear turned to Bud and gave him a nod. This pit stop was going to be sudden. The Ballet Company casually took their places as if nothing was set to happen. Paolo reached down and picked up the jack to examine it like a lady would a mislabeled pot roast at the supermarket. Bear laughed up his sleeve. *They've eased into position and the media folks don't have a clue. Maybe the competition doesn't either.*

Orly held his line going into turn three, then halfway through the corner he dropped to the inside, feathered the brakes, threw his hand in the air, and dropped down onto the pit lane. The Ballet Company moved into position behind the pit wall, and as Orly came sliding to a stop, they were over it in a flash.

Paolo was halfway around the car before it stopped moving. Alicia was watching from her seat on the war wagon and gave an involuntary jump, thinking Paolo might have been hit by Orly. *Good thing he still has some brakes left.*

Initially it was a good plan. But then it went sour as the #2 car blew a motor going down the front straight—spilling parts and fluid practically under the flagman's nose. He had no option but to reach down and grab the yellow flag and wave it in front of the field.

Jimmy's voice echoed in everyone's ears. "Yellow flag, yellow flag. Drat, a dingbusted yellow flag."

Bear's voice came right over the top of Jimmy. "Okay, everybody, do your job. We'll lose a lap but we can get it back. Finish up, guys, let's get him out of here."

The Ballet Company finished the job and Paolo dropped the jack. Orly pulled back out to catch the pace car a lap down. Not only that, but the rest of the field now had the luxury of pitting under the yellow flag. Orly would now have to race himself back on to the lead lap, which meant he had to pull out in front of the field and go all the way around the two-mile track and back through the field to join the leaders. It was a bad break.

"Whatta you got, Hoss?" said Bear in Orly's ear.

Orly had his left hand out the corner of the window net trying to funnel some air into the car and cool his hand at the same time. The race wasn't even half over and his shoulder was starting to throb. He knew what Bear was asking, and as he rode behind the pace car he was thinking through his answer. Bear wanted to know if he had enough race car to make a serious effort to get his lap back or whether he should maybe just ride in the hope of catching a break. Just riding meant that they were, in essence, giving up any chance of a win, but at least they would come away with some points. If he raced hard they could blow a motor or hit the wall or any number of things could go wrong . . . but all those things could go wrong anyway.

Orly clicked the mike twice.

Bear smiled. *Well, this ought to be something. Hang on folks, because Orly Mann is going to teach a class on how to wring the most out of a well-built race car.*

"One more lap, Orly," said Jimmy in his ear.

Orly clicked the mike twice and settled himself back in the seat. He put his shoulder out of his mind and hunkered down to race. He had to be quick and precise. If he could stay out front, maybe, just maybe, there would be another caution and he could circle the track and get his lap back.

Once again the pace car headed for the safety of the infield and the pack thundered off the fourth corner. The starter waved the green flag and Orly took the lead. Like a racehorse with the bit in his teeth, Orly used every drop of his skill to stretch his lead. He chose his line through the corners carefully, letting the car run free, using just enough brake to keep him in the fastest groove. In three laps he had a twenty-car-length lead, and those running behind him gave up the chase. They were like a pack of dogs that realized the fox was not going to be caught today, so they squabbled amongst themselves.

Bear watched in admiration as Orly continued to lengthen his lead, running the same exact line lap after lap as though he were on rails. What made it effective was that he was doing it without abusing the car.

Loren stood beside Harry and watched the monitor showing Orly's in-car camera. She shook her head in admiration. Orly was not only good, he was fantastic.

Harry leaned over and said, "Are you seeing what I'm seeing?"

195

Loren answered, "Do you mean the way he's using the fastest line every single lap with no mistakes? Yes, I am. Look there. See that mark on the fence going into three? He's using that mark to brake every time. Never deviates from it."

In ten laps, Orly was starting to pick off back markers and his driving style changed. He could no longer use the same line lap after lap but instead was working his way through the traffic like a broken field runner.

Jimmy's voice echoed through the room with a constant litany of phrases, "Clear, watch the left side, left side, clear, right side, right side, watch the #13, he's got no handling left, clear."

In thirty-five laps Orly had managed to work himself into the middle of the pack and was running twenty-second in a forty-two car field. The closer he got to the front, the more difficult it was to pass. He could feel the handling starting to go away. The push was coming back, and it was getting more and more difficult to keep the front end down. The car wanted to go up the racetrack instead of turning. If Orly would have had the luxury, he could have adjusted his line and moved around on the racetrack to compensate. But that was impossible in the midst of all the traffic. The car was still good and far better than most, but it was no longer cutting edge.

Orly keyed the mike, "How many?" Meaning how many laps until he pitted.

Bear looked over at Doug. Doug held up some fingers then waved his hand twice. "Bout . . ." He was interrupted by Jimmy.

"Stay low, stay low, clear, go high, go high . . . you got it. You all right?" Orly clicked the mike twice.

Three cars right in front of Orly sailed into the corner, three abreast, and in the process, did a little paint swapping. It was a normal event in the course of close combat. But this time the middle car got a little sideways and cut a tire down, taking the outside car right up to the wall. Orly was able to avoid most of the fallout and, with Jimmy's help, steer his way through the tire smoke and twisted sheet metal.

Bear didn't have to say a word as the Ballet Company got ready to perform once again.

Orly's voice echoed in Bear's ear. "Give me a half turn and bump the pressure, Bear. The push is starting to get serious."

"Got it," said Bear. Then he turned to the Ballet Company. "All right now, let's get him some track position. Every one of these guys we can pass in the pits, he don't have to pass on the track."

On the next lap, the pits opened and practically the whole field came down pit lane. In the midst of the chaos, the Ballet Company gave an exemplary performance; they were, in fact, so quick that they had him up in sixth place. It was done. He had his lap back and he still had a shot at a win.

Up in the box, Alphonse forgot himself and slapped Harry on the back. Harry didn't mind and in fact stuck his hand out so they could exchange fives. Hildy hadn't said a word, but if body language was any indication, she had helped the crew change the tires and fuel the car.

The field bunched up in preparation for taking the restart on lap 192. Fifty-eight laps left, which meant they would have to do at least one more stop. The starter waved the green flag and the pack shuffled as everyone jockeyed for position. It was getting on toward crunch time and things were getting serious. Every driver had the same goal, and that was to get past the guy ahead of him. Orly tucked in behind the first five cars, biding his time as he searched for a weakness in the car ahead that would allow him to get by.

Orly felt it more than he saw it. Just a quick metallic bang that didn't belong in the realm of normal racing sounds. Something alien, something just a little off. Then he felt the results and knew exactly what had happened. With unthinking reflex, he fought to keep the car off the wall in an absolutely hair-raising slide. Fortunately, those around him managed to get by as he fought the car. Bad shoulder or not, he was able to gather it in and brought the car across the track to the low line.

Jimmy's voice was in his ear. "You got it, Orly, nice save. . . . He's cut down a left rear tire, Bear. Left rear for sure. Run over something I think. Caution ain't out yet, Orly."

Orly was faced with a decision. If he pitted right now, he would lose a lap for sure. He had maybe one lap or less to run on the inner liner inside the tire before it gave up completely and dropped the rim on the ground. He stayed low coming out of four, but went right on by the pit lane entrance. Cars were passing him, but maybe, just maybe, a caution might come out. He was under control—but just barely. Then what he was hoping for happened. The tire separated from the inner liner and began to throw chunks of rubber onto the track. The starter reached for the yellow and waved it as the leaders passed under the start-finish bridge. Orly came limping along behind—still on the lead lap. Now, if he could just make it to the pits. The tire shredded completely, tearing out the crush panel and beating on the side of the car. Orly ignored the sound and drove the car as fast as he dared. In what seemed like an eternity, he finally managed to get the car into pit lane and came wallowing down to his pit box.

Bear and the Ballet Company were ready. Bear himself went over the wall this time. Paolo, thinking quickly, handed the jack off to Matt. Experience told him that the car would be sitting too low with the tire gone to slip the jack underneath. They were going to have to manhandle the thing high enough to get the jack under it. The rest of the crew knew the drill, and as soon as Orly hit the pit box, they were over the wall with their backs against the quarter panel, lifting the car. As soon as there was room, Matt pushed the jack under the car and Paolo jumped for the handle. Bud already had the lugs off of the smoking rim as the car went up. He snatched it off and Bear had his head in the wheel well checking for damage. He made a motion and a short-handled sledge hammer was placed in his hand like a scalpel in the hands of a surgeon. A few well-placed bangs and the crush panel was knocked back into shape, good enough to allow fresh rubber to fit under the wheel well.

In the meantime, the rest of the crew changed the left front tire and fueled the car.

Jimmy's voice spoke in everybody's ear. "Pace car is coming. Better turn him loose."

A new tire and wheel was thrown on and Paolo dropped the jack. Orly accelerated down the pit lane at the mandated speed and screamed out onto the track ahead of the pace car. He ran as hard as he dared and then came flying back into the pits.

This time the crew changed right side tires, and as Paolo dropped the jack, Orly repeated the procedure, pulling out ahead of the pace car once again. The third time he came down pit lane, the car went up again on the left side, but only the rear tire came off. Bear stuck his head in the wheel well once again and banged the crush panel with half a dozen well-placed blows. He looked it over carefully, gave a nod, and the tire was bolted back on the car.

"Good to go, Orly," Bear said as Orly fell into line behind the pace car.

"We still on the lead lap okay?" Orly asked.

Bear looked down at Alicia who gave him a thumbs-up.

"What place?"

Doug's voice came over the radio, making Loren smile. "Eighteenth, Orly. Going to get the green next time around and you got thirty-eight laps to move up. Fuel is good to go."

"Whatta ya think, Hoss?" asked Bear.

"Don't know if we straightened out the push. I might've bent the exhaust pipes, dragging the body on the flat, but so far it feels okay. I'll tell you when we get up to speed."

"We won't see you again unless we get another yellow. We'll make that call when it happens."

Orly's mike clicked twice. *Every time I think about my shoulder, it feels like it's on fire. I'll try not to think about it. Eighteenth. Not too bad, considering that I was in the pits three times in a row. Hopefully I can get by the lapped cars.*

The rules said that they must stay to the inside lane during the restarts, but once they crossed the start-finish line they could move up. Some were easier to get by than others. He would have to go suddenly if he had any chance at all of getting to the front.

The starter waved the green flag. As Orly sailed into the first corner, he smiled to himself. He literally turned left in the middle of the corner and drove the car down to the inside line, passing three cars in the process. It seemed that whatever Bear did to the crush panel in the left rear fixed his push. The car was handling. He was even more pleased as he came off the corner onto the back straight. With the fresh rubber, he was really hooked up. He settled back in the seat and went to work.

Alphonse couldn't stand the tension permeating the air in the box. "Think he has a chance, Mr. Hornbrook?" he said in a tight voice.

Hildy overheard the question and much to everyone's delight said, "You bet he does. Just watch."

The sweat was running down Orly's face as the afternoon sun added to the heat of metal in close combat. As he came off turn two yet again, he flipped up his visor and wiped his forehead with the back of a gloved hand, then flipped it down again.

"Twenty laps left, Orly. You're in tenth," Bear said.

Orly knew that, but the ninth-place car was blocking him and he couldn't afford to wait around for this clown to get out of the way. The lead cars were getting away. He was blocking Orly both high and low and Orly was getting irritated. Finally, he ran completely out of patience and eased into the guy's rear bumper at 175 miles per hour going into the first corner. It was just a love tap, but it was enough to upset the balance of his car and he sawed at the wheel to keep off the wall, going high in the process. Orly ducked low and picked up another spot. It took him three more laps to close up on the next group of cars. He used his momentum and picked them off one by one. And then he was in fifth.

Bear could no longer sit down. Neither could anyone else. The crowd of over one hundred thousand were on their feet as the race wound down to the closing moments. Everybody knew that Orly was coming, including the cars ahead of him. The big question was whether he was going to have enough time to get to the front.

Orly pulled even with the fourth-place car coming off the second corner and simply outaccelerated him going down the back chute. The first three cars were arguing among themselves as they swapped positions for the lead of the race. Orly eased into the fray, inviting himself to the dance.

"Seven laps left," said Jimmy.

Orly paced himself for two laps, letting his tires cool a little and taking a few deep breaths. His shoulder was absolutely screaming in agony, but Orly pretended he was deaf. *Five laps left,* he told himself as he flew past the start-finish line. He was like a boxer looking for an opening, searching for any tiny weakness or place where he could take advantage. The third-place car decided to block him rather than race the other two for first or second. He went low and Orly didn't even look at him as he went high and drove around him.

"Clear," said Jimmy in his ear.

Bear was standing on the war wagon, twisting a red rag in his hands as he tried to follow Orly around the track. The Ballet Company, jostling each other for position, were gathered around the TV monitor on the pit box, watching the race from the satellite feed. Paolo was standing next to the war wagon just below Alicia, watching in silence with his arms folded.

Everyone in the suite was standing in front of the window. They were blocking Harry's view from his chair, but it didn't matter. He was watching both the satellite feed and the in-car camera. Hildy was trying to stay calm but she couldn't keep still.

It was down to three cars . . . but Orly's car was handling the best. *There's no way they can hold me back.* With two laps to go, the first- and second-place cars were side by side going into turn four. Orly simply dove under them, nearly to the apron, and took the lead. There was an audible roar from the crowd as Orly made this incredible move. The car fishtailed a little as Orly gently fought the wheel. Then he rolled into the throttle—locked solid in first place. One lap later, he took the checkered flag for the win.

O Lord, the king rejoices in your strength. How great is his joy in the victories you give! You have granted him the desire of his heart.

Psalm 21:1–2

"This one was real special. We've had some rough ones but I knew we could get back into victory lane and we proved it today."

Jeff Gordon, Winston Cup driver
(upon winning the California 500)
car #24 DuPont Chevrolet

ORLY CROSSED THE START-FINISH LINE with the hammer down as hard as he could.

Bear's excited voice rattled in his ear. "You got it, Orly, you got it. We won this thing. What a piece of driving. Whoooeee! Good job. Thank you, Lord. Good job, everybody. I'm proud of you. Jimmy, you done great today. Good job, Thunderfoot boys." Bear was effusive in his praise. "Hey Hildy and Harry, how you like them apples? That man can drive, can't he?"

Orly didn't roll out of the throttle until he hit the back straight. He was so deep in the zone that it took him a minute to come to reality. Bear's voice helped. Yeah, he'd won the thing. It's about time they had another win. They needed this one. He slowed and pulled to the inside of the track

202

as some of the competitors pulled up beside him to give him a wave of congratulations. Orly loosened his belts and dropped the window netting. He wriggled in the seat and audibly groaned as the pain in his shoulder overwhelmed him. There was no blocking it out this time. The race was over and even with the victory, the adrenaline was fading. As it did, the pain came washing over him. He managed to get the car down the pit lane to victory circle, and cut the motor as they pushed him through the crowd. He undid the chin strap on his helmet with one hand and worked it off his head. It was all he could do to raise his right arm.

A media guy started to stick a microphone in the window, but somehow got shuffled out of the way by the crew as Bear looked in at Orly. One look told him what he needed to know. Bear popped the steering wheel off with the disconnect lever and threw it up on the dash. Then he carefully pulled Orly's belts away from his body. Somebody handed him a wet towel and he gave it to Orly. Orly took it with one hand and wiped his face. Then he looked up at Bear and grinned.

"Hey, Bear, we got this one, didn't we?"

"Sure did, Hoss. Sure did."

"Do you think they would just let me sit here for an hour or two and catch my breath? I don't think I can get out with this shoulder."

"No, you got to get out. We need that check for the winner's share of the purse," said Bear with a laugh in his voice.

🏁

As soon as Orly took the checkered flag, Hildy turned and looked over her shoulder at Harry sitting up behind her. He jerked his head as if to say, "Go on, get out of here." She was out the door and down the stairs in a flash.

A few minutes later she was waiting patiently behind Bear in the crush of people surrounding the car. Paolo saw her and reached over to gently push Bear over a little. Hildy eased up beside him and put her head in the window. Bear took his cue and stepped back, giving her room. She stuck her head in and Orly reached up with his good arm to hug her neck as she kissed him full on his dirty face.

"Now that is the way a sponsor should greet a winner," said Orly.

It took a while to get him out of the car. Paolo finally went in through the right side window to help Orly get out of the seat. He was spent and so weak at this point he could hardly move, but he finally made it. In the postrace interview, he dedicated the win to Harry and the years of faithful support that Speed King had given to the team.

He added, "I'm looking forward to working in close contact with the new boss and CEO."

Everybody laughed when he said this because he had his arm wrapped around Hildy and gave her a squeeze for emphasis.

Finally the party was over and the Orly Mann Racing team joined the rest of the competitors in packing up the haulers for the long trip back to Charlotte. They would be pulling out as soon as they were buttoned up. There was another race next week in Richmond, Virginia, and they had to get back to Charlotte to do it all over again. The team plane was leaving that night from the Ontario airport. Doug, Paolo, and Alicia would be on it, getting home to Charlotte Monday morning. They would take the day off for a little sleep and then come straggling into the shop Tuesday to get ready to go again.

Alphonse also had an evening flight, but he would be back in San Francisco in nearly an hour. He already had his stuff in the car and was ready to go.

The suite was empty now except for Alphonse and Harry. Loren had gone down to talk to Doug as the team packed up.

"I want to thank you, Alphonse. It has been my pleasure to meet you and get to know you a little. I think you are a very talented young man, and I'm sure the Lord will use you in mighty ways. In fact, I am certain of it."

"Thanks, Harry. You're one special dude, if you don't mind me saying so. You've done so much for God's kingdom with your foundation and all."

Harry smiled. "Alphonse, you're going to get a call this week from some folks that would like to talk to you about your filmmaking and media career. They'll be asking you if you might consider transferring to USC or UCLA and working with them on some major projects we have in the works. I'm telling you now so you have a chance to pray about it and think a little before they contact you."

Alphonse was speechless. He didn't know what to say. Tears formed in the corner of his eyes.

Harry reached out and patted his arm. "You have talent, young man. Use it for the Lord. He will honor it." Harry pulled the wrap closer around his shoulders. Even though it was warm outside, he was feeling a little chilled. "One other thing I wanted to say to you, Alphonse. God will honor your commitment to Ricky. As long as there is breath, there is hope. Keep praying. You never know what God may do in that young man's life."

"Yes sir, I know that. I just wish he would have taken the chance to get straight. I would have helped him."

"Well, you and I both know that God never gives up."

Loren, Alicia, Paolo, and Doug stood in front of the team motor home, saying good-bye. Loren gave Alicia a hug and Alicia hugged her back. "Thank you, Alicia, for being my friend. God used you in a special way. I am so glad I got to know you."

Alicia dabbed her eyes. "You take care, Loren. We'll be talking to you regularly with your new job. Probably be seeing you at the track now and again. At the least, we'll be on the phone a lot."

Loren nodded then turned to Paolo. She reached up and gave him a hug. "Thanks, big guy. Alicia loves you, you know," she whispered in his ear.

"Yeah, I know. I'm not so dumb as folks think."

She turned to Doug. She put her arms around him and gave him a hug. "Stay in touch, Doug. You're a very special guy and I can't tell you what you have meant to me these past few days." Doug couldn't trust himself to speak, so he just hugged her back. She kissed his cheek and turned to go. She stopped and waved at the three friends. They waved back. She turned, tears running down her face, and jogged to rejoin Harry and Hildy.

Two hours later, Jimmy carefully steered the big hauler out of the garage area. As he exited the racetrack, he made a left turn toward Interstate 10. He was in the outside lane, and as he passed a weed-filled lot, he saw a group of young men leaning in various postures against a couple of beat-up cars, watching the race traffic go by. They were mostly Hispanic and dressed in black. Some had stocking caps and bandannas around their heads. Jimmy didn't pay them much mind as he joined the traffic. It came to a stop and he applied the brakes to the big rig and sat there idling, waiting to move forward. One young man, a little smaller than the rest, gave him a tentative wave. Jimmy ignored him.

"What're you doing, Ricky, waving at that dude?" said one of the bigger guys.

"I know them guys," Ricky said.

"You don't know nothing," the older guy said as he cuffed the back of Ricky's head, knocking off his stocking cap.

"I do too," said Ricky as he bent over to pick it up. "I know them guys," he said under his breath so no one would hear.

The traffic moved and Jimmy released the brakes with an audible blast of compressed air and rolled forward.

Ricky watched him go—a wistful look in his eye.

It was mid-morning Monday and the small group was enjoying the sunshine on Harry's veranda. Bear and Orly had been to the bank and were discussing what to do with what they found in the safety deposit box. Hildy had already been to the office but was home to join in the decision-making process. She was in the house making a phone call.

Bear had a piece of white binder paper spread out on the table. "Read it again, Bear," said Orly.

Bear,

    If you are reading this, then I am dead. I figure I won't last too much longer because my heart has been giving me trouble lately. This is what I want you to do. Inside this box is the deed to a place just outside Bozeman, Montana. It is a little ranch where I thought I might retire. I tried to live there but did not like it much. I don't know nothing about horses and such. There is an old couple living there, taking care of the place. There is another house on the property. I have deeded the place to that foundation you and Harry and those other people have. It has been notarized and done legal. Maybe you can do good with it somehow. There is also some cash in this box. Do whatever you want with that.

I hope I can trust you. I think I can. You have always been fair to me.

Ernest Brewster

"And how much cash was in there again?" Harry asked.

"Exactly $101,272," Bear said.

"Good grief," said Harry. "What was he thinking?"

"Well, you know he had the key marked 'R' for a rainy day. Maybe he was thinking that it might come someday and wanted to be prepared," Bear replied.

Hildy came out on the veranda. "Well, I talked to the husband of the couple that is living out there. Delightful folks. He said they have about twenty horses and a few head of cattle. Apparently Doc set up a trust for them and they get paid a monthly salary to keep the place going. They say the other house is in good shape, furnished and everything. They have taken good care of it. The problem is that they would like to move closer to their children in a few months. So I suppose the foundation would have to find someone who knows horses and ranching to take over the place. Do we know anyone like that?

Loren came out of the kitchen with a tray of glasses filled with ice tea. "Did someone say horses?" she asked.

EPILOGUE

And we know that in all things God works for the good of those who love him.

Romans 8:28

THE RANCH IS CALLED MORNING STAR and is owned by a Christian foundation managed by a young lady named Loren Janine. But it is more than just a ranch. It is a haven for young girls who are coming out of difficult situations, and at any one time there may be four to six of them living in the big house. The fresh air and safe atmosphere seem to facilitate the healing process. That, plus the regular prayer and Bible study. Loren is happier than she has ever been in her life. She still corresponds with Doug and the team on a regular basis, but she doesn't see them much. Doug has been to visit twice.

Two months after the California 500, Harry died quietly in Hildy's arms. The church was overflowing and Orly was one of those that eulogized Harry. Orly and Hildy still manage to see each other on a regular basis, despite their hectic schedules. Rumor has it that something permanent might be in the works. In the meantime, the Orly Mann Racing Team continues to do what it does best, and that is to race hard and *run in such a way as to get the prize.*